An Audience for Einstein

Winner of the
Fountainhead Productions 2002/03
National Writing Contest

Winner of the
2003 Authorlink New Author
Award for Science Fiction

Finalist in the
Writemovies.com International
Writing Competition, 2003

An Audience for Einstein

Mark Wakely

Mundania Press

A Mundania Press Production

Mundania Press LLC
6470A Glenway Avenue, #109
Cincinnati, Ohio 45211-5222

To order additional copies of this book, contact:
books@mundania.com
www.mundania.com

Cover Art © 2005 by Stacey L. King
Book Design and Layout by Daniel J. Reitz, Sr.
Production and Promotion by Bob Sanders
Edited by Rie Sheridan and Jennifer Scholz

Hardcover ISBN-13: 978-1-59426-385-9
Hardcover ISBN-10: 1-59426-385-X

Trade Paperback ISBN-13: 978-1-59426-096-6
Trade Paperback ISBN-10: 1-59426-096-6

eBook ISBN-13: 978-1-59426-037-0
eBook ISBN-10: 1-59426-037-0

First Trade Paperback Edition • January 2005
First Hardcover Edition • September 2005

Library of Congress Catalog Card Number 2004113978

Production by Mundania Press LLC
Printed in the United States of America

10   9   8   7   6   5   4   3   2   1

Dedication

For my wife, Pam,
and our three children,
Sarah, Eric, and Kevin

and

In fond memory of my grandmother,
Mildred "Muzz" Gorndt
1900 - 1974

Your faith in me early on made all the difference.

This book is for you.

And many thanks to the following for fact-checking my manuscript:

Richard C. Siebert, M.D. (Neurosurgeon, retired)

Marie Baehr, Ph.D. (Physics) Professor and Associate Dean of the
Faculty at Elmhurst College, Elmhurst, Illinois

Gina Consolino, R.N., M.S.N., C.N.P.

Prologue

Cambridge, England 1924

In all of his fifteen years, nothing mattered more to him than this.

The poolside bleachers were filled to capacity, the students intense in their crisp red and white uniforms, the faculty men serious in their school sweaters and sturdy black bowlers. They clapped and cheered as he lined up with the rest of the swim team qualifiers for the final race. He faced the end lane, having barely earned a berth.

"I didn't sleep very well last night," he said over the din to the taller, more muscular teen next to him. "Did you?"

The teen scoffed, stretched up on his tiptoes as if to emphasize the physical difference between them then rolled his shoulders to loosen up. "I slept like a baby. That comes from having confidence. Something you must not possess."

Another school cheer went up from the tightly packed crowd, echoing in the cavernous, tiled room. One of the swimmers dipped his foot in the smooth water, sending ripples on their way to the other side.

The smaller boy waved his arms about to limber up. "It's not that, it's just that it all comes down to this, our last and most important race of the season. School champion." He looked at the mass of spectators on either side of the pool with scarcely concealed trepidation.

The teen regarded him with a brief sneer. "That's right. And frankly, I'm shocked you actually made it this far, Marlowe."

"Well I did, didn't I?"

"Doesn't matter. Everyone's certain you're going to lose, you know. You're just a brainy underclassman, not a true athlete like me." He flexed prominent biceps to make his point. "Go back to your books, bookworm. You're no threat."

Percival drew himself up, his expression dark. "We'll see about that, my good man."

The teen sneered again as he twisted from side to side. "I suppose we will."

A group of teenage girls clapped in unison, and then one of them held up a paper sign with the tall teen's name scrawled on it.

The teen waved to them. They squealed and waved back, bouncing up and down.

"See that, Marlowe? How can I possibly lose with them cheering me on?"

Percival stared wistfully at the auburn-haired girl with the sign as he now twisted. "I could win it."

The teen scoffed. "Not likely. This is for all the glory. I'm not going to let it get away. The rewards will be great and many, if you know what I mean." He nodded at the girls then glanced at Percival with scorn. "But then again, I don't think that you do."

The swimming coach stepped forward, satisfied with the team's preparation.

"Ready, lads."

The young swimmers assumed their start positions as the crowd quieted down.

"May the best man win," Percival offered.

"Yes," said the teen. "And that will be me."

The coach raised a silver whistle, a stopwatch in his other hand. "Steady now, gentlemen."

The swimmers leaned forward, muscles tensed.

The sound of the whistle launched them.

He flopped into the water, a terrible start. All Percival saw were the feet of the other swimmers as they sped away.

He dug in, his arms flying and legs kicking furiously. They all reached the other side and turned around at nearly the same time.

His lungs aching, he swam with an intensity he never had before, determined to prove everyone wrong.

He drew even with the leader, the tall teen next to him. The teen looked startled to see him, and in that instant, lost his rhythm and faltered.

Percival took advantage of the teen's mistake, and took the lead.

The teen swam frantically to close the distance in the last few feet, but Percival lunged forward and touched the wall half a heartbeat before the teen did.

The coach stood in front of Percival's lane, staring at the stopwatch with surprise and delight. He raised his hand to silence the excited chattering in the room, everyone now on their feet. The only sound was that of the swimmers' labored breathing.

"The winner, with a new school record, Percival Marlowe!"

Percival's arms shot up out of the water as the bleachers erupted in a roar of approval.

The tall teen turned his back to him, and the other swimmers huddled to whisper in amazement.

They all climbed out and grabbed their towels to dry **off for the** award ceremony. Percival acknowledged the congratulations from several of his teammates—solid pats on his back and playful shoves—then stepped up to the top of the three-level award stand for the first time. He bent down to allow his coach to slip a medal on a red and white ribbon over his head. A fresh chorus of cheers went up from the crowd. As he shook his coach's hand, he saw the group of girls applauding for him now.

He straightened up, boldly raised his right arm to point at the one who still held the sign with the vanquished teen's name on it. Aware they weren't the chosen one, the girls around her leaned away. With an innocent look, the auburn-haired girl grasped the sign in the middle with both hands, then grinned and tore it in half.

On the second tier, the tall teen scowled and lowered his head.

Percival raised two fists in the air as he listened to the crowd chant his name, absorbing their adulation. Then he held out the medal for them to see, looked closely at it himself, even took a whiff of it before letting it drop back down to his chest. He wondered how, in all of life still stretching ahead of him, he would ever equal or surpass this moment, and could only conclude that would be impossible. This was, and would forever be, his one best, defining moment—the time when his life truly began, forever and ever and ever...

Chapter One

Sometimes he envied the dead.

There was once a fierceness in him that radiated to every corner of a room; now, all that was left were the steel-gray eyes that could still flash at injustice great or small, like the great injustice of growing old.

He set the wheelchair in motion, out of the musty, oppressive bedroom to the cool sanctuary of the red brick patio. The brief whir of the electric motor made the seabirds resting nearby take wing in shrill protest. A sharp ocean breeze sent his thin white hair straight up, and his ill-fitting shirt flapping against his shrunken arms and neck. Like the bright, earnest young men who sought him out, then left visibly distressed at who they found, the old man could not believe what had become of him; how, in what seemed like the mere snap of his fingers, he went from the dynamic, premiere scientist of his era to nearly bed-ridden and obscure. Even teachers who made their living reciting his theories that forever changed the world often spoke of him in past tense, the bright young men reluctantly confirmed—their eyes averted— as if those mere reciters could ever shoulder the mantle of scientific eminence that still rightfully belonged to him.

The professor clenched his jaw, and his eyes flashed again. "Afraid you're not quite rid of me yet."

As the seabirds cautiously returned and circled above, he stared down at the moon-like landscape of rocks and sand mounds and the white foam waves that raced ashore less than fifty yards away. The wind took days to move the mounds noticeably, like surf in slow time.

He saw a small sand pile forming at the edge of the patio, burying the bottom of the rusting iron fence partially enclosing the weathered bricks. The professor shook his head. Years ago, he wouldn't have hesitated to grab a coal shovel and toss back the invasion; now he wondered why on Earth he had been so eager to fight such a losing battle. In a few days, the wind would sweep the patio clean and another sand mound would begin to grow. He liked the steady, dependable rhythm, that could appreciate it now his youthful impatience was gone.

The professor gasped, sat up straighter in his wheelchair. He noticed a small but startling distant bump on the ocean, shimmering with festive lights like a city in celebration. But that was impossible, he thought in confusion. Could atmospheric conditions bend light that far? He had seen mirages before—dozens of them—but this was far more focused and clear. Why, the shores of Europe were two thousand miles away, he marveled, yet it seemed he could almost reach out and touch...

...and he realized he was staring at a ship on the horizon, its image wavering where the boundary between sky and water blurred.

The professor dropped his trembling arm, and slumped in defeat. Why hadn't he immediately realized it was only a ship, as any fool could plainly see? Was his eyesight failing him now too? *My God*, he thought, *leave me something!* And even though it was an insignificant mistake, he closed his eyes and sobbed once, despising his relentless decline.

He turned and propelled himself back into the bedroom, aware his feelings of hopelessness meant only one thing: he had forgotten to take his anti-depressant.

As he took a pill from one of the open amber vials on the crowded nightstand, the thousand-red-hot-needles pain in his chest that was becoming more frequent and severe struck him again, pitching him forward unceremoniously out of the wheelchair, to land hard on his side on the worn carpet. He fought for every breath, clutching his throat not just for air, but also to keep from making a sound. As before, the needles withdrew as fast as they had come, leaving him panting, forehead wet with sudden sweat, and eyes burning with determination to keep hidden from Natalie for as long as he could how he fought these little skirmishes with death.

He did not want to be taken from here to die in a far away place, his slim chance to live again lost because his memories had degraded beyond Dorning's ability to save them.

He grasped at the wheelchair, straining to pull himself up until he was finally sitting again. His shoulders heaving from the effort, he suddenly realized, to his slight amusement, he was still clutching the pill he meant to take in the palm of his left hand.

There were three familiar soft raps on the bedroom door behind him.

He closed his eyes a moment to compose himself and blot his forehead with a handkerchief before answering.

Much too close that time, he thought.

The professor tried to sound nonchalant as he hastily tucked his handkerchief away. "Dorning? Is that you? Go ahead and let yourself in. I can't help."

The door swung inward, revealing a plump, perspiring man in a taut blue suit and a coffee-stained tie. The man held white-knuckle tight to the handle of an overstuffed briefcase.

"Morning, Professor!" The voice boomed with enviable baritone strength, and just the slightest shadow of a German accent. "Did you sleep well last night?"

"Of course," the professor lied. He fumbled to slip the secret pill into his shirt pocket then maneuvered to face his visitor.

⁊ ⁊

Carl Dorning was relieved to see the old man looked about as well as could be expected. Dorning towered over the wheelchair and its frail occupant, loosening his tie in the warm, stale room.

He smiled primly. "Well, then. Did you remember to take all your medicine this morning?"

The professor bristled with open resentment. "Yes, yes."

Dorning bowed his head; he knew he shouldn't always open their conversations with the same condescending questions. But despite the housekeeper's steady assurances, at least every other week he had to see and hear for himself how well the old man was doing.

Dorning wasn't quite prepared for the professor to die. Not yet.

He waved his free hand to dismiss the professor's resentment, smiling weakly again. "So! Your birthday is in a couple of weeks, isn't it? I imagine the cards and letters are already pouring in. Another milestone, Professor." He sat down on the corner of the sour-smelling bed and swung the heavy briefcase up onto his lap.

The professor shrugged. "A year older, but not any wiser, I'm afraid." He motored past his guest and grabbed a glass of water from the book and paper cluttered dresser before turning away.

Dorning said nothing as the professor clumsily tried to hide what he was doing—swallowing a forgotten pill. As guilty as Dorning felt for thinking about it, he couldn't help but imagine he was watching a crude marionette as the professor's arms shook, head bobbing on a ridiculously thin neck that looked ready to snap under the weight. It was almost as if someone horribly unskilled was making the old man perform the jerking motions. Cut the strings, and the figure would never move again.

Done, the professor wiped his mouth with an unsteady hand and rolled back around to face his guest. "So, tell me. How is that great experiment of yours coming along, Dorning? I take it your visits are to make sure I'm still well enough to take part in your future Nobel Prize-winning procedure, but the older I get, the more you fret since you're still not ready after all this time. Isn't that right?"

Dorning fiddled with the latch on his briefcase. "The experiments are going just fine. In fact, I've made considerable progress recently."

He spoke quietly. He disliked talking so directly about his life's work since it ultimately required the professor's demise to be proved or disproved in humans.

"Ah." It was the professor's turn to be dismissive. He whirred back towards the patio, away from his guest. "I don't know what the point is, Dorning. It's not going to work nearly as well as you think it is, you know. You're just wasting your time and mine. Not to mention all my money."

"What do you mean?" Dorning stood up and followed the professor outside. "All indications so far are that it should be a great success."

"Indications? Not good enough, Dorning. Besides, you haven't experimented with anything higher up the evolutionary ladder than mice. How would you know?"

"Guinea pigs," he corrected the professor. Dorning loosened his tie further, grateful for the fresh ocean breeze. "And I have two primates coming. Don't ask me how. I'm going to try...something new."

His confident, almost smug expression faltered for a moment, then returned.

The professor rejected Dorning's comments with a wave of a hand. "Come back when you have success with the primates. Then I might finally believe your scheme will work."

Dorning huffed. "Scheme?" He especially disliked this part of their conversation, when the professor played Devil's Advocate. It was almost as if the professor enjoyed mocking him, as if that proved the professor's intellectual superiority. "This could be the secret to nearly eternal youth, assuming the procedure is repeatable indefinitely, which it might be."

"Yes, but at what cost, Dorning? Tell me again whose life you take away in the process, and who would volunteer for such a thing?"

"No one's life is taken away. You already know that. Someone else, someone younger, will simply ...accommodate you. It's a chance to live again, to finally finish your life's work. Lots of people would be willing to become a whole lot smarter practically overnight if they could. You're still highly regarded and admired, you know. I assure you, if it weren't for the narrow age restriction, there would be no shortage of volunteers, no end to the number of people lined up to help Percival Marlowe any way they could."

The old man was quiet. That bit of reasoning, Dorning knew, always silenced the professor. The chance to continue being revered by so many people was the real reason why the professor was not only willing to finance, but participate in the untried procedure.

"Besides, you will have just died when I attempt the procedure," Dorning added dryly. "What difference will it make to you then whether it works or not?"

Marlowe cast an angry glance at him. "Thank you so much for reminding me. You know, I'm still surprised the authorities are going to allow you to experiment on humans. There must be considerable ethical debate going on about this, but it's funny how you never even mention it. And where are all these eager volunteers you keep talking about, Dorning? Except for a few naive graduate students who can't wait to leave when they see how impaired I am, I haven't seen anyone." He stared at Dorning with a challenging gaze.

Dorning reddened a bit, but said nothing immediately. He took off his tie, clearing his throat. "Yes. Well. Let me deal with the authorities, and select who will be lucky enough to accommodate you, all right? Those are things you don't have to worry about. In fact, you don't have to worry about anything at all."

The professor looked away. "Except dying." The voice was soft, full of sadness.

Dorning folded his tie, stuffed it in his suit pocket, and stared down at the professor with pity. "Which will be a meaningless event, if everything goes according to plan. That's the whole purpose behind what we're trying to accomplish. Oh!"

Dorning lightly tapped his forehead. "I almost forget. I have some more papers for you to sign. That's another reason why I came here today." He opened the bulging briefcase and extracted a slim manila folder and a pen.

Marlowe rolled his eyes. "Not more papers! Haven't I signed enough? When will it stop?"

"This should be just about it, Professor. It's just a legal form that prevents any heirs you don't know about from suing me for the experiment."

The professor clutched the pen and struggled to sign his name. "Unknown heirs. Yes. I'm sure some alleged distant third cousin twice removed will come out of the woodwork once my death is announced, trying to claim what's left of my money. If by some miracle your experiment does works, Dorning, I'll be glad to thumb my new nose at them."

Dorning shifted his weight uneasily. "Speaking of money, you need to sign a check for me today as well." He pulled the professor's checkbook out of the briefcase, hastily presenting it to him for another signature.

Marlowe glanced at the amount then struggled once more with the pen. "Well, you can't take it with you, as they always say." He looked at the amount a second time and gave a faint little laugh. "My goodness, I think I've given you all of my own Nobel Prize money by now and then some, haven't I? You better share some of yours with me when your procedure finally works, that's all I can say."

Dorning froze briefly in surprise. That was the first time in a long time the professor had suggested the experiment might not end in failure. "Of course, Percival. You will be very well taken care of indeed." He took back the checkbook with the signed check.

The professor nodded. "Thank you, my boy."

They shook hands.

"I must leave now, Professor. I have to get back to my lab."

"All right. Keep me posted."

"Of course." Dorning backed away. "Shall I ask the housekeeper to get you anything on my way out?"

Marlowe shook his head. "No, I'm just fine," he said without conviction. Then he straightened up as if he had just had a sudden thought and turned towards Dorning. "Speaking of Natalie, let me ask you something. She's been very good to me all these years. If it's at all possible, I would like her to be included in any future plans."

Dorning smiled slowly, glad to hear the professor was finally talking in such positive terms. "That's already been arranged. She could be of great assistance bringing you back to us after the procedure since she's so familiar to you."

"I see. Very well then. Oh, and one other thing, Dorning."

"What's that?"

"I don't intend for any of this to happen anytime soon." He looked defiant.

Dorning laughed. "That's fine, Professor. More time for me to make sure it will work, especially since I only get one shot at this. Just one, you know."

Percival turned away briefly to consider that, and when he looked back to respond, Dorning was already gone.

Chapter Two

He practically lived on the city sidewalks, sunup to sundown, absorbing all the teenage talk both serious and joking, mimicking the postures and gestures of the homeless young men who, like him, had nowhere else to be. They gathered near bus stops but never got on any buses; huddled under store awnings when it rained but never went in to buy anything; waved to the cabbies they knew by name but never paid for a ride. He enjoyed it all immensely.

Missing two teeth—one above, one below—the boy rarely smiled, and spoke with his lips drawn tight to hide his assumed shame. Head craning, his eyes would dart from one pimply or stubbled face to another as the teens tried to outdo each other with stories of their unlikely past exploits, and their elaborate plans for the future.

After a while, they rarely acknowledged him, except to chide him for not being in school like he should be, even though not one of them had made it through school either.

"You know something, bud?" one of the teens told him one drizzling day as they crowded together under an awning. "You didn't just fall through the cracks, you jumped in."

They all laughed, including him.

"Yeah," said another, not to be outdone. "You know what your real problem is, Miguel?"

Lips barely moving, expression earnest: "No, sir."

"The real problem is, you don't know that you're poor."

They all laughed again, but the boy wasn't sure why. He didn't feel poor at all.

At night he took refuge with his father in one of the church shelters if they weren't full, and if his father wasn't drunk and loud. Otherwise, he slept in the park in a hiding place he kept secret from everyone, especially his father, who always demanded whatever money the boy had panhandled out of passersby that day. His father would always spend the money on himself: for meals, liquor, lady friends. His mother, who he saw less frequently, was always in court-ordered rehab somewhere for heroin abuse.

When he was a few years younger, Miguel had thought her precious heroin helped turn her into some kind of heroine since the words were so close, that his mother's addiction was actually something to be proud of. But the sad, quiet faces of everyone he used to boast to about her finally told him she was not. Now he just told people she was sick and hoped someday she would get better so they could be a family again, and let it go at that.

But at the moment, as it drizzled and the wind blew and all the traffic and somber people streamed by in a great rush to get where they were going, the boy never felt happier to be a part of the lively group who were a fixture in the neighborhood. The people in a rush came and went, unhappy visitors at best, but it was as if, as one of the homeless young men, he belonged here, as if he owned the very best part of the city.

≈≈

Dorning left the bank after depositing the professor's check. Once again, the funds were just enough to cover his expected expenses for a few more weeks, and then he would have to ask the professor to sign another check. People might consider his experiments ethically questionable, he mused, but at least they could never accuse him of embezzlement or fleecing the professor of his life's savings. Every penny went for research, and the part-time teaching position Dorning had at the local community college went to keep body and soul together.

A wife and family were totally out of the question. Even friends were hard to keep; his work was his one true love and his best friend.

He sighed, turning off the highway towards the ramshackle district of the city where his modest house was. He could only wish his lover and best friend didn't have so many nagging little problems— and one enormous one, as the professor had so pointedly reminded him that morning.

The recipient.

He gripped the steering wheel tighter as he headed straight through the center of town.

Of course he had mulled it over from the beginning. Without a recipient, the entire project was meaningless. But where to find one was a looming problem he knew he would have to resolve, and soon. The professor's health had declined noticeably in the past few months, and he might have to be prepared to work quickly at any time.

The real stickler, he knew, was it had to be someone young. All his experiments clearly demonstrated juvenile subjects would achieve the best results of permanent memory transfer. Not toddlers, not older teens, but somewhere right in between. And what parent would ever give permission to let their ten-year-old be a guinea pig for an unproved experiment?

He slowed down as traffic approached some bottleneck he couldn't see up ahead, pondering the unfortunate answer to the question.

Regrettably, in order to obtain a suitable subject, he knew he might have to embrace questionable methods again, like the ones he used to obtain the smuggled primates. It bothered him a little not to be straight-forward and follow all the regulations, but after years of steady progress, no one could be allowed to deny him or the professor the right to succeed.

The project had clearly taken on a life of its own. It demanded to be carried through to its ultimate conclusion now, no matter what was required. It had become much bigger than him, or anyone.

Dorning braked as traffic slowed to a crawl.

He had considered looking overseas, many times. Perhaps South America, perhaps Eastern Europe or Russia, where child welfare seemed not to be such a high priority. Race didn't matter, but gender might, as his experiments hinted. So a foreign boy would be best. But the expense and risk—not to mention the time away from his work—made that impractical. Certainly there were poor areas in America, but again, his time right now was better spent in the lab perfecting his groundbreaking techniques before addressing the questions of who, and how, and from where. And all without involving the narrow-minded authorities who would never understand this was far above any of their petty regulations, or that it would benefit society immensely in the long run.

Traffic stopped.

Dorning sighed, tempted to beep the horn. Then he saw the prob-lem; there was a fender bender at the intersection up ahead, and a group of unruly-looking teenagers were taking advantage of the situa-tion to beg drivers for handouts.

He shook his head, more in pity than anger. He had driven by them nearly every day for months, but until now, had been lucky not to be approached.

"Hooligans," he whispered as they came nearer to his car. "Go back to school where you belong."

A tall, skinny teen tapped on his window. He rolled down the window just a crack.

"Hey man, how about it. Help a poor boy out?"

The other young men gathered round now too. One youngster in particular caught Dorning's attention. The boy seemed much too young to be a part of the rough-looking crowd, Dorning thought, but appar-ently he was.

The doctor sighed as he pulled out his wallet. It was a small price to pay to be done with them and get home; he was hungry and had yet to prepare for tonight's class.

He grabbed three dollars and pushed them out the barely open window. "Here. It's for him."

"What?" The lanky teen pulled on the bills.

Dorning didn't let go. "Him. Over there." The doctor nodded towards the shortest of them, standing forlornly in the back. "He looks like he could use it the most."

The teen hesitated then let go. "Yeah, I guess so." He glanced behind him. "Hey, Miguel, come get your money."

His sad expression oddly unaffected, the boy came forward and took the three bills.

"Thank you." The boy's mouth barely opened.

"You're welcome. Now if you don't mind, I have a class tonight. Unlike all of you."

But the gang had already moved on to the car behind him. In his rearview mirror, Dorning saw the woman driver ignore the boys with more than a hint of fear in her eyes, windows rolled up tight.

Dorning laughed to himself, then it was his turn at last to steer around the two crumpled cars and their loud, arguing drivers.

※ ※

"Time is up, ladies and gentlemen. Pens and pencils down please, and pass your papers to the front."

The class collectively murmured in dismay as the papers made their way forward to Dorning's waiting hands.

Dorning put the stack of papers aside, stood before the two-dozen slouching students and held up a hefty textbook. "All right, we have seven minutes left. Quiet now, please. Let's consider what Darwin and his rival Herbert Spencer had to say about natural selection. This assumes, of course, you read the assignment last night. I imagine I'll find out who did or didn't when I grade the quizzes. Any volunteers to get us started?"

No one moved or spoke. The industrial-looking fan in the corner quietly churned the warm, humid air.

Dorning flipped through the book. He hadn't really expected anyone to respond. This was not exactly the most enthusiastic class he had ever taught; not one of them was a biology or even a science major.

As he hunted for the passage he wanted to read, he spoke to break the languid spell the summer evening had cast over the students.

"Well, what more should I expect from those here just to fulfill their science requirement for graduation? Physics is filled with too much esoteric math, and the chemicals in chemistry stink and can stain your clothes. I guess that means biology is the one true savior of the liberal arts student, isn't it?"

There was a smattering of nervous laughs.

A slouching, sizable young man tentatively raised his hand. Dorning was stunned.

"Jacob! Well, there truly is a first time for everything. Go right ahead." He lowered the textbook, curious as to what the student had to say.

Jacob struggled to sit up straight as his classmates looked at him with curiosity too, all of them alert now. The young man's chair squeaked in protest under the strain.

"Doctor, I read the section about survival of the fittest, and think none of it applies to modern humans. At least, I hope not."

Dorning raised an eyebrow. "Really? Please elaborate."

He closed the book and sat down on a corner of the teacher's desk behind him, intrigued by this sudden interest from a student barely passing his course.

The young man grimaced, as if unsure how to comply. "Well, humans aren't strictly animals, are we? We can reason and solve problems. It's not just the strongest that survive; it's the smartest. Even a physically weak person can be very successful if he's smart."

Dorning rubbed his chin, pretending to be deep in thought. "Hmm. I see. So what you're really saying is being smart is also an advantage. Is that correct? If so, it seems to me that agrees perfectly with what Darwin had to say. Brains or brawn, either way you can win out over others, can't you?"

Jacob looked embarrassed then resigned. "I just meant we're better than animals, higher up. We're not savages anymore. We're civilized; we follow rules. We have charities, and help each other in times of crisis. Animals are never so altri...altrus..."

"Altruistic?" Dorning suggested.

"Yeah, that's it!" Jacob looked triumphant.

Dorning opened his mouth to argue how few truly altruistic acts had been recorded in human history, and then remembered the meager handout he had given to the homeless boy just a few short hours earlier.

He spoke more softly. "When we can afford to be altruistic, sometimes we are. But when conditions call for it, we can be very self-centered indeed, rules be damned. Being self-centered isn't always such a bad thing, you know. Sometimes it's essential for survival. That's the lesson from Darwin."

"Yes, Doctor, but don't we go to great lengths to help others survive sometimes, even if it means we have to make a lot of personal sacrifices or risk breaking the rules? That's certainly altruistic." Jacob replied.

Dorning immediately thought of the professor, taking a sharp inward breath in surprise at the relevance of the young man's words. "Yes, Jacob. It most certainly is."

He stared into the distance, his desire to argue with the student gone.

A young woman squirmed in her chair then finally raised her hand. "But you can't justify breaking rules or stepping on other people just to save your own neck, or the neck of someone you happen to like."

"Justify it? To whom, Cynthia? Many of our greatest leaders and heroes often did whatever it took to achieve goals that ultimately benefited humanity, even if at the time it meant having to step on other people." Dorning paused. "Or perhaps just...merely inconvenience them."

The young woman firmly shook her head. "I'm sorry, Doctor, but I don't buy it. Look what happened to the American Indians. White European settlers, with their brains *and* brawn, treated them like cattle to advance 'civilization.' I don't consider those people my heroes."

"Oh, but you miss what the Doctor is really saying," Jacob said. He turned around to face the young woman. The chair squeaked again. "I remember when my grandfather was dying. I would have done anything to save him if I could, anything. If we didn't think and act that way, try to help each other as best we know how, we really would be savages, now wouldn't we?"

The young woman frowned, but didn't respond.

Dorning secretly grinned then glanced at the clock. Time was up.

"That's all for today, ladies and gentlemen. See you Monday."

The class shuffled to its feet.

"And thank you, Jacob, for your interesting observations. I thoroughly enjoyed your remarks. Let's have more of those in the future, shall we?"

Jacob nodded pleasantly as he lumbered by.

Dorning noticed the young woman who disagreed with him was waiting to say something as the rest of the class quickly departed.

"Yes, Cynthia?" Dorning stuffed the students' quizzes into his briefcase and closed it. "You wish to continue the argument? Go right ahead. I won't flunk you for speaking your mind. You of all people should know that by now."

Emboldened, the young woman stepped forward. "I still disagree, Doctor. The ends don't justify the means. Just because we personally benefit from something illegal or immoral someone did years ago still doesn't make it right, even if it was done on our behalf." She folded her arms defiantly.

Dorning stared at the young woman with faint disdain. "Noble sentiments. But the truth of the matter is that civilization has benefited tremendously from not-so-nice events throughout history, and there's no reason to suspect that won't continue to happen. Besides, many of those people who were 'stepped on,' as you put it, are ultimately revered by people such as yourself precisely because of the sacrifices they had to make for society—yes, often unwillingly."

Cynthia glowered in silence.

Dorning smiled. "Cynthia, these are very complex issues you and I aren't going to resolve standing here after class. There are exceptions to every rule; times when laws should be closely observed and times they should be thrown out the proverbial window. And there have been plenty of bad laws and unfair regulations that no one should ever have to follow, as I'm sure you're aware. That's just the way life is."

The young woman dropped her gaze then slowly lowered her arms. "Well...maybe you're right."

Dorning laughed. "Of course I'm right! Now go and have a nice weekend. I'm glad you're taking this course so seriously. That's more than I can say about some of your fellow students."

Cynthia grinned as she picked up her books to leave. "See you Monday, Doctor." She hurried from the room.

Buoyant now, Dorning followed the young woman out into the balmy, inviting night, reassured he was planning to do absolutely the right thing not only for the professor, but also for the good of all humanity. He found the thought profoundly comforting, his determination to do what must be done only further strengthened.

Chapter Three

Natalie opened the bedroom door.

"Time to wake up, Professor."

The room was musty and warm. Sunlight filtered through the dirty windows, illuminating a somber explosion of books on the desk, dresser, and floor. Dust rode the currents down in lazy circles, turning the heavy mahogany furniture gray. Things rarely moved anymore in the room, she mused. Even the professor's open books, the ones Natalie remembered him paging through furiously, were now covered with fine, thin grit.

The bedroom—like the professor—was slowing down.

Natalie frowned. This was the only room in the small house she wasn't allowed to invade with her rags and buckets and brooms, all the scraps of paper lying about filled with the professor's cryptic notations contained possible answers to everything. Since Natalie didn't want to be held accountable for throwing away any priceless solutions to universal questions, she cleaned only as far as the professor's door, eyes open for any unusual junk her buzzing vacuum cleaner might eat.

She switched off the machine. "You have to get up now, Professor. Otherwise you won't get to sleep tonight. Come on now, nap time is over."

Natalie put the day's mail on the cluttered dresser, on top of the rest of the week's unopened mail. The tall stack wavered a moment then spilled to the floor. Natalie cursed under her breath as she scooped up the envelopes, some with exotic foreign stamps and postmarks, once again resisting the urge to open them to discover the secrets they contained. Only the fear that the professor might realize what she had done stopped her. And she was too shy to ask him to open them so she could read the letters when he left the room as she had done for years, when he still shared her curiosity for what the mail might contain.

Natalie saw the professor was still asleep, wrapped tight in his linen sheet. She clutched the mysterious envelopes for a few seconds more and then reluctantly put them back where they belonged.

She moved across the room, stared down at a dust-covered page of an open heavy volume on the professor's desk, and clucked her tongue over the incomprehensible symbols that spilled down the page like a waterfall.

Marlowe stirred, a long, low groan chased her away from the book.

"Really, Professor, it's time to wake up." She tentatively shook the great man's shoulder; a shudder ran through his entire length. "Dinner will be ready in about an hour."

"I don't..."

"What it is? You don't want to eat? But you must."

"Don't feel so good." He rocked his head on his pillow. "Not so good. No choice now but to finally tell you."

Natalie backed away in small, uncertain steps. "Should I call the hospital? Should I call Doctor Dorning? Tell me what to do."

Marlowe coughed violently, his stick frame shaking the bed.

A spot of blood appeared on his chin.

Natalie ran from the room.

≈≈

He was not ready, not ready, not ready, not ready.

The windshield wipers beat in time to the refrain, much faster than they had to in the light mist. Dorning gripped the steering wheel unnecessarily tight.

"This can't be happening," he muttered again. "Not now. Not yet."

The worn tires on the old Mercedes squealed as he took a sharp left turn through a yellow light in the center of town.

At least the housekeeper had the good sense to call him first, he thought. Perhaps the professor would make an adequate recovery, or better yet, perhaps it was a false alarm. But from Natalie's description—the rolled-back eyes, the labored breathing—Dorning feared the worst, so he had no choice but to call for an ambulance.

He simply was not ready, and could only hope the clinic could save him.

Traffic slowed to a stroll; Dorning saw the street light at the next intersection flashing red in a malfunction, and banged a fist on the dash. "Come on, come on. Not today."

He noticed the gang of young beggars that had accosted him yesterday was taking advantage of the snarled traffic once again.

Dorning glared at them as they worked their way towards him, car by car. "Go away, you unwanted scum." He rolled up the windows, staring straight ahead so as not to be bothered.

The same lanky teen that knocked on his window before knocked again.

"Hey, man, remember me?"

Dorning refused to look at the young man as traffic inched forward. The teen easily kept pace.

"Hey, don't you want to help out Miguel again? Just look at this poor boy."

The teen reached behind him, grabbed Miguel by the back of the collar and pulled him up to the closed window. "Now how can you possibly say no to a face like this?"

The other teens behind him laughed.

Dorning turned to merely glance at the boy, but stared at him instead. The boy had a fresh-looking bruise on his face yet seemed strangely calm despite his rough appearance.

He heard a horn behind him; Dorning looked ahead and saw the car in front was speeding through the intersection a quarter block away. He stepped firmly on the gas to close the distance. The Mercedes lurched forward.

There was the softest of knocks against the side of the car, then a gentle side-to-side rocking that under normal circumstances he would have ignored. But the sudden sharp cries of the youthful gang and the fact he no longer saw Miguel beside or behind his car made Dorning gasp, and then slam on the brakes. He threw the car into park and hopped out, looking down where the jolt seemed to originate.

The lanky teen pointed to where the boy lay motionless. "Look what you did! What if you killed him?"

As if to prove that wasn't true, Miguel struggled to sit up, clutching the top of his forehead with one hand.

Dorning started breathing again and relaxed a bit. Then he huffed. "I did nothing. He slipped and fell into the side of my car, and you know it. What is this, some kind of insurance scam? I'll have none of it." He scowled at them all.

"No, sir. I just fell," Miguel said. "But my head hurts, and I'm bleeding." He tried not to cry, but tears betrayed him. "I think I might need stitches or something."

Dorning went and peered down at the boy's wound, seeing to his dismay it was true. Then he looked up and noticed several people in the cars behind him were watching him intently, as if waiting to see if he would stay and help, or turn and run.

Dorning huffed again. "All right. I'm in a hurry to get to the medical clinic outside of town to see someone who's gravely ill. I can take you with me. Do you know if your parents have you covered under their medical insurance?"

The older teens looked at him and laughed, loudly.

Dorning scowled at them again. They fell silent.

"So. Perhaps not. Who's coming with us?"

No one stepped forward.

Dorning nodded. "Fine." He opened the back door of the Mercedes. "Let's go. I've wasted enough time here. Come on, you're well enough to get in by yourself. I'll drop you off at the emergency room. What they do with you after that is up to them."

Miguel hesitated then meekly slipped into the back seat.

Dorning got back behind the wheel. "Last chance to come with us if you're concerned about your young friend, gentlemen."

The youthful gang warily backed away.

Dorning stared at them, incredulous. "You mean your young friend is being driven away by a grown man you don't know and none of you care?"

The lanky teen shrugged. "Not really. Sorry." He looked into the back of the car where Miguel sat, still holding his head. "I mean, it's got nothing to do with you or anything. We just can't get involved. You know, what with maybe the cops and all. See ya."

"Suit yourself," Dorning said. It was his turn to shrug. "See ya," he mocked the teen, and sped away from the curb.

Dorning hunched over the wheel, his youthful passenger in the back nearly forgotten already.

"Hang on, Percival," he said firmly. Then it was his turn through the intersection.

Puzzled, the boy finally lowered his hand, glad to see there wasn't too much blood. "Did you just call me Percival?" He fell back in the seat as the Mercedes rapidly accelerated.

Dorning glanced at the boy in the rearview mirror, laughing at how ridiculous that sounded.

"No, I wasn't talking to..."

He fell silent as he alternated between staring at the road ahead and at the homeless boy in the mirror, his mouth hanging open in astonishment.

He slowed down a bit. "How old are you?" he asked.

The boy lowered his head as if ashamed. "I think I'm eleven, but I might be twelve."

"I see. And what's your name again, if you don't mind me asking?"

"Miguel Sanchez."

"And where are your parents right now, Miguel?"

He dropped his head further still. "I don't know."

"Could you find them if you had to?"

The boy hesitated. "Just my mother. She's...in rehab again." The answer was faint. "But she's getting better. She really is."

"That welt on your face. Who gave it to you? Your father?"

Miguel hesitated then nodded.

"That's what I thought. So it's probably better you not find your parents if that's what happens when you do."

The boy didn't answer.

Dorning tapped his lips, his thoughts racing. He cleared his throat and sat up straighter. "Do you know why I'm going to the clinic, who it is I'm going to see?"

"No, sir."

"Does the name Percival Marlowe mean anything to you?"

"No, sir."

Dorning nodded. "That's all right. It doesn't matter. He's only the greatest scientific mind of the century, if you ask my opinion. He's brilliant, a genius."

"Oh."

Dorning shot another glance at the boy in the mirror as he turned off the main road. "Would you like to meet him?"

Miguel was confused. "Sure. I don't know. Why?"

"Because it would be an honor for you to meet such a great man."

The boy touched his head, felt fresh blood. "Oh. Okay. But can I see the doctor first?"

"Of course, of course."

The clinic finally came into sight; Dorning felt his optimism continue to rise. If the professor pulled through, and just one more hurdle was overcome with his experiment, he might finally be ready.

It was amazing to him how everything seemed to coalesce, to fall right into place just when it needed to happen, as if preordained.

Dorning laughed lightly as he pulled into the clinic parking lot, and then glanced back with a grin at the boy. "And to think I almost ran you right over! Instead, I think we'll be taking very good care of you, Miguel. Very good care of you indeed."

If his head didn't hurt so much, Miguel might have jumped out and run after hearing those suspicious words. Though he knew some of the other boys had joked about selling themselves for a night when they needed something like he did now, he stayed with the man whose name he didn't know because things would be worse without the man's help, even if he had to betray the man later and run to avoid something unpleasant expected from him in return.

Dorning felt positively cheerful now. "Professor," he said, "our biggest problem might have just been solved. Your salvation's on the way. Actually," he corrected himself, with another glance back at Miguel after parking the car, "you're the one who will gain the most, if everything goes according to plan."

"What will I gain?" Miguel was still suspicious, and put his hand back on his head to staunch another trickle of blood.

Dorning got out, opened the car door for the boy and held it like a proper chauffeur. "The gift of a truly superior intelligence." He beamed.

The boy didn't know what to make of that answer as he tentatively followed Dorning into the bright lights of the emergency room to get the stitches he needed.

Chapter Four

He ran his finger over each stitch, feeling all six of them. In the mirror a nurse held up for him, his partially shaved head and the short row of tied black plastic loops on the front of his scalp looked unreal, as if he were wearing the top half of a Halloween mask.

"Don't touch them," the nurse chided him. "Your hands aren't sterile."

She applied a carefully sized bandage over the closed wound to hide it and his missing hair. "That's it, little guy. You're all done." She smiled at him. "Come on. You can go home now."

He hopped off the examination table and followed the nurse through the maze of back rooms to the lobby where the man who had brought him to the clinic waited.

"He's all yours, Mister Dorning," she said, and headed back into the maze.

Dorning glanced around to see if anyone was looking, then carefully peeled back the bandage.

The boy was alarmed. "What are you doing?"

"Quiet. I want to see if it will interfere...I mean, I want to see how good a job the doctor did. I don't know any of them here." Dorning eyed the stitches. "Good. Not too tight, not too many like some doctors' use. I couldn't have done much better myself. I'll take them out when the time comes."

"You? Are you a doctor?"

Dorning was silent a moment as he smoothed down the edge of the bandage. "Yes, I've kept my license, but I don't have time for patients anymore, I'm afraid." He stood staring over the boy's head at nothing in particular, then roused himself and smiled weakly down at Miguel. "The good news is that the Professor is no longer in immediate danger, but the bad news is that in his current condition, there's nothing more they can do for him. Are you ready to meet the great man?"

The boy shrugged. If all he had to do for the ride to the clinic and the stitches was meet some guy, he would go along with it. "Sure."

He followed the man down the corridor, onto an elevator, up to the next floor and into the room where a thin, white-haired man lay motionless in bed, sleeping with his arms raised over his head.

The boy peered at the man from behind Dorning. "Are you sure he's alive? I don't see him breathing. Man, he sure is old."

Dorning grunted. "Of course he's alive. He's terminally ill and now he knows it, but yes, he's alive. The best news is it isn't spreading into his brain. Thank God, not his brain. I've managed to convince them to let me take him home. All they can do for him is give him more painkillers. He'll be discharged soon. We'll wait here."

The frail stick figure stirred slightly, as if by a breeze.

"You're taking him home now?"

"Yes. And you're coming with us."

The boy froze. "I am?"

"Yes." Dorning crouched down to look straight at the boy. "Listen to me, Miguel. Here's what we can offer you. The Professor has a spare bedroom in his house. You can stay there free of charge. He has a housekeeper, a woman who will give you three home-cooked meals a day—again, free of charge. The house is by the beach, with a magnificent view. You can play on the beach anytime you like, if you're careful. I could even arrange for the housekeeper to buy you a few playthings— perhaps a bicycle, or a video game." He looked square at the boy, who stared back at him wide-eyed. "I assume all that would be far better than living on the streets, begging for money, getting beaten by your father. Is that correct?"

The boy thought a moment. "So what do I have to do in return?"

A faint smile flitted across Dorning's face. "Do? Nothing, really. Just be there to keep him company, get to know him in the time he has remaining. Soon enough you'll get that gift of genius I promised you. Is it a bargain?"

The boy looked at the frail figure in the bed and realized the old man couldn't possibly hurt him in any way.

"Okay. It's a deal. But you can keep the genius gift. I don't need it." He held his head high.

Dorning nearly laughed. "Oh, but you're wrong. That's part of the bargain. You'll be glad when you get it, I assure you. Your life will have so much more meaning, so much more purpose than it does now. You'll become a respected and admired member of society, instead of a burden. I promise."

The boy had a terrible suspicion. "This doesn't involve going back to school, does it?"

Now Dorning did laugh. "No, not at all. It will truly be a gift. You don't have to do anything but let it happen. It's not a difficult procedure, at least not for me. It won't even require more stitches, just a simple bandage." His expression turned darkly serious. "Listen to me, Miguel. There are people out there who would give anything to be a pioneer like this. You'll be the very first, like Lindbergh across the

Atlantic or Armstrong on the moon. It could change your life for the better practically overnight."

The boy wavered uncertainly, finally deciding Dorning meant him no harm. "Well...why me? Why did you pick me? Why am I so special?"

"Fair questions. It's because you're the right age, you're available, and you need to be a part of this just as much as the Professor does. In fact, given your present lifestyle, you might need this even more than the Professor. It's a golden opportunity Miguel—a wonderful, rare, fantastic opportunity. I'm offering you the chance to participate in a historic, groundbreaking procedure, one that will make you famous someday beyond your wildest imagination. Don't pass this up and regret it for the rest of your life, Miguel. You need to be a part of this, more so than you can possibly realize right now. Is it a deal?"

Miguel looked away; he had only one more question. He grimaced slightly. "Will it hurt?"

Dorning shook his head emphatically. "Absolutely not. You'll go to sleep, and then when you wake up, it will all be over. A few days or weeks after that, your gift will begin to appear, bit by bit. It won't happen overnight. But in time, you will be perhaps the most brilliant mind on the face of the Earth, as the Professor once was. Now wouldn't that be nice?"

The boy nodded solemnly, mesmerized by Dorning's offer and persuasiveness.

Dorning held out his hand. "Is it a deal, then?"

The old man in the bed stirred again, as if disturbed by something.

The boy made up his mind. "Deal."

They shook hands.

The boy started to let go, but Dorning held his hand firmly. "I'm counting on you for this, Miguel. So is the Professor. A deal is a deal, after all. This is far too important to take lightly. Do you understand? You must live up to your part of the bargain. You absolutely must."

For a moment, as Dorning continued to squeeze his hand just a bit too hard, Miguel wondered if he wasn't making a mistake, if he should say no thanks and run away. Only the realization he had no particular place to run to kept him in the room.

"I promise."

Dorning let the boy's hand go.

"Excellent. You've made the right decision, Miguel, one you'll never regret."

The boy turned and stared at the old professor, hoping the words were true.

Chapter Five

The beach house was small and further from the city than Miguel had thought it would be. But he had his own room for the first time ever, with a comfortable bed, pillow and a blanket without holes. All the worn, filthy clothes he had owned were gone now, replaced with new ones that actually fit. The food was the best he'd eaten in a long time, although he ate exactly what and when the old man in the room next to him ate, measured portions with no seconds. Still, he didn't complain, since the food was brought to him and the empty plates whisked away by the housekeeper, who also cleaned his room every day. He was careful not to say or do anything to upset the old man or the housekeeper in any way, afraid all this special treatment would be yanked away from him in an instant.

As the days went by, he eventually realized he could never return to life on the streets, which only made him even more cautious to behave. The only thing he really missed was visiting his mother in the rehab center, and at times, when the weather was bad, he wondered how his friends were doing.

Miguel was certain of one thing, though—if they could see how he was living now, his mother would be as grateful as he was, and his friends would be both jealous and amazed.

No longer having to beg for coins to survive, or be ever watchful for the police, he was finally free to enjoy himself. He found the beach particularly alluring. He would challenge the foaming surf, timing his charges towards the departing waves and retreating just as fast as they reared up and returned; sometimes he would win, sometimes his feet or legs got wet, to his never-ending glee. He found a large rock he would climb up on and just lie back in the sun, or stare far out across the ocean, wondering what could possibly be on the other side. Every now and then, the crashing waves would wash ashore some unusual piece of wood, gray and twisted in a way he found pleasing. He collected a few, along with the seashells that poked up out of the sand on those days when the surf had been unusually heavy and thunderous.

Since the man who brought him here—Doctor Carl Dorning, he

finally learned—had encouraged him to start talking to the professor now the old man was out of bed and feeling somewhat better, he decided one day to show the professor his burgeoning beach collection.

"Can I please eat lunch with the Professor?" he asked the housekeeper one morning, after working up the nerve.

Natalie seemed surprised by the suggestion. "Well, I don't see why not. You're supposed to get to know him for some reason, aren't you?"

The boy nodded eagerly.

At lunchtime he followed Natalie into the professor's bedroom, which had a stale smell his own room didn't. Natalie skillfully wheeled the professor up to the folding wood tray with his waiting meal, and then brought in the boy's identical meal on an identical tray. They ate in silence, side by side, until the professor finally seemed to notice with a start that he had company.

Finished, he put his fork down. "So. You're the one, are you?" the professor asked.

"Yes, sir."

Marlowe harrumphed and wiped his mouth. "Never thought of being Hispanic."

"I'm Mexican," Miguel said proudly. "But I was born here."

"That either," the professor said.

There was an awkward pause.

"I heard about your stitches," the professor finally said. "Too bad."

Miguel giggled then shrugged.

Marlowe turned and stared at the boy, leaning towards him for a closer look. "Why are your lips closed so tight? Is there something wrong with your mouth? Let's see."

The boy felt the professor's dry, rough hands on his face. Miguel tentatively revealed his partially toothless grin, fervently hoping it wouldn't mean the end of their agreement.

Marlowe laughed once then withdrew from the boy. "So! Finally lost your last two baby teeth, did you? That's all right. You'll get your new ones soon enough."

Miguel was astonished. "I will? You mean they all grow back?"

"Of course." The professor stared at the boy again. "My God. Didn't Dorning explain that to you when he gave you your physical?"

"No sir. He ran lots of tests on me when I came here, but he never told me what any of them were for."

Marlowe harrumphed again, then nodded sympathetically. "Typical for a doctor, I'm afraid. Well, you're still here, so all the results must have been just fine." He lifted a glass of water towards his lips.

Miguel slumped a bit in relief. "Good. I was afraid..." He didn't finish the thought.

The professor paused with the glass near his mouth and looked sideways at the boy. "Afraid of what?"

Miguel was sorry he had started to say anything. "Afraid you wouldn't let me stay here anymore."

Marlowe took a drink. "Nonsense. You're the right age, and apparently healthy. After Doctor Dorning tries his little procedure, you'll be all set. All this," he waved a hand, "such as it is, will be yours."

Miguel gasped, looking around the cramped room. "It will?"

"Of course. You're my heir apparent. Didn't you know that? That's your reward for the inconvenience. And thanks to my textbooks, which are still quite popular, it's a considerable amount."

The boy didn't understand. "Your hair? Like, on your head?"

"No, no. My heir, like a family member. The one who will inherit everything I own."

"Don't you have a family?"

"Nope. I've outlived them all."

"So I'm like...your son?"

The professor considered that. "According to Doctor Dorning, it's even better. You're going to be me."

Miguel thought a moment. "How can two people share one brain? That doesn't seem possible."

Marlowe laughed once and set the glass down. "Well. Out of the mouths of babes. That's exactly what I always thought."

Miguel shifted uneasily. "So you don't think Doctor Dorning's plan is going to work?"

The professor paused. "No, not really. At least not the way the Doctor thinks it will work. I'm afraid I don't share his unbridled confidence. All his test results so far show very limited success. I just don't see how he's ever going to do any better than he has."

Miguel was silent a moment. "Then, why am I here?"

"Because...because..." Marlowe's voice dropped. "Because if you can retain even a few vague memories of how I used to be, and can share those memories with others for years to come, it will all be worthwhile. Worth every penny."

Miguel slumped a bit further. "And you think that's all that's going to happen?"

The professor grinned, but there was no joy in his expression. "My boy, you aren't going to wake up and suddenly know astrophysics. That's just not going to happen."

"Will I at least be any smarter, like Doctor Dorning said?'

The professor looked at the boy. Now his expression was one of amusement. "I think you're already pretty smart. You asked some intelligent questions. With some schooling, and some life experience, you'll do just fine."

Miguel looked down, feeling strangely disappointed. "But I wanted to be as smart as you."

Marlowe laughed robustly then sputtered a bit at the effort. "You and all my competitors. I mean colleagues, of course." He gave a sly wink.

Miguel had another thought, and gasped that he hadn't considered it before. "Will anything bad happen to me if it doesn't work? Could I get injured, or something worse?"

The professor emphatically shook his head. "Absolutely not. Either the procedure will work—to some small degree—or it won't, and that's it. I've read every single one of Dorning's test results, even though he doesn't think I care much for the details of his research. None of the subjects he's experimented on have ever shown any ill effect whatsoever. If they had, if there was even the slightest doubt as to its safety, I would have put a stop to this immediately." He sat back and shrugged. "Besides, he was a highly regarded neurosurgeon who had a substantial reputation, so I guess we should give him some credit for knowing what he's doing."

Miguel nodded, reassured.

Natalie came into the bedroom. "Are you two finished eating?"

Before either could answer, she yanked their nearly empty plates away.

"Good. You two can keep visiting, but don't tire the Professor out now. He had quite a scare last week and needs his rest." And she marched away with the dirty dishes.

Miguel remembered his beach collection, his reason for wanting to dine with the professor in the first place. "Would you like to see what I found outside on the beach?"

"Why sure."

Miguel raced to his room, pulled a box out from under his bed, and then raced back to the professor.

"See?" He proudly pulled out a piece of driftwood and handed it to the professor.

Marlowe grinned. "Why, it's beautiful." He held it up for a closer look.

"I've got more, and seashells too. Here." He carefully poured out the contents of the box on to the professor's tray.

The professor's expression turned brighter still. "Wonderful, wonderful." He picked up a shell, cradling it in the palm of his hand.

Miguel was pleased the professor liked his offerings, and stood proudly with his arms folded on his chest. "I can get you more anytime you want," he promised.

Percival carefully set the seashell down and buried his face in his hands. He began to sob—deep, wracking sobs that rocked the wheelchair. "Thank you, thank you. It's all just beautiful."

Miguel was alarmed, and couldn't think of anything else to do but pat the professor on his spiny back to console him. "There, there," he heard himself say.

The housekeeper appeared at the door and clamped her hands to her face. "What's happening here? Are you all right, Professor?"

Percival looked up, tears running down the creases under his misty eyes. He turned his head to Miguel, who was still gently patting him on the back.

"Try to remember me," he said plaintively. "Please, just...try to remember."

Miguel stopped patting and took a step back. He balled his fists, determined to help.

"I will. I swear, I will."

Chapter Six

Dorning waited until the end of class to tell them.

"Just a moment, ladies and gentlemen. Before you go, I'm afraid I have something very important to announce."

The class chatter died down, and those already out of their seats sat back down in them.

"Unfortunately, today was my last day with you. I have resigned to attend to other, more pressing duties."

The class murmured in dismay.

"You will have a new teacher here next Monday, of course. I don't know who that will be, so I can't give you any impressions or warnings. It's been my pleasure to stand here and try to enlighten you, and I can only hope some of what I've said has affected you in a positive way and helped you to understand science is more important than most people will ever realize. I doubt any of you will now go running to the registrar to change your major, but I would like to think you now have a finer appreciation for science and will at least remember some of what I've said in the exciting years ahead." He bowed slightly. "Thank you, and goodbye."

After a moment of silence, one student began to clap, then another, and another, until they were all clapping and on their feet.

He bowed again, pleased.

The class filed out, each student pausing briefly to thank him. Dorning picked up his briefcase, stuffed the last homework assignments he had to grade under a side flap, and then realized Jacob was behind him, still standing by his chair.

"Yes, Jacob? Can I do something for you?"

He approached him with a stoic expression. Dorning instinctively backed off half a step from the imposing young man.

"Doctor, I just want you to know you were one of the best teachers I've ever had. I know my test scores weren't the best, but I think a lot about what you've said in class."

Dorning was touched. "Why, thank you, Jacob. I appreciate that." His gaze softened. "I particularly appreciated your heartfelt comments about your grandfather's death. I'm afraid I'm facing a similar circumstance right now, although not involving a family member. This is some-one who I admire greatly, someone who, regrettably, doesn't have too much longer to live."

He nodded, brow furrowed. "Oh. I'm very sorry, Doctor. Is that why you're leaving?"

"Partly. An experiment I've been working on has recently entered a critical phase. I must devote my full time to it now. If I'm successful, and I think I will be, the results might help save this individual. Money will be a little tight for a while, but..." He stopped, wondering why he was revealing all this to Jacob when he hadn't even said as much in his letter of resignation to the Dean.

The young man grabbed Dorning's hand and shook it vigorously.

"Doctor, you're so smart, I'm sure you'll succeed."

"Why, thank you."

"Don't let anyone stand in your way, Doc. You know a lot more than any critic."

"Yes."

"I'm sure anyone who doubts you will regret it someday."

"Yes."

"Thanks again for being such a good teacher, Doctor. Goodbye."

"Thank you, Jacob. It's been my pleasure."

Jacob finally let go of the doctor's hand. He stepped back and nodded, then turned abruptly and strode away, his large shoulders still stoically squared.

Dorning watched him go, surprised to feel admiration for the young man, and sorry now he hadn't gotten to know him better. He blinked in amazement, then shrugged and grabbed his briefcase. As he headed for the door, he slowed, and then stopped just before turning off the lights in the room. Instead, he set his briefcase down, opened it and pulled out his class attendance book. He grabbed a pencil, erased the D after Jacob's name and wrote a C in its place. Then he put the pencil and book away, picked up his briefcase and swiped at the wall switches, plunging the classroom in darkness.

He walked out of the building for the last time, with a spring in his step, humming a happy tune.

≈≈

Dorning descended the basement steps in his modest bungalow to his two laboratories. The first one, well lit and clean, was set up as a hospital operating room, with all the monitoring equipment and instruments needed for surgery. There were two operating tables side by side, oxygen and anesthetic cylinders, an autoclave, a scrub sink, and the same model cranial drill and workstation Dorning had used to gain his reputation as an acclaimed neurosurgeon.

Behind that room was a less impressive one where Dorning spent most of his hours. The walls were lined with racks of animal cages, most empty now except for a few mice that scratched relentlessly, looking for a way out. The surgical instruments here were smaller, as was the space where Dorning operated. Although clean, the room had an oppressive quality to it, and seemed bleak in comparison to its impressive next door neighbor.

In one tall cage was the remaining monkey of the two he had obtained. The other was dead now, and kept frozen in a chest freezer in a corner of the room with the yet to be examined corpses of guinea pigs and mice.

All Dorning's hopes were now pinned on that last living monkey, which sat on a fake tree branch clutching a teddy bear, a bandage wrapped around its head and wires trailing from underneath to a computer terminal facing Dorning.

The doctor approached the monkey with a calculated stare, holding a stuffed toy dog in front of him. He glanced at the computer screen and saw normal brain activity in the form of multiple red lines rising and falling rhythmically, like steady waves.

"Hello, Miguel," he said. "It's been a week now. You know, I don't think you've been feeling like yourself lately, have you? In fact, I'm sure of it." He held out the toy dog for the monkey to see. "Look. Is this familiar? I think it is, isn't it? It should be by now. It most definitely should be."

The monkey chattered menacingly then settled down.

"What's the matter, Miguel? You don't like change? Oh, but you must. Change is good, especially for you."

He held the toy dog closer to the cage. The monkey followed his every move.

"Come on, little man. You don't want that old toy. You want this other one, don't you?" Dorning cradled the dog in his arms the way the dead monkey used to cradle it for hours. "Remember now? This is your toy, not that one. Come on, Miguel. Don't let me down today. It's been a week, more than enough time for you to begin to remember. Think, little man. Think hard." He brought the stuffed animal right up to the bars of the cage. "This is yours now, isn't it? Show me it is, show me it is."

The monkey seemed mesmerized by the sight of the dog. He loosened his grip on the teddy bear and lowered it to his feet.

Dorning looked at the monitor and saw that the monkey's brain waves were changing, dampening out a bit.

Dorning's eyes widened. "Yes, that's right. That's right, little man. You're beginning to remember something now, aren't you? That's good, that's very good."

The teddy bear fell to the bottom of the cage. The brain waves grew more pronounced.

Dorning's eyes were at their widest. "Come on, you can do it. You can remember. I'm counting on you, Miguel. We're all counting on you."

The monkey trembled as if about to have a seizure. His head went back, and his eyes rolled up.

"I know you're in there, Percival. Come out, come out, wherever you are." He watched the monitor as the red waves peaked and grew closer together, as if an earthquake was underway.

And then the monkey leapt to the door of the cage, hand pushed through the small opening, demanding the toy Dorning held. The doctor relinquished it and the monkey pulled it inside, scrambling to a different fake branch where the dead monkey used to stand.

Dorning looked at the monitor; the brain patterns had returned to normal, but they didn't seem quite the same as before.

He hurried to the keyboard and tapped in a few commands. The stored brain wave patterns of the dead monkey appeared beneath the one coming from the monkey in the cage. He synchronized the signals, and then overlaid them.

They matched perfectly.

Dorning jumped to his feet, let out a yell and punched the air with his fists.

"Good to have you back, Percival," he said. "It's so very, very good to have you back." He immediately used a set of tongs to carefully reach inside the cage and remove the discarded teddy bear; the doctor knew from his experiments with guinea pigs that removing all traces of the monkey's former life would help prevent a relapse.

The monkey paid no attention to the teddy bear as he tightly cradled his familiar dog instead.

Chapter Seven

Dorning kept a watchful eye from the bedroom patio as Miguel scampered on the beach, concerned about the boy's welfare. Fortunately, none of the outcroppings of rock the boy seemed to frequent were tall enough to cause serious injury in a fall; the ocean itself was another matter. Dorning disliked the game of tag Miguel played with the crashing waves, and wished the boy at least knew how to swim should he one day lose his gamble and get pulled in. He was fast enough to avoid the waves entirely most of the time, but still Dorning fretted. He had stalled on his promise to buy the boy a bicycle because of the safety issues, but now it didn't seem like such a bad idea.

He clasped his hands behind his back. "Well, Percival, I'm glad you like him."

"He's a good boy. I've got to leave my money to someone; might as well be someone young enough to enjoy it."

Dorning looked down at the professor, who was wrapped in a light blanket for protection from the steady ocean breeze. "You know, you're actually leaving the money to yourself, after the procedure."

"Hmm? Oh yes, yes. Of course."

Dorning wondered again if Percival truly believed in everything they were trying to accomplish, or if—as he suspected—the professor was merely treating the whole thing as a crapshoot: long odds, but worth it.

He decided to wait a little longer before making his startling announcement.

Dorning cleared his throat and changed the subject.

"I'm very sorry about your final diagnosis, Professor."

Marlowe didn't respond.

"It would have been nice if it had just been dehydration as you originally thought, but you know, that spot of blood you coughed up..." Dorning left the rest unsaid.

The professor pulled the blanket around him tighter. "You must be nearly done with all the details of your experiment, Dorning. Before you were desperate to keep me alive; now you don't sound so sad I'm about to go."

Dorning couldn't help but grin, a wide grin that nearly made him laugh out loud.

"Yes, Professor, I'm ready. I know exactly what to do now. I jumped the last hurdle, found the last piece of the puzzle. We have the boy and we have the procedures. This will work. I guarantee it. It will work like an absolute charm."

Marlowe snorted. "Or what? I get my money back?"

Dorning refused to let his happy mood be shattered. He turned and grinned down at the professor, who stared back at him darkly. "That's always what you've really thought, isn't it, Percival? That this was probably a waste of time and money?"

"No, not a waste. I think you've advanced our understanding of memory enormously. Why, with what you've discovered so far, there might be a Nobel Prize of your own waiting for you, even if your results are limited."

Dorning's stubborn grin remained. "Limited? Really? Well then, let me tell you some astonishing news that might finally change your mind. The results of my latest experiments were an unqualified success. When I tried my newest technique on the primates, I achieved complete memory transfer for the first time. Do you hear me? Total and complete transfer. I have since successfully repeated the experiment on other animals. It works, by God. It works."

Marlowe's eyes widened. "That's impossible," he said quietly. "I've read every one of your research reports. The problems you've had transferring all the delicate memory proteins intact seemed insurmountable. How the devil did you do it, Dorning?"

He ignored the professor's question, gazing out over the ocean instead. "Just imagine. You get to live another complete lifetime—nearly from the beginning. You can finish things left undone and strike out in totally new directions. This one time, nothing will be wasted on youth." He paused. "I envy you, Professor. I doubt I'll be given a second chance. Perhaps no one else will ever again, once the do-gooders with their misplaced ethics realize what we've actually accomplished. You'll be unique in all the world. Think of the possibilities! It may not be immortality, but it's pretty damn close." He grinned again as he watched the boy skip happily across the sand. "Soon, that will be you." He nodded.

The professor looked away and took a deep breath. He closed his eyes. "Something the boy said, 'How can two people share one brain? That doesn't seem possible.' He's right, Dorning. It doesn't seem possible, despite what you think you've achieved."

"You don't understand. There won't be a boy. There will be only you."

Marlowe's eyes widened again, this time in alarm. It was a moment before he spoke. "What do you mean, 'there won't be a boy'?"

"I mean for all practical purposes, he'll be gone. Your personality, your memories, every thought that makes you, well, *you*, will eventually supplant Miguel's meager experiences and memories. I've proven that in my experiments. That's what I've worked for, that's what I struggled so hard to achieve. And I have. In time there will only be you, Percival Marlowe, the greatest mind since Einstein. Miguel will essentially...vanish. And as long as we keep you away from anything familiar to the boy that might trigger a relapse, he will stay vanished."

He looked at the professor, puzzled. "I thought you understood. It was clearly spelled out in my initial proposal, you know."

The professor gasped. "No, I didn't understand at all, or at least, didn't believe it." There was open fear in his eyes now. "My God, if I hadn't read your slow but steady results all these years, I would think you quite mad."

Dorning shrugged, unfazed by the professor's remark. "Mad? No, I'm not mad. I'm realistic. What contributions to society could the boy make, being homeless, uneducated, and without any hope for meaningful employment? This way, at least he serves a noble purpose. Oh, it's possible from time to time some vague memory of his former self might surface, but that's unproven. After all, I can't tell what the animals are thinking. I can only see how they assume the lives of the animals whose memories were implanted in them, abandoning their former lives. That's what you're going to do, Professor, assume control. You'll see."

Marlowe stared out at Miguel, his eyes still wide with apprehension. "I thought it would be exactly the opposite, that I would be the vague memories from time to time. That was more than enough for me. Poor Miguel." He looked at Dorning as if seeing him for the first time. "Dorning, I'm not sure anymore we have the right to do this. Maybe those do-gooders *should* be involved."

Dorning vigorously shook his head. "Absolutely not. They would only cause needless delays while the matter was debated over and over. They would raid my research, demand federal or even international regulations to control the procedures. By the time they decided to do anything, I'm afraid you would be long dead and buried. I can't permit that. Why do you think I scrupulously avoided all government funds for my work? I can't have them meddling in things they can't fully comprehend."

"Oh, but you do?"

Dorning firmly clapped his hands together. "Yes! I'm the only one who does."

The professor looked warily towards the boy. "You've wrestled with the procedures and won, but not with the long term consequences, Dorning. Don't you see? If you're successful, you might have found a unique way to create a new class of slaves."

Dorning gasped then looked perplexed. "Slaves? What are you talking about? The boy will be free to go anywhere he wants, anytime he wants. He won't be denied any freedom."

Marlowe held up a bony index finger from under the blanket. "Except the freedom to be himself, to create his own life memories. You said there won't be a boy anymore, remember?"

Dorning sighed impatiently, frustrated by the professor's new objections. "Semantics, that's all this is. Besides, it's a little late now to harbor any doubts. I've been absolutely upfront with you about my research and my intentions. You've had the chance to read all my test results, and you did. You just said so yourself."

The professor nodded. "Yes, I did. What I didn't realize until now, however, was your inability to weigh all the moral issues." He stared hard at Dorning.

Dorning drew himself up, towering over the frail figure in the wheelchair. "Not true. I've had nothing but your best interests in mind from the beginning, Professor. I'm doing this for your ultimate benefit, not mine."

"Really? Just mine? So who has the boy's best interests in mind?

Dorning sighed again, and then glanced towards Miguel, who was once more running from the surging waves. "Well, certainly it's for his benefit too. The quality of his life will improve dramatically. He'll want for nothing instead of maybe being killed in the streets."

"But he won't have much say in the matter, will he? No freedom of choice."

"He's just a child. He will do as he's told. He's too young to make any decisions about his future."

"But he won't be a child forever. Or for much longer, if your experiment works as well as you claim it will. That's what you're taking away from him."

Dorning opened his mouth to loudly protest then slowly closed it. He grinned again. "Well, let's just say I respectfully disagree with you, and let it go at that. Obviously we are not going to agree, so what's the point of arguing?"

"The point of arguing is to make sure what we're about to do is acceptable to society."

Dorning nodded respectfully. "And it most certainly is. Society will benefit greatly. Besides, everything is in place. We can't alter our plans now; there's too much at stake."

Marlowe hesitated. "I don't suppose I could refuse to go along?"

Dorning slowly shook his head. "No, Percival. You've signed all of the legal papers quite willingly, you know. I must hold you to your commitment. It's for you own good. You'll see. I refuse to let one of the most brilliant minds that ever lived perish needlessly. There's no reason to. We have the hard-fought means to give you a second life, and we must see it through to completion. We must, and we will." He paused. "Besides, thanks to your years of generous financial support, you're as responsible for my discovery as I am. Or at least, nearly so."

The professor shrank down in his wheelchair. "Then this is my fault, isn't it? Until the boy showed up, I never seriously considered what your ultimate success might do to someone else, particularly someone so very young." He watched Miguel climb a rock near the water's edge. "Had I ever suspected you might fully succeed, had I not been so caught up with the idea of my life being remembered—even if only in brief flashes—I don't know if I would have agreed to this, despite my desire to somehow live on."

He wheeled himself around to face Dorning directly. "I could say congratulations, Dorning, but I wouldn't really mean it. So I guess you were right. I didn't think your experiment would ever actually work the way you intended. Not in my lifetime, at least."

Dorning smiled brightly, his years of frustration gone for having finally bested the great Percival Marlowe. "Glad to prove you wrong, Professor. So very glad indeed."

As the evening faded to twilight, Miguel noticed the doctor who brought him here was gone from the patio. Only the thin figure of the professor in his wheelchair was visible in silhouette. Miguel waved to the professor, who barely stirred in acknowledgement, then the boy turned his attention to pulling half-buried seashells out of the sand before it became too dark to see them. The beach was unusually deep today, like the ocean had shrunk. When he had mentioned it to the professor at lunch—they always ate lunch together now—he said it was low tide, and to take full advantage of it. And so the boy was, running back and forth with the meager rise and fall of the surf, grabbing handfuls of shells and carrying them up to the rock where he had them spread out to dry.

As he arrived with another armful of shells, he heard an unfamiliar noise behind him, one that made him pause. It was a shuffling noise, like something being dragged across the beach towards him. Miguel slowly turned around.

The shells went clattering back down to the sand, forgotten.

Miguel shrank back against the rock, unable for a moment to breathe. There on the beach, only a few yards away was the professor, crawling towards him, reaching for him like some sort of impossible, giant crab. Miguel saw the wheelchair abandoned on the patio, the blanket the professor had been wearing now being dragged behind him as if refusing to let go.

The boy could only whisper: "No. No. No."

He finally found the courage to run to the professor's side, sank to his knees, and took the old man's hand. It was cold and limp, and shook as if afraid.

Miguel knew he had to help, saw his own hands were shaking too, felt his heart racing not in fear for himself, but for the professor.

Marlowe tried to lift his head up, but failed. Miguel cradled him as best he could and pulled the blanket back up and over the gasping figure.

"Professor! What are you doing out here? Are you all right?" He looked towards the beach house, hoping the housekeeper would see what was happening and come rushing to their aid. She wasn't in sight. "Help us!" he yelled as loud as he could.

With that, Percival stirred, opened his eyes and looked at Miguel as if surprised to see him. "I'm sorry." His voice was coarse. "I'm so very sorry. I didn't know. Didn't know."

"There, there," the boy heard himself say once again to the professor. "Everything's going to be just fine." He brushed back the professor's sparse, windblown hair.

"Help us, please!" he shouted towards the house.

This time, the housekeeper appeared on the patio. Miguel heard her wail, then saw her come running down the wavering path the professor had cut through the sand.

Miguel breathed out in relief. "See? You're gonna be all right." He nodded towards Natalie.

Percival stared steadily at Miguel, ignoring where the boy wanted him to look. "But are you?"

Miguel shook his head, confused by the question. "What? What did you say?"

And then Natalie was there. She took the professor from him, cradling his head better than Miguel was able to.

She turned to him. He was surprised to see her crying.

"Go back to the house. Call Doctor Dorning at once. The number is on the phone." She helped the professor sit up as she draped the blanket around his shoulders. "Hurry."

Miguel raced back to the house. He wanted to believe what he told the professor was true, but wondered what was happening to the poor old man, why he would do such a crazy thing and why he was talking nonsense. To his surprise, he felt tears pour down his cheeks and he had to fight not to cry as he dialed the number.

"Hello?" The man's voice was unmistakable.

Despite his best effort, Miguel began to sob.

"Hello, hello?" the familiar voice said.

"The Professor..."

That was all he could manage before his voice broke down again.

"I understand. Stay there. I'm on my way. Don't call anyone else, okay?"

The line went dead.

Miguel hung up, still sobbing, glad the doctor knew immediately what was wrong. He stared across the beach to where Natalie and the professor sat together in the near darkness, barely visible now, as if they were fading away with the light.

"Please don't die," he whimpered. "I really didn't want you to die. Not really."

Chapter Eight

Miguel was astonished at the remarkable room in the doctor's house. From the street, the house looked liked most of the other houses on the block, and had the usual kitchen and living room and bedrooms like he had seen on television. But the room in the basement was surprisingly like the hospital room where he had gotten his stitches. There were two operating tables side by side, all kinds of mysterious electronic equipment and surgical tools on carts, bright overhead lights and steel cylinders like the ones used to fill balloons at traveling carnivals.

One of the tables contained the motionless professor, strapped down with a mask over his nose and mouth. Most of the professor's head had been shaved clean, making him look even frailer. The mask was connected by a long tube to one of the electronic machines, which in turn was connected to a tall cylinder. The professor's chest rose and fell with each click and hiss of the machine.

Miguel noticed the same arrangement was waiting next to the other operating table; he wondered why the doctor wanted to fill them up like balloons.

He stood next to the professor, hands folded in prayer like he had seen his mother do years ago over his dying grandmother. He didn't remember all the words to the prayers, but repeated over and over the words he did know:

"Our Father, who art in Heaven, hallowed be Thy name. Forgive us our trespasses as we forgive those who trespass against us. Pray for us sinners, now and at the hour of our death, and lead us not into temptation, but deliver us from evil, Amen."

The door to the room swung open, and the doctor quietly walked in.

Miguel looked up. "Is he going to be all right?" he asked earnestly, hands still folded.

Dorning was quiet a moment, but there was more than a glimmer of satisfaction in his eyes. "No, I'm afraid not, Miguel. He's dying, and there's nothing we can do about it but make him comfortable. It won't be long now until he's gone."

Miguel dropped his arms to his side, wondering if prayer ever really saved anyone.

Dorning bent down in front of Miguel.

"It's almost time, Miguel. Time to receive the gift I promised you."

"You mean to be as smart as the Professor?"

Now Dorning grinned, unabashed. "Yes. Precisely." He stood up, pulled a small green gown out of a drawer underneath the empty operating table and handed it to Miguel. "Here. Go in the next room and put this on. Come back when you're ready. But hurry; the Professor's condition could deteriorate at any moment."

Miguel went into the room and closed the door. As he hastily changed into the robe, he suddenly realized he wasn't alone.

The monkey stood transfixed, staring at him with both tiny hands grasping the bars of the cage.

Finished, Miguel tied the robe tight, self-conscious now.

He cautiously approached the cage. "Hello," he said to the quiet animal.

The monkey seemed to nod once in response, and the wires trailing from its swathed head swayed gently back and forth.

Miguel stared wordlessly into the monkey's deep liquid-brown eyes for a few seconds, then blinked several times and backed away. He paused briefly at the door to look back at it in wonder one more time before he left the room.

Dorning motioned to him impatiently, patting the vacant operating table, all business now. "Come now. Hop up here and lie down. It's nearly time to begin."

Miguel obeyed. He turned his head and looked over at the professor a few feet away. "Is he...dead?"

Dorning turned the knob on a steel cylinder next to Miguel. "Hmm? No, not yet. But we have to be well prepared before that event. We have to be absolutely, one hundred percent prepared."

He went to put a mouthpiece in Miguel's mouth; the boy held up a hand to stop him.

"Wait. Are you sure this won't hurt me? You said it wouldn't, remember?"

Dorning laughed. "No, it's not going to hurt. The procedure will be absolutely painless, just like I promised. Just a bandage, remember? And you should be happy to hear it's finally time for those pesky stitches to go as well." He lightly tapped the bandage just above the boy's forehead.

Miguel lowered his hand to allow Dorning to put the mouthpiece in. Then the doctor slipped a clear plastic mask like the professor's over his mouth and nose, and glued some cold metal discs trailing electric wires to him, on his chest and temples.

"Now, breathe deeply. Deep breaths. You'll go to sleep now for a while, and when you wake up, it will all be over."

Miguel inhaled, felt as if he was getting lighter, almost as if he could float up and away; he was just like a carnival balloon after all. He turned for one last look at the professor.

I won't let you down, Professor, he thought. *I won't.*

And then sleep took hold.

Dorning saw Miguel was under and all the readings were normal. He wheeled a cart full of surgical instruments between the two tables. As he put on a surgical cap and facemask, he paused to look at the professor.

"Talk to you later," he said. Then he had a startling realization as he glanced at the clock on the wall. "My God, in just a few more hours it's your birthday, isn't it? Well, here's a nice little gift for you, Percival. You're about to be reborn."

He looked at one of the monitors; the professor's heart rate was becoming more erratic.

He deftly shaved the top of Miguel's head, then cleaned the boy's scalp with an antibacterial scrub and dried it with a sterilized towel, just as he had done earlier with the professor.

"Almost," Dorning said. "At last, we're almost there." He tore open a new package of towels and set them at the ready on the instrument cart, then went to the sink in the corner of the room to scrub and put on surgical gloves. He watched and waited, pacing in front of the professor's table, poised to take action.

An alarm sounded on Marlowe's monitor; Dorning nearly shouted in glee.

"To begin!" he said, and did.

⁊≈

The two operations were finally over; they had gone exactly as he had planned.

Dorning fell heavily into a chair in the quiet lab on the other side of the basement, a cup of cold bitter coffee in front of him. It was now five a.m., and his eyes were starting to play tricks on him. He kept thinking he saw ghostly apparitions of his former test animals in the empty cages that lined the far wall. They seemed to flit back and forth, as if oddly agitated. At his elbow, Percival the primate was asleep in his cage, and in the other room, the boy was still under the anesthetic. Marlowe's body was dressed and ready for the final ride to the clinic, where he would arrive having "just" died, as everyone expected at any time. He had copies of all the signed papers to prove the professor had indeed donated his body to science, and more specifically, to him; that, he knew, would deflect any questions about the professor's missing brain tissue, should anyone discover his stealthy operation at the morgue. But since he had taken great pains to restore the professor's appearance after the operation—complete with secured toupee—not only was he unlikely to be questioned, there was no reason not to have a glorious wake, which would be attended by hundreds of scientists and admirers from around the world, all eager to outdo each other with eulogies of high praise.

He chuckled to himself, and then quickly swallowed the gritty dregs at the bottom of the paper cup.

"My, my. When they finally learn the truth, won't *they* be surprised?"

Chapter Nine

Miguel woke slowly. He blinked to clear his blurry vision then saw the doctor standing next to him. He realized they were back at the beach house, only he wasn't in his own bed; for some reason, he was in the professor's. Behind the doctor was the housekeeper, Natalie. The doctor looked pleased; Natalie looked as if she had been crying for hours, her eyes heavily red-veined.

The boy felt groggy, like from too many rides on a roller coaster, and his head hurt—a careful examination with his right hand revealed a second bandage on the top of his head, behind a new, smaller bandage covering the wound where his stitches had been.

He tried to speak, but could barely make a sound.

The doctor smiled. "Take your time, young man. You have all the time in the world."

Miguel tried again. "Water," he finally managed to say.

The doctor turned to Natalie. "Get him some. Cool, not cold. And only a little for now. I don't want him to vomit."

She did as she was told, and handed the doctor a small, half-filled glass.

He brought the glass down to Miguel's waiting lips.

"Can you sit up? Sorry, the bed isn't adjustable. I thought about moving a regular hospital bed in here, but decided it would be best not to change the Professor's room. I wanted everything to be as familiar as possible. Here, I'll help you."

Miguel struggled to rise, finally settling instead for merely lifting his aching head to accept the water.

"You lied to me," he whispered hoarsely to the doctor. "It does hurt."

"Oh?" The doctor came closer, looking genuinely concerned. "It shouldn't, really. I thoroughly numbed the entire area so it wouldn't. I'm afraid I can't give you any painkillers. They might interfere with the recovery. The only medications you must take for a while are the antibiotics I obtained. How does it hurt exactly?"

Miguel struggled to find the words to describe his discomfort. "Well, my head feels...I don't know...full, I guess. Like a balloon." He thought again of the steel cylinders back at the doctor's house, and wondered if they had anything to do with how he now felt.

The doctor's eyebrows went up. "Really? Interesting, interesting." He grabbed a notebook out of his briefcase by his feet, hastily jotted a few notes. "You know, it might be beneficial to keep a daily journal about your recovery, since you can talk and my previous subjects could not." He rubbed his chin as he stared at the notebook. "Yes, this could have some future scientific and historical value."

"So, the Professor..." Miguel didn't dare say it.

The doctor looked indifferent. "Yes. I'm afraid he expired."

Natalie sobbed once then covered her mouth.

Miguel nodded. "So I'll be as smart as him now?"

The doctor gave a quick, furtive glance back at the grieving house-keeper. "Let's not talk about that right now. Just rest, and in a day or two, you'll be up and about, feeling just fine."

Miguel nodded again and settled back on the professor's pillow.

The doctor smiled brightly again. "Rest now. Rest." He picked up his briefcase and took the still weepy Natalie gently by the arm to usher her out of the room. "Remember, you have all the time in the world. All the time in the world."

The boy closed his eyes and drifted back into a deep, dreamless sleep.

✍ ❧

Miguel was familiar with the church where the funeral was being held; on cold nights, there was a free shelter in the basement where he had slept with his friends from the streets, or sometimes his father, if his father was permitted in. But he had rarely been on the main floor where the altar was, except to peek in when it was quiet and mostly empty, with only a few old woman scattered throughout the pews, who occasionally crept down the aisles to drop coins in the wooden collection box and light fat prayer candles in their red glass containers.

Today though, the church was jammed, the organ thundered, and the mourners milled about on the front steps for a breath of fresh air, or to have a quick smoke. Dorning led him in by the hand, not to pretend he was family, but to prevent him from being swept away by the jostling swarm that came to pay last respects.

Miguel was surprised they had reserved spaces so close to the front, before remembering the professor didn't have a family to mourn him. But hundreds of strangers wanted to, he thought to his utter amazement as he surveyed the noisy church. He wondered where all those people were when the professor was dying practically alone. Several of the people stared in sympathetic curiosity at the two bandages on his head, then whispered to one another and shrugged.

He sat down stiffly in the pew, fidgeting with his tie.

Dorning leaned over to help him loosen it a bit. "It is a little warm in here," he said.

"I'll tell you something if you promise not to laugh. I never wore a tie before," Miguel confessed.

"That would have been my guess," Dorning replied.

From where he sat, Miguel could see only the professor's hands folded peacefully on his chest above the top of the open gold-colored casket in the center aisle.

The minister arrived from a side door near the altar and climbed the steps to the pulpit that towered imposingly over the crowd. He stood silently until the animated conversations and even occasional laughter died down as people realized he was waiting.

"Friends, today is both a sad day and a joyous day, in Heaven and on Earth."

The speakers high on the wall screeched hideously; hands throughout the crowd flew up to cover ears as the minister pushed the microphone back in its holder. The screeching faded away.

A few of the mourners resumed fanning themselves with church bulletins left behind from the early morning services.

"Today is the day God shows us no matter how intelligent, how beloved, or how important someone is, when He calls us home, we must heed His call, no matter who we are or who might grieve. Percival Marlowe was a giant in the scientific community, but in God's eyes, all of us are equal, and all of us must contemplate the end of our existence in this world, whether we're rich or poor, famous or forgotten. Only by admitting our mortality can we be humbled, only by realizing our time is limited can we understand the importance of living according to His word every precious day. But grieve not for Percival, because the end here is only the beginning there, in the company of those who went before him. Percival had a rewarding life, a full life, and so was blessed by God, who meant for him to achieve those great things he achieved, and now, has brought him forward to his next life, a better life by far. We may grieve the loss for mankind, but we must also celebrate God's will has been done, according to His plan for all of us, and this is how God meant for it to be, no matter who we are. He did not mean for us to live forever; He meant for us to share in the heavenly glories that await those who accept His plan, who live each day with the knowledge that it might be their last. That day finally came for Percival Marlowe, and at the end, God's plan was fulfilled, and Percival moved on to that far better life, a life that frees him now from the physical infirmities that inflicted him in his old age. For that we should be thankful, for God's plan is also a merciful plan, and we can now think of Percival Marlowe not as he was, but how he is right now, no longer a prisoner of the daily struggles he faced, but renewed and free from the years of suffering and cruel constraints he so courageously endured. Praise be to God."

Dorning glanced at Miguel sitting quietly next to him then answered with the rest of the crowd.

"Amen."

The minister climbed down from the pulpit, and the organ came back to life. The ushers signaled to the front rows to line up for one last view of the professor, and Dorning and Miguel made their way to the already crowded aisle.

"What happens after this? Are we going to the cemetery?" Miguel asked just above the organ music.

"No. I think it's more important you go home and rest."

They made their way slowly to the front. When they finally passed by the casket, Miguel saw the professor looked remarkably lifelike, as if only asleep.

"He doesn't look dead," he said only as loud as necessary to reach Dorning's ear.

"No, he doesn't," Dorning agreed as they headed out the church down a side aisle. "They did a remarkable job on him. And thanks to the extreme care I took, they never even knew I…" The doctor stopped, letting the thought go unsaid.

They found Dorning's car in the jammed parking lot, got in, and headed for home.

"I hope you didn't find that too disturbing," the doctor said.

"No. I've seen lots of dead people. In the streets. You know, drunks and gang bangers." Miguel yawned and rubbed his eyes.

Dorning nodded sadly. "I should have known. That could have been your fate, but fortunately, the Professor needed you. In that regard, you literally owe him your life. I hope seeing him today reinforces the promise you made to remember him. You heard what the minister said we should do. He said, 'Think of Percival Marlowe, think of Percival Marlowe.'"

"Yes," Miguel answered. He made a fist, his expression stern, brought it down repeatedly onto the palm of his other hand. "I will remember him. I will. I will. I will."

Dorning settled back in his seat, pleased with the boy's answer and apparent determination. "Good, very good. I knew we could count on you, Miguel. I knew it all along."

Chapter Ten

"Nothing?" Dorning asked. "Are you absolutely sure? Nothing at all?"

The boy took another bite of his lunch as he shook his head no.

Dorning sighed, sat back and considered the nearly blank notebook page. He sighed again, abruptly closed the book, then capped his pen and stuffed both back into his ever-present briefcase.

"Very well. Perhaps tomorrow then."

Miguel swallowed. "It's been more than a week. I don't feel any smarter."

Dorning huffed as he ran a hand through his hair. "Yes, yes. I'm aware of that."

Miguel scooped up another spoonful of food. "Maybe it just didn't work." He stared down at his plate.

Dorning stirred uneasily. "Nonsense. This is still well within the timeframe I predicted for the first recovered memory. I'm not the least bit worried. Not in the least." He drummed his fingers on the kitchen table.

Miguel kept eating.

Dorning studied Miguel's motions, reluctantly concluding he saw nothing of the professor in the boy's simple mannerisms.

His patience wearing uncomfortably thin, he knew he would have to take a much more direct approach to revive the professor instead of waiting for the familiar surroundings to do the job for him.

Dorning cleared his throat. "I've decided it would be best if I lived here with you, at least for a while. I will sleep in your old bedroom."

"Why? Natalie takes good care of me."

"Of course she does. But I want to be here when the Professor's memories assert...when the Professor's memories begin to return." He leaned closer and pursed his lips, choosing his words more carefully as the boy continued to eat. "I'll be honest with you, Miguel. You might find some of the Professor's memories a little...intense, maybe even incomprehensible. I will be here not only to record those memories, but also to help explain them so you won't be worried or afraid. Okay?"

Miguel shrugged. "Okay."

Dorning nodded. "Good. I'm moving in tonight."

The boy's face brightened. "Hey, maybe we can run through the waves together."

Dorning's expression immediately turned dark. "Run through the waves? Out of the question. You can't get your bandage wet, remember? Don't tell me you've been in the ocean!"

Miguel put his spoon down as he sank a bit in his chair. "Well, just up to my knees. I didn't get my head wet."

"Unacceptable! Is Natalie aware of this?"

Miguel hesitated. "No." His voice was small.

Dorning took note of the hesitation. "That's what I thought." He turned to the open kitchen door. "Natalie!" his voice boomed, "come here, please."

Natalie appeared, drying her hands with a kitchen towel. "What is it, Doctor?"

"I understand the boy has been in the water, despite my explicit orders he avoid getting wet. Is this true?"

Natalie and Miguel stared at each other. She suddenly broke into laughter then covered her mouth with the towel to stifle it. "Oh, Doctor, he's just a boy! What else is there for him to do but have a little fun outside? He's not getting his bandages wet."

Dorning was immediately on his feet, facing Natalie, his eyes burning with anger. "You will listen to me. The boy is to not go anywhere near the water. Is that clear? There is much too much at stake to risk Percival's...to risk Miguel's safety in any way. If I find out he's so much as gotten his ankles wet out on the beach, you will be out of a job and never return here again. I don't care how important you are to my plans or the boy's recovery, we will simply have to do without you. Do you understand?"

Natalie stood shoulders hunched. She answered quietly. "Yes, Doctor. I'm sorry."

He nodded, his anger spent. "It's for the boy's own good. Please don't take it personally. And I don't want him climbing on any of those tall rocks anymore, either. I don't want him injured in a fall. He must be allowed a full, safe, and complete recovery."

"Yes Doctor. If you insist." She stood there contritely.

"I do." He grabbed his briefcase, confident the housekeeper would now follow his orders. "As I told the boy, I'm moving in for a while to assist with his recovery. I'll be back later today with some personal belongings. Please provide some clean linens for the spare bedroom." He turned to go, stopped, then slowly turned back around. "And one more thing. I would like the boy to go through all the Professor's belongings in his room. Have him look at everything. That would be much more productive than frolicking on the beach. It's important he become thoroughly familiar with...his inheritance. It was very munificent of Percival to select an underprivileged boy to eventually receive the bulk of his estate. We must make sure the boy thrives here. That's all I'm saying."

"Yes Doctor."

"Good. Then it's settled."

Dorning abruptly left.

Natalie and Miguel followed him to the door and watched him drive away.

She gently squeezed the boy's shoulders. "I'm afraid he just took away all your fun, didn't he?"

"That's all right. He just wants me to be as smart as the Professor someday."

Natalie stared down at the boy's two bandages and laughed a little. "If you keep banging your head, you'll never be as smart as the Professor. Maybe the Doctor's right to limit your activities. You must be horribly clumsy."

Miguel was silent. He remembered what the doctor said about not telling Natalie yet about the true nature of the experiment.

For now, it was supposed to be just their little secret.

⁂

That night, Miguel had a vivid dream.

He dreamt he was in the ocean, far from the shore, swimming towards one of the brightly lit ships he often saw in the distance. Each stroke propelled him faster and faster, until suddenly he found himself on the deck of the ship, surrounded by a crowd of admiring people. At first he thought they were admiring him because of this amazing feat, but then he realized he was an adult like them, and they were anxious to meet him because he was someone famous. He looked down as he shook the hands of his guests one by one, and saw his hands were large and strong. He shook the hand of one man who didn't easily let go. When he looked up to see who the man was, he was shocked to find himself looking into the anxious eyes of the doctor—only the doctor looked years younger.

"Hello, Professor Marlowe. I'm so glad to finally meet you. I'm Carl Dorning."

"Oh yes! I remember the letter you wrote. You're the neurosurgeon with the interesting theories about memory preservation."

"That's right. I would like the opportunity to talk to you about my research."

He backed away slightly from the doctor, still smiling. "Well, my schedule is pretty full nowadays. Besides, that's not my area of expertise, you know. Maybe you would be better off presenting your ideas to your peers. I found your research intriguing, but perhaps a little beyond a mere astrophysicist such as myself."

Both men laughed amiably.

"I came to you, Professor, because I think my research may eventually benefit you personally. I read your comments about needing another lifetime to truly finish your work. My research may actually provide you with that opportunity."

He backed away still further, and made a point of looking eagerly towards the other guests waiting their turn to meet him, hoping the doctor would get the hint. "That sounds fine, just fine. Perhaps we can get together some other day. Write me again, will you?" He nodded politely to the woman standing behind the doctor then tried to extend his hand to shake hers.

The doctor didn't move out of the way. "To be perfectly honest, I came here today because I need your help, Professor. I'm afraid I'll soon be deeply in debt because of my costly experiments. Naturally I had to quit my job to devote my full efforts to my research, but even a neurosurgeon's savings only go so far." He stepped forward to close the growing gap between them. "Professor, the results I've achieved so far are nothing short of amazing, as modest as they have been. Quite frankly, my research could be your salvation, if we could only discuss it further." Dorning stepped closer still.

The professor saw two uniformed security guards approaching with concerned expressions and motioned them to hurry.

They quickly flanked the doctor.

"Is everything all right, Professor? Is this man bothering you?" one of the guards asked.

"Let's just say his welcome has worn out. Others are waiting their turn. Please escort him from the room, quietly. Good day, Doctor Dorning."

There was a look of betrayal in the doctor's eyes. "I don't deserve to treated like this, Professor. You're my idol. I merely wanted to share my research with you."

"Yes. Well. And apparently, you want me to pay for it. Doctor, there's a time and a place for everything. This is neither. Now good day."

The guards took the doctor away. Dorning continued to glance back at him, looking sadder still.

Miguel woke with a start and sat up bed, his heart racing.

"¡Ay, Dios mío!"

He jumped out of bed and raced into the bedroom next door, where the doctor slept soundly.

Miguel turned on the bedroom light then shook Dorning's shoulder.

"Por favor, Doctor, wake up!"

Dorning snored loudly and rolled away from him.

"Please, Doctor! I had a very strange dream."

Dorning finally turned over and look at the boy, blinking from the light.

"What? A strange dream? You mean a nightmare?"

"No, it was like a vision about the Professor. And you, years ago."

Dorning immediately sat up. "Wait a minute. This might be important." He grabbed his notebook and pen from the nightstand. "Go on. Tell me as much as you can remember." He flipped the notebook open and uncapped the pen.

Miguel took a deep breath. "I was swimming out to a ship at sea, swimming real fast, and suddenly I was on board. Only I wasn't just me anymore, I was the Professor too, in some big room. There were all these people waiting in line to talk to me, and one of them was you, only you looked younger. You said some things I didn't understand, and the Professor said some things I didn't understand then the Professor had two policemen take you away. He was mad at you for some reason, but I didn't really know why."

Dorning dropped his pen, but paid no attention. His eyes bulged, and his mouth hung open. "These things I said, and Percival..." His voice was no more than a whisper. "Try to remember some of the conversation. You must."

Miguel thought. "Well, you had written him a letter, and the Professor had read it, only I think he didn't really understand it. And you said you could help him someday, and I...I mean the Professor," the boy laughed, "backed away as if he didn't believe you. That's when he went like this." He motioned in the air. "And the two policemen came. They asked him if you were bothering him, and I said...I mean, he said..." Miguel screwed his eyes tight, trying to recall the words.

Dorning's voice was still soft. "Nineteen years ago, the first time we ever met, the Professor said, 'Let's just say his welcome has worn out.'"

Miguel opened his eyes, and his face brightened. "Yes! That's it!" He snapped his fingers. "And you said you didn't deserve to be treated like that!"

Dorning dropped the notebook and let out a yell as he jumped up and down on his bed, his arms raised triumphantly.

Startled but amused by the unexpected sight, Miguel stood back and laughed.

Natalie appeared in the doorway. "Doctor! What's the meaning of this? Are you all right?" She looked in bewilderment from the doctor to the boy to the doctor again, holding her night robe shut.

Dorning stopped jumping and stared at her, his face beaming with joy. "The meaning? It means success, that's what it means! The boy is making precisely the kind of recovery I predicted! This is only the beginning!"

Natalie shook her head, still baffled. "Well, I'm glad to hear he's going to be just fine, but really, Doctor, aren't you overreacting? You scared me half to death!"

"Sorry, dear madam, let me make it up to you." He sprang from the bed and grabbed Natalie around the waist, spinning her down the hallway in an impromptu waltz.

Now Natalie laughed along with the boy. "Doctor, really! Don't be so silly!"

She pulled herself away from him and retied her loosened robe. "Do you know what time it is? It's three o'clock in the morning."

Dorning waved a finger in the air. "Three o'clock! Good point. I must record when these moments occur." He bowed to Natalie, who giggled. "Now if you'll excuse me, madam, I have work to do."

"You do what you want, Doctor. I'm going back to bed." Natalie waved a hand to dismiss him then returned down the hall to her room. She glanced back at him from her doorway, still surprised and puzzled by his sudden, unexpected good mood.

"Come with me, young man." Dorning guided Miguel back into the bedroom and retrieved his fallen pen and notepad. "I must get this down while it's still fresh in your mind, then we can all go back to bed, although I doubt I'll be able to sleep anymore tonight." He directed the boy to a spot in front of him and sat on the bed to write. "Now, I want to know how you felt when you had this dream." He waited for an answer, pen poised over the page.

"Felt?"

"Yes. Were you scared, happy, mad, sad..." The doctor shrugged.

Miguel raised his chin up. "I wasn't scared. Not a bit."

"Excellent." Dorning began to write. "What else?"

"Well, I was little confused about who I was."

Dorning looked up at him sharply, the pen suddenly motionless. "Oh? In what way, exactly?"

"I felt like I was the Professor when I was talking, and I even sounded like how the Professor used to talk, but somehow I knew I wasn't really the Professor. It was like I was just having the dream for him, even though he's dead. Maybe he used to dream that dream, I don't know." He stopped, brow knitted in frustration from trying to explain it, to sort it all out. "Does that make any sense?"

Dorning nodded slowly, pleased by the answer. "Yes. Thank you for that description. That's exactly what I need to hear from you. Anything else?'

"No."

"Fine. You can go back to bed now. Just be aware you will have more dreams like that, and soon you should start remembering things about the Professor's life when you're awake. Goodnight now. Try to get some sleep." He continued writing.

The boy silently turned to go.

"One last thing, Miguel. I'm glad you're not scared of what's happening. There's no reason to be afraid. You're doing a wonderful thing for the Professor, you know."

Miguel nodded wordlessly, his head low.

Dorning noticed the change in the boy. "Is something wrong? Something you're not telling me?"

"No. Well, yes. Just one other thing. When I woke up, I felt..." He stopped.

"Go on. You can tell me."

"I felt...sorry for you."

Dorning gasped at the unexpected answer. "For me? What on Earth for?"

"Because the Professor was mean to you, that's why. I thought he was a nice man, but he sure wasn't nice to you. All you wanted to do was to help me...I mean, him...and he forced you to you leave." The boy pouted. "He shouldn't have done that."

A grin came slowly across Dorning's face. "You know, Percival, I'll take that as a long overdue apology. You were quite mean to me." A distant look came into Dorning's eyes.

Miguel shook his head, confused. "I'm not Percival. I'm Miguel."

"Hmm?" Dorning roused himself and looked at the boy. "Oh, of course. Well, goodnight, Miguel. Thank you for waking me to let me know about your dream. Don't ever hesitate to do so again."

Miguel quietly left the room.

As he listened to the boy walk down the hall, Dorning grinned once more, and then spoke quietly to himself. "No, you're not Percival, but he's got his foot in the door, and soon he's going to kick it wide open."

Dorning capped his pen and put it back on the nightstand with the notepad. Despite his initial excitement, he pulled the covers up around himself, feeling pleased and vindicated, but now also exhausted.

"Wide open," he said again with a yawn.

Soon the house was quiet except for the sound of gentle breathing from the three bedrooms, as if nothing unusual at all had just occurred.

Chapter Eleven

"Do I have to go through this again?" Miguel asked.

"I'm afraid so," Dorning replied.

Miguel buried his head in his arms, weary of all the professor's things, and of going through them over and over. He hardly understood any of the books, could barely read the handwritten letters with their faded, florid handwriting, and thought the mementos the professor owned—diplomas and proclamations and brittle newspaper clippings—were boring, and meant nothing to him. The doctor kept promising reading and handling all these things would eventually make him as smart as the professor, but he was beginning to have his doubts.

Ever since that one vision almost a week ago, no other memories of the professor had surfaced, and Miguel knew the doctor was worried once more.

"Come, come. The sooner you're done, the sooner you can go out and play."

The boy sighed then decided it was best to just get it over with. "All right. Where should we begin?" He sat up straight behind the professor's old wood desk.

"Good question. Let's see." Dorning tapped his chin as he looked around the crowded room. "I think we should try going through the medals again. Certainly they held special meaning for the Professor—since he kept so many—and may have the best chance for triggering an old memory."

Miguel resisted a groan. "Okay."

Dorning reverently took the Nobel Prize medal out of its glass case on the wall and carried it over to the desk. "Are your hands clean?" he asked, eyeing Miguel's fingers.

Miguel nodded and held out his hands to prove it and take the medal.

Dorning put the medal in the boy's open palms. "Remember now, be very careful with this one. It is the Nobel Prize, after all." He sat down across from the boy and pulled his chair up close. "If any one thing was especially significant to the Professor, this has to be it. I can't help but believe this will eventually trigger some truly wonderful memories."

Miguel turned the medal over several times.

Dorning grinned with anticipation. "Well? Anything?"

The boy shrugged. "It's kind of heavy. But I don't remember any-thing about it."

Dorning's expectant look faltered. "You mean you don't remem-ber his short but pithy acceptance speech, the formal dinner after-wards with the King, the bumpy flight home through bad weather that made the Professor quip it might be his last reward ever?"

Miguel shrugged again before handing the medal back. "No. Noth-ing like that. Sorry."

Dorning frowned in disappointment, then took the medal back to the case and hung it up again. "Odd. I really thought this would finally do it." He closed the small glass door. "Well, let's see what else we can try again."

He looked around, saw the pile of lesser medals on the nightstand, scooped them up and dumped them in a heap in front of the boy. He noticed they were nearly all of different metallic colors, and caught a whiff of their heavy, tarnished odors clinging to his fingers.

He lowered his hands from his face. "I have an idea. Look at each one like you did before, but this time, I want you to try something new. I want you to smell them."

Miguel looked up at the doctor in disbelief. "Smell? You're kid-ding. Aren't you?"

"No, I'm not. Smell is often a powerful memory trigger. Certain smells remind me of my own childhood. Roast duck, fresh cut hay, horse sh...well, you get the idea."

He handed the boy a small brass award and sat down again. "What they smell like exactly should vary by their composition, what they're made of. Even a subtle odor could make a big difference. It's called a 'sense memory,' I believe, if I'm remembering my psychology correctly. Try it; it can't hurt you."

Miguel sighed, knowing it was useless to resist. He grabbed a medallion, raised it to his nose, sniffed it, and put it aside.

He tried hard to keep a straight face, but failed miserably.

The doctor straightened up with sharp interest. "Yes? What is it? Are you remembering something?"

The boy kept laughing to himself as he shook his head. "No, it just seems funny, that's all."

Dorning sat back, annoyed. "There's nothing funny about it. This is quite serious. I don't care if you do laugh, keep trying."

Miguel picked up medal after medal, smelling each one in turn. Tears welled in his eyes, and his shoulder's shook from the absurdity of the task.

Miguel tried not to giggle, but couldn't prevent it. "This is too stupid."

"Don't tell me that. Tell me instead what you smell."

He pulled one medal after another from the shrinking collection, weeping and shaking with laughter, tossing each one aside after a cursory glance and a pass under his nose.

"Nothing, nothing, nothing, nothing, Cambridge, nothing, nothing..."

"Stop!"

Miguel froze. "Why?"

Dorning was on his feet. "Don't move." He selected one of the medals from the pile of discards next to the boy's elbow and examined it closely. He saw it was a first place finish medallion from the 1920s for some unnamed swimming event.

"This one. Smell it again." He thrust it in the boy's face.

Miguel sniffed it several times. "Nothing."

"Again."

He did.

"Nothing."

"Once more."

He complied. "Nothing. No. Wait. Let me see that." He took the medal from the doctor's hand and stared keenly at it.

His gaze grew hazy. "Cambridge, 1924," he said quietly, the words measured and precisely spoken, just as the professor used to speak, the cadence identical, and the inflection unmistakable. "It says Cambridge. That's what I said, didn't I, and I hadn't even read it." His mouth hung open. "I remember this medal. I was so proud to win it, so very proud. My first one. I wore it for days, even to class. I guess the ribbon must have fallen off. It had a red and white ribbon, you know."

Miguel shook his head and dropped the medal. It hit the desktop with a sharp clang, and the boy blinked as if the spell it had over him was broken.

"Wow. Was that strange. For just a moment, I thought I *was* the Professor, even more than when I had that dream." He stared at the medal, but didn't touch it. His voice was his own again, although he seemed unaware of its return. "I guess the operation worked after all. Man, that was really freaky." He looked up at the doctor.

"No." Dorning's eyes shone in victory. "That was wonderful."

Chapter Twelve

"Okay, you can open your eyes now."

The boy's eyes fluttered open. Then he flung his arms out in the direction of his surprise.

"My own bike!" He lunged toward it.

Dorning grabbed him by the shoulders, holding him back.

"Not so fast, young man, not so fast. I have something else for you, something I insist you always use with your shiny new bicycle. Natalie?"

She pulled a white helmet from behind her back.

Dorning pointed a stern finger at the boy. "If we see you riding your bicycle without wearing your helmet, I'll take the bicycle away and you'll never see it again, understood? We don't want to send you to the hospital for more stitches, now do we? You are to avoid all traffic, obey the rules of the road at all times, only ride during daylight hours, stay in our immediate neighborhood, avoid talking to any strangers, and finally, absolutely do not try any daredevil stunts. Again, if you disobey any one of these rules, I will take the bicycle away from you at once. Now, let's see if the helmet fits properly."

Miguel reluctantly took the helmet and put it on.

Dorning adjusted the straps. "There. Don't change anything."

"Can I go now?"

"By all means."

Miguel raced to the bike, hopped on and began doing lazy figure eights on the hard-packed gravel driveway. He gave a thumbs-up sign to Dorning and Natalie as he went by.

"Keep both hands on the handlebars at all times, please," Dorning admonished him.

Natalie smiled. "That was nice of you to give the boy something to play with, Doctor. He was getting so bored. I felt sorry for him."

Dorning scrutinized the boy's riding skills. "Yes. Well, he seems proficient enough. I decided this was far better than allowing him to play on the beach. He gets much too close to the water sometimes. That makes me very nervous. At his particular age, this is statistically much safer. A scraped knee can be bandaged, but there is no cure for being swept out to sea if you can't swim, now is there?"

Natalie looked at him kindly. "It was good of you to take him in, Doctor. I appreciate someone else to care for since the Professor died. I don't know where I would have gone if you had dismissed me. At first I wasn't sure I could keep up with someone so young, but it hasn't been too difficult. He's very precious, but I tell you, sometimes I still miss the Professor." She gave a heartfelt sigh. "I miss him very much."

The doctor turned slowly towards her. "I'm not sure Percival is really gone, Natalie." He stared steadily at her with a humorless expression, knowing he took a risk.

"What do you mean? That he lives on in our hearts?"

"No, I mean you may soon see and hear him again."

She laughed uneasily. "How is that possible? Recordings? That's really not the same thing, now is it?"

He opened his mouth then closed it, deciding instead to reveal the truth in small doses. "I mean I want you to start watching the boy very carefully for me."

She shook her head, unsure what he meant. "Why? Haven't I been doing a good job?"

"Of course you have. What I mean is, the boy is being carefully groomed and prepared to...take the Professor's place in due time. You should notice a change in him before too long. Please inform me when you do. Some of the things he says or does should most definitely remind you of Percival."

Natalie gasped and put a hand to her throat. "You mean he's that smart? I had no idea. No wonder you and the Professor took him in." She looked at the boy in awe.

Dorning relaxed. "Precisely. And that's why I might seem somewhat overprotective of the boy at times. Nothing must be allowed to interfere with his full recovery from his...unfortunate accidents. I have very big plans for him."

Natalie nodded promptly. "Of course, Doctor. Now I understand."

Dorning smiled. "Good. Now, you might as well know I've also arranged to go on a short trip with the boy in the near future. We're going to a place that was very familiar to the Professor. I'm anxious to renew some of Percival's former ties, particularly the academic ones. I expect they'll come in handy when the boy is...older. We should only be gone a couple of days."

"Whatever you say, Doctor." She turned her attention back to the boy, still riding his bike up and down the long driveway. "Miguel. Miguel! Not so fast! Slow down."

Dorning nodded, pleased with Natalie's heightened sense of responsibility. That was precisely what he had intended her response to be.

In time, he knew, she would realize the truth, and be thankful the professor was back among the living.

Chapter Thirteen

Miguel flew smoothly down the street, deftly swerving to avoid a pothole. The white crescent moon, hanging high in the Sunday twilight sky, seemed to grow brighter by the minute as he raced home before darkness could fully settle in. He did not want the bicycle taken away from him, though knew he might be in trouble already for wandering so far away from home. The late summer air rushed past him as he pedaled furiously, hunched over the handlebars. He turned a corner, taking it wider than he intended. Up ahead, he saw a parked pickup truck by the side of the road, and a man walking steadily towards it from another beach house just blocks from the professor's house.

Miguel glanced up again at the darkening sky, saw a handful of stars shimmering through and thought about the professor. He briefly wondered how many stars there were, and how far away they were, and how old they were, and then he wondered if all the white and brown dwarf stars that had expended their nuclear fuel and were now cold and invisible could indeed help account for a significant portion of the missing matter in the Universe as a number of his colleagues had postulated.

As he fought to keep the speeding bike on a straight path, a strange sensation swept over him, and his eyelids began to flutter.

The bike started to wobble, and he felt oddly uncoordinated, as if all his bicycle-riding skills were rapidly fading away.

"Heaven help me. Where am I?" he whispered. "What the devil's happening?"

He saw the back of the parked truck coming up fast, but was powerless to do anything but close his eyes.

The bicycle hit the truck's back bumper with a loud, solid thump. He flew up off the bike and sailed through the air, landing on his stomach in the thick reed grass by the side of the road. He immediately knew he wasn't hurt, and breathed a deep sigh of relief.

He heard rapid footsteps coming in his direction.

"Hey!" The voice was deep, filled with angry concern.

He rolled over and looked up at a man he vaguely remembered.

"You crazy kid, you could have been killed! Are you all right?"

He nodded and sat up, realizing he was wearing some kind of helmet.

The man looked at the spot where the bicycle hit his truck. "You're damn lucky. Not a scratch."

"I'm terribly sorry, really I am. I...I don't know what I'm doing here." He was surprised at how high and oddly pitched his voice sounded, and wondered why he felt so small. The reed grass seemed ridiculously tall all around him.

"That makes two of us. Geez, you were flying down the road like a madman. Look what you did to your bike." The man held it high in the air for him to see; it was nearly twisted beyond recognition. "No way this can be fixed, you know. No way. And it looks brand new. Whoever bought it for you isn't going to be too happy." He tossed the broken bike aside. "Where do you live?"

"Why, in the beach house a few blocks from here, where I've always lived."

The man raised an eyebrow. "You mean the Professor's old house? Are you his nephew or something? Sorry to hear he died."

"Died?" Percival laughed. "I think I would know if I were..." He stopped, remembering something about an experiment, then abruptly stood up in gap-mouthed wonder.

"Dorning," he whispered.

The man gave him a quizzical look. "Are you sure you're feeling all right?"

Marlowe looked down at his arms and legs, and then patted himself on the chest. "The boy. It's me. It worked. It actually worked."

And then he felt lightheaded again, put his hands on his helmet, and fell to one knee with a soft moan.

When he looked up, Miguel stared at the man in front of him as if seeing him for the first time. "What happened? Who are you? Where's my bike?"

The man came forward, a worried look etched on his face. "Geez, you must have taken a harder knock on the head than I thought." He helped the boy to his feet. "Come on, let's get you home. I think you might need some medical attention."

He ushered Miguel into the truck, then got behind the wheel and sped the short distance down the road to the professor's house. The man helped Miguel out and guided him to the front door.

A note was hanging by the doorknob. The man read it out loud.

"Miguel. We are out looking for you. Stay right here. PS. You broke one of the bicycling rules. Afraid you must be punished."

The man sadly shook his head. "Uh-oh. Looks like you're in big trouble, buddy. Wait till they see what you did to your bike."

Miguel moaned again. His eyes rolled up and his head went back. He shuddered once, and when he lowered his head and his eyes refocused, he smiled widely at the sight in front of him.

"My house! Splendid, just splendid! Dorning? Are you here? I have some smashing news for you, Doctor, simply smashing."

"Wait a minute." The man examined the helmet then took it off the boy's head. "My God." He dropped the helmet at the sight of the two bandages; it wobbled down the front sidewalk. "You already have a head injury, maybe two of them."

"Injury? Nonsense. This is amazing," Marlowe said. "Why, I haven't felt this alive in ages!" He looked at his hands, then flexed his small fingers and laughed. "This is marvelous, but just look at how short I am now! It's sure going to take some getting use to, I'll tell you that." He laughed again.

The man threw his arms up in the air. "Okay, that's it. You're talking gibberish now. I'm not taking any chances—we're going straight to the emergency room." He steered the boy in the direction of the truck. "Don't argue with me."

"The emergency room?" the professor said as the man led him away from the house. "Yes. Dorning's a neurosurgeon; he might be there. Let's try it. I won't argue."

The man helped him into the passenger side and carefully strapped him in.

Marlowe looked at him. "I know you. You're Jordan, aren't you? Jordan, the architect chap. You helped design a new science building for the university where I used to teach. What was that, thirty years ago?"

Jordan stared at him in disbelief. "How the hell did you know that? Ah." He made sure the straps were tight then waved a hand. "The Professor must have told you." He hurried around to the other side, got in and sped back down the driveway.

The truck lurched down the unimproved side streets, made it to the smooth coastal highway and roared towards the medical clinic on the outskirts of town.

"How are you feeling?" the man asked without taking his eyes off the road. "You doing okay?"

Marlowe stared at the bright lights of the city far down the road.

"Just fine," he said. "My, they've certainly built up over the years, haven't they? It's no longer the sleepy little town I remember."

Jordan gazed at the sky glow from the city up ahead and shrugged. "That's progress, kid." He thought about what the boy just said and glanced at him. "Wait a minute. You're way too young to remember the city when it was just a sleepy little backwater. *I* barely remember that. How could you?"

The professor gazed out the window at the streetlights as they flitted by. "I remember it well. Like it was yesterday."

"Not likely," Jordan scoffed. "Is that another thing the Professor told you? Sounds exactly like something he would say."

Percival smiled faintly, but didn't answer him.

"Hey, what's your phone number? I should try calling whoever's watching you and let them know what's going on, or at least leave a message." He pulled a cell phone out of his shirt pocket and waited.

"My phone number? Why, I don't know. I haven't used a phone in at least five years."

The man sighed. "Never mind. You're still babbling nonsense." He put the cell phone away and glanced at the boy with more than a little concern. "After I drop you off, I'll swing by your house and tell them what happened and where you are."

They finally arrived at the clinic. Jordan pulled the truck up to the emergency room doors. He hopped out, grabbed an empty wheelchair nearby and helped the boy into it.

"I hope to hell they don't ask me about your insurance," Jordan said, then wheeled the boy into the quiet emergency room foyer.

A blonde nurse was the only one on duty behind the admittance desk. She looked up from her paperwork as they came in.

"Oh no!" she said, with a cautious laugh. "Not you again." She came around the desk. "Now what did you do to yourself, young man?"

Marlowe looked up at her. "I...I'm not sure, exactly. This gentleman brought me here." He nodded towards Jordan.

"I'm a neighbor of his. He had a pretty severe bicycle accident. I saw it all happen. I think he might have a concussion or something," Jordan explained. "The things he's been saying don't make any sense."

She bent down and slipped off her glasses, looked into the boy's eyes. "Well, your pupils aren't dilated. Do you remember me? You were here for some stitches on your head, and judging by this new, clean bandage, it looks like you've already had them taken out." She smiled and briefly touched the first bandage, then looked confused at the much larger one behind it. "Now that's odd. I don't remember a second bandage. Your name's Miguel, isn't it? Miguel Dorning, I think."

The professor's face brightened. "That's it! Dorning. That's who I came to see. Is he here?" He looked around. "I have to tell him it worked."

The nurse looked up at Jordan with trepidation.

"See what I mean?" he said.

"Yes, I do. He's already in the computer, so we'll take care of the paperwork later. The doctor will probably want an X-ray, just as a precaution. I'll take him from here." She took command of the wheelchair and pushed the boy down the hall. She glanced back at Jordan. "You can wait right there if you want," she said.

Jordan shook his head as he backed towards the exit. "I can't. I have to go find his folks and tell them where he is. They're out looking for him. I'm sure they're worried sick."

"Okay. If I don't hear from them soon, I'll try calling. I'm sure I have his father's phone number. Thanks for bringing him in." She casually waved goodbye.

Jordan watched them go. "Poor kid. Hope he'll be all right," he said to no one in particular, and then hurried from the emergency room.

The nurse found the doctor on duty near the X-ray station. He was studying a freshly developed negative by the fluorescent lights above.

"Doctor, we have a boy here who apparently struck his head in a bicycle accident. He's not bleeding externally, but he does seem mildly incoherent. What would you like to do?"

The doctor looked down and gave the boy's head a cursory examination, still clutching the X-ray in one hand, then thrust his free hand into a pocket of his lab coat and peered more intently at the boy.

"Hey, weren't you here not too long ago for some stitches?"

"Why, I don't know," Marlowe said. "I suppose I might have been." He looked blankly around the room and shrugged.

"Yes, he was," the nurse answered for him. "The funny thing is, he has two bandages now, one right behind the other, but I'm positive I only put the first one on." She pointed accusingly at the boy's head. "I'm not sure why he has a second one."

The doctor looked unconcerned. "So? Maybe he banged his head again and his folks just slapped on another bandage, too embarrassed to bring him back here. It happens."

The doctor nodded wordlessly in the direction of the X-ray machine behind them as the nurse had thought he would, then stared back at the ghostly black and white images on the film he held.

The nurse wheeled the boy over to the table and helped him up on to it. "Now just relax and hold perfectly still. This won't hurt a bit." She gently positioned his head.

"Short wave electromagnetic radiation? I suspect not."

The nurse was taken aback, and laughed uneasily. "My, how educated you are." She moved the camera into position.

"Stars emit X-rays, you know, including our own sun. You should see how beautiful the sun looks in X-ray light. I always thought it was like seeing the Universe through the eyes of God. It's just that beautiful. It really is." His far-away gaze was one of awe. "You should see it sometime."

The nurse's thin smile disappeared. She hurried over to the doctor and spoke quietly to him.

"I think he's definitely delirious. We can't rule out possible head trauma."

The doctor finally put the film down and rubbed his eyes. "Okay. Let's get on with it."

They went together into the X-ray control booth and shut the door behind them.

The doctor rubbed his stiff neck as he groaned weakly. "Man, I hate Sunday nights at this place. We have to do everything but cook the meals and take out the trash. Too bad I told Williams I was an X-ray technician before I became a doctor. But then again, I guess that's one of the reasons why he hired me. I had added value."

He adjusted the controls then triggered the machine.

He sighed. "There. Back I go into the darkroom."

"Oh, the joys of working weekends at a small clinic in the middle of nowhere," the nurse offered. She grinned.

"I guess," the doctor wearily replied, and went to develop the film.

Chapter Fourteen

Dorning drove wordlessly, Natalie by his side. They slowly cruised down a street they had already traveled three times that night.

Natalie finally found the courage to say what she knew they were both thinking.

"Doctor, maybe we should call the police."

Dorning shook his head firmly.

"No. Not yet. I don't want the police involved if we can avoid it."

"But we've been looking for him for almost an hour."

"And we will keep looking for him until we find him."

"But what if he was..." She couldn't speak the word.

"What? Abducted? Unlikely. There's never been a stranger abduction in the Professor's neighborhood. That's much too improbable to seriously consider."

"Then where is he?"

"Lost. But he won't be once we find him. That's what we're out here trying to do."

"What if he's hurt somewhere by the side of the road?"

"Entirely possible. Or the bicycle malfunctioned and he was forced to walk home. He might even be waiting for us there right now. Let's check one more time."

He swung the car down their street.

"I should have just waited for him at home," Natalie said.

"No. I needed another pair of eyes, especially in this gloom."

Natalie wrung her hands in her lap, wishing the doctor would just call the police. As concerned as he was for the boy's well being, she couldn't understand why he didn't immediately involve the authorities.

Dorning's head suddenly swung to the left, and he hit the brakes. The car slid on the impacted gravel, sending some flying.

"What is it, Doctor? Do you see him?"

"I thought I saw something. Wait right here. I'm going to take a closer look." He got out of the car.

She ignored his demand and followed him through the tall grass to a spot near the side of the road.

In the dim moonlight, they both stared down at the mangled remains of the boy's bicycle.

Natalie put a hand to her throat. "Oh, Doctor!" she said softly. "Maybe you should never have bought him that bicycle after all."

Dorning rubbed his forehead in disbelief, ignoring the suggestion he was somehow at fault.

He carefully lifted the bike up with both hands for a closer look. "This should not have happened. Statistically, this simply should not have happened. Recreational bicycling is much safer than skateboarding or rollerblading or those scooters all the kids have nowadays. Much safer." He dropped the bike and turned completely around, scanning the area. "He must be here somewhere; help me find him. He probably would have headed straight home if he wasn't too hurt."

They searched frantically through the tall grass. Headlights appeared down the road, and a noisy pickup truck came to a stop behind Dorning's car.

"Hey!" the driver called out to them. "You aren't looking for a kid on a bike, are you?"

"Yes! Is he with you?" Dorning crashed through the grass to the vehicle and looked inside. He didn't see the boy.

"No, I took him to the medical clinic. He had an accident, but I think he's going to be all right. I see you found the bike, or what's left of it."

Natalie closed her eyes in relief, able to breathe again.

Dorning froze at the man's words. It was moment before he could respond. "You took him to a clinic? Which one, the small one outside of town?"

"That's the one."

Dorning felt his face redden. "Why, how *dare* you? Only *I* can take him to the clinic!"

The driver's expression turned dark. "Hey listen, pal. Even though he was wearing a helmet, I think he might have hit his head pretty hard, so I took him as a precaution. He was saying some pretty strange things for a kid."

Dorning paused, stunned by the news, then reached into the truck and grabbed the driver by the arm.

"What kind of things? Tell me quick."

"Geez, let go! I don't know. Crazy things about how the town has grown, and how he knew me thirty years ago, and how he hasn't used a telephone in years. All kinds of odd comments. Will you let go of me? I'm warning you." Jordan tried to pull his arm out of Dorning's solid grip.

Dorning finally let go and took a step back. The look on his face was one of surprise.

"It is my fault." He spoke to himself, too quietly to be heard. "The Professor. I don't know if he ever learned how to ride a bicycle. Why didn't I think of that before?"

He roused himself and spoke louder. "I must apologize. I was just worried about the boy."

The driver's angry expression quickly faded. "Sure. I guess it's understandable. Apology accepted. I'm Peter Jordan, by the way. I live right here. Good to meet you." He stuck his hand out for Dorning to shake. "So you're living in the Professor's old place?"

Dorning ignored the extended hand. "Sorry. No time to chitchat. I must get to the clinic right away. Natalie? Come along."

She quickly followed him to his car. They sped off into the night, leaving Jordan sitting alone in his truck.

The architect shook his head in disgust as he rubbed his arm where Dorning had grabbed him. "So that's the thanks I get. Geez, some people."

Dorning drove hunched close to the steering wheel, wondering what kind of tests the doctors were performing on the boy, and what they would think of his handiwork once they found it. He thought hard to come up with an acceptable explanation for what he had done.

The last thing he needed, he knew, was for his mistake of giving Miguel a bicycle to trigger some sort of medical investigation that would point straight to him, and reveal the experiment to the world when the world still wasn't ready to accept it.

Chapter Fifteen

The young doctor stared at the new X-ray under the fluorescent ceiling lights, his mouth hanging wide open.

He lowered the negative and rubbed his eyes. "Wait a minute."

He went over to the viewing board mounted on the wall, thrust the X-ray up into the holder and switched on the bank of lights behind the frosted white glass. They flickered to life.

He blinked at the sudden brightness. "That's better." He studied the plate closely again.

The strange pattern of holes drilled through the boy's cranium was still there.

He shook his head in disbelief. "What the hell is all this?"

The doctor glanced around the empty room, wishing for the first time since he had started working weekends in the emergency clinic there were other doctors on the graveyard shift with him so he could get their opinion.

He stepped into the hall and looked towards the nurse sitting behind the admittance desk, eager to show someone what he had found.

"Nancy?" he called. "You got a minute? I want to show you something really mysterious here."

She got up and hurried to him.

"What is it, Doctor?"

"Look what's underneath that second bandage on the boy." He pointed at the X-ray.

The nurse adjusted her glasses. "What is that? Some kind of brain surgery?"

"Yeah, but for what? I've never seen anything like it. I'm not a neurosurgeon, but this is too strange. It's just a series of small holes. It doesn't make any sense."

She peered steadily at the image. "Too bad you can't do more tests to see what it's all about."

The doctor slowly turned his head and looked at her. "I can't? Or you mean I shouldn't?"

"You shouldn't." She saw the look on his face and shrank a little. "But you are going to, aren't you? I know you too well already."

He nodded mischievously. "Do you know if he's had anything to eat in the past few hours?"

"I don't think he has. He said he was hungry."

"Good. Don't feed him. Let's put him through the PET scanner. I want a different look."

"The PET scanner? You're on thin ice, Doctor. Can't you wait until tomorrow morning and go through proper channels? If Doc Williams finds out..."

"He won't. It will be just our little secret. Go ahead and prep him with FDG. That radioisotope reveals a lot of different things about brain activity. I want to see if I can figure out what's going on here."

She hesitated. "I'm not so sure about this, Doctor. We have strict rules and regulations here you know, and..."

"I know you do. This is a very nice little clinic Williams has. But since I'm here and he's not, we're still going to do it." He turned back to study the X-ray. "Besides, body scans were all the rage not too long ago. Why shouldn't the boy have one, even if it's just his head?"

Nancy wavered a moment, debating whether to consult with the young nurse on duty on the second floor who was monitoring their few overnight patients, then realized the other nurse would know even less what to do than she did. If this were going to happen, she realized to her chagrin, it would have to be just between her and the doctor.

She finally sighed. "Yes, Doctor." And she reluctantly went to do as he instructed.

Twenty minutes later she wheeled the boy into the room where a machine composed of a sliding table poised in front of a large, upright metal ring stood waiting.

"The doctor wants to do another test. That's what the shot I gave you was for," she explained to the boy as she helped him up on the table and strapped him down. "Now, you have to hold perfectly still again as you go in." She noticed he looked worried. "There's no reason to be afraid. This machine won't hurt either, but it is going to take a while. Try to relax. It just makes a faint humming sound. Actually, it's kind of boring." She smiled pleasantly to put him at ease.

He squeezed her hand. "Have you found Dorning yet for me? It's very important."

She realized he wasn't worried about the test at all. "No. I'm...still looking."

"Good. I must talk to him as soon as possible."

"I'll...do what I can."

The nurse joined the doctor in the console booth nearby. He sat down behind the controls.

"I sure hope you know what you're doing," she said. "If you break anything, Williams is going to skin you alive. This is his pride and joy, you know. Not too many clinics have one of these things. It might be a used model, but it still cost a fortune and we just had it installed."

The doctor brought the console to life with the flip of a switch. "I know, I know. Even the big city hospital doesn't have one, as Williams loves to say. Don't worry, these things practically run themselves. I've helped do this dozens of times at least." He looked the console over with a smug expression. "Ah. Now here's exactly why I like working weekend nightshifts at places like this. With no one breathing down my neck, I get to do whatever I want." He grinned as he adjusted a series of knobs. "You know, this one only creates still images, but the newest PET scanners and the functional MRI machines can even produce movies of brain activity."

"I bet you'd love that, wouldn't you?" She watched his every move, realizing with some relief that he seemed to know what he was doing.

He rubbed his hands together. "You bet. I'm the ultimate gadget freak. I figure if we've got it, we might as well use it, or what's it doing here, right? I'm glad Williams bought this rather than a plain old CAT scanner like everybody else has. It might not be as medically useful, but it's a hell of a lot more interesting, that's for sure." He turned another set of controls; the front of the table moved smoothly into the center of the ring and stopped. "The hardest part is learning to interpret the results. It takes years of study to become an expert. I just want to see if there's anything really unusual happening in the boy's brain. My hunch is that there is." He looked at his watch and saw thirty minutes had passed since the FDG had been administered to the boy. "Well, here we go."

He turned on the radiation detectors; they began collecting a stream of data.

She shook her head in exasperation. "You're like a kid in a candy store with all this expensive equipment."

He grinned again. "No. More like a fox in a hen house when the farmer's away."

She stirred uneasily, still bothered that the clinic rules were being so blatantly ignored. "I better return to the front desk, Doctor. I'll come back when you've got something to show."

The doctor waited until the detectors shut themselves off and the images were ready to be displayed on the computer screen. He turned a knob and brought the table with the boy on it out from inside the ring.

He stepped out into the hall. "This is it, Nancy."

She left the front counter and went to unstrap the boy, then helped him back into the wheelchair.

"Now that wasn't so bad, was it?" she asked him.

"Not at all. Any sign of Dorning?" He looked past her, still anxious.

She backed away and shook her head. "Uh, no. Not yet. Wait here; I'll be right back."

She went to join the doctor in the booth again.

Just as she stepped in, a ghostly gray picture of the boy's brain came into view on the monitor. They both stared at it intently.

"Now. Let's see what we've got." He rotated the image several times.

"Looks normal enough. But take another look at this." He held the X-ray over the monitor, superimposing the image of the boy's skull over the brain image. "Look at how many almost microscopic holes were drilled into his skull. Whoever did this was very skilled. Very skilled. These holes are just millimeters apart, in perfect alignment in some sort of elaborate, symmetrical pattern." He tapped the X-ray. "Too bad I have absolutely no idea what they're for."

He rubbed his chin, studying the images again, and then took a sudden inward breath. "You know, if I didn't know any better, I'd almost say it looks like these holes were drilled so something could be injected directly into specific areas of the boy's brain. But that's absurd, isn't it?" He laughed uneasily, shaking his head at the very idea. "What would you inject, and why?"

He set the X-ray aside and used the computer mouse to slide a scale at the bottom of the screen. "I'm going to add some false color to the image and see if that reveals anything."

He froze. "Uh oh. That can't be right."

"What do you mean 'Uh oh'? Don't tell me you broke it. If Williams finds out, I'm telling you..." She shook her head firmly.

He slid the scale back to gray. The normal-looking image returned.

"No, everything's working just fine. Come on, Nancy, have some faith in me here."

He moved the scale back to false color. The image glowed brightly again.

He sat back, baffled. "This can't be."

"What can't?"

"Let me print out a few of these scans and I'll show you."

He rotated the color image several ways. Pages poured from the side of the console.

He gasped as he studied them one by one. "This is incredible, just incredible."

"What is? So tell me already, will you?"

"Look over there." He pointed at a laminated poster on the wall. "See that series of pictures? Those are transverse and coronal views of an 'average' brain in false color, whatever average is supposed to be. The scale rises from black, through purple, blue, green, yellow, orange, and finally red. Some parts of the brain are highly active, others, not so. Now, look at the boy's brain scans." He handed her the sheets.

She paged through them. "Why, they're mostly red and orange, with just a little bit of yellow here and there."

"Precisely. This kid's brain is on fire. I've never seen such an active one. This is amazing." He took them back and went through them again. "He's burning up the glucose in the FDG at an astonishing rate. Just look at the parietal, temporal and frontal lobes, the sections of the brain associated with learning and memory. In most people, they're a little green, mostly yellow, maybe a touch of red, but here they're mainly red. That doesn't seem possible, but here it is. And the odd thing is, we didn't ask him to perform some mental task to make those areas active. In him, they just are. I can't explain it."

"So what does it all mean?"

He stared at her. "I don't have a clue. But I'm willing to bet the operation he had—whatever it was—had something to do with it."

"So, are you saying it hurt the boy, or something was improper or irregular?"

He shrugged. "No. I was just curious, that's all. But it is damn peculiar." He examined the scans again. "I've never seen a brain so alive."

The nurse put her hands on her hips in renewed exasperation. "Well, did you at least determine if the boy has *any* serious problems, due to the accident he had or anything else?"

He finally looked up from the scans. "You said neither of his pupils are dilated, and he hasn't thrown up?"

"No. But I still think he's mildly delirious. He keeps asking me if his father's here, but he's calling him by his last name. It's sort of amusing."

The doctor's gaze dropped back down to the printed images. "Under normal circumstances I would say he might have a mild concussion, but based on his scans, he doesn't seem to have any mental impairment at all. In fact, just the opposite seems to be true. He must be phenomenally alert." He shrugged again, finally put the scans aside. "Well, I know it's outdated advice, but tell his parents to keep him awake for about eighteen hours just as a precaution, and he should be fine. That way they'll think they're helping somehow. We don't really have any reason to keep him."

"Well for God's sake." She rolled her eyes. "I've got to get back to work. Here I thought there was some big medical mystery, and it's just some operation you're not familiar with. If I had know that, I never would have agreed to go along with this." She turned and walked out.

"Hey, I said I wasn't a neurosurgeon." He held the X-ray up to the lights again. "My God, this looks like real Frankenstein stuff," he said quietly. "I'd sure like to know what the hell's going on."

He turned off the machine then fell back in the chair with a groan when he realized he hadn't saved any of the data. "Damn! Well, at least I have these." He stood and scooped up the printed scans and X-ray plate.

The nurse went to wheel the boy out of the room, knowing she should hurry and get back to the front desk where she was supposed to be.

"Come on, Professor. You're just fine."

He looked up at her sharply. "Why did you call me that?"

She stepped back, surprised by the intensity of his gaze. "I don't know. You were talking about electromagnetic radiation before. I guess I just thought the name fit."

"Oh. Of course." He regarded her warily then decided he should be more careful from now on about what he said, and to whom.

"I hope someone's coming to take you home soon."

"So do I. With any luck, it will be Dorning."

"Yes, of course. My thoughts exactly."

She wheeled the boy back down the hall towards the admittance desk. It was then she heard the counter buzzer sound repeatedly.

"Oh no," she moaned. She hoped whoever it was hadn't been waiting too long, and now regretted leaving the desk unattended while the doctor led her on the wild goose chase. "I'm going to put you right here for a moment," she told the boy, and parked the wheelchair. "Be right back. Don't go to sleep on me now."

She hurried to the desk, and immediately recognized the man standing there as the same one who had brought the boy in for the stitches.

"Oh thank goodness," she said. "Hello, Mister Dorning."

"Hi. A neighbor told me my son is here. He apparently fell off his bicycle. Is he going to be all right? I hope we can take him home to-night." Dorning's right eye twitched.

"Yes, he should be just fine. The doctor said he doesn't need to be admitted."

Dorning visibly relaxed.

"I just need you to sign some insurance paperwork for me, and he can go. The doctor's instructions are that—"

"—The boy be kept awake for the next eighteen hours, just to play it safe. He might have a mild concussion, but probably not," the doctor finished for her. He carried the X-ray and PET scans with him into the room, walked up to Dorning, and warily shook his hand. "Good to meet you." He stared steadily at Dorning, the handshake becoming slower and slower. "You look familiar. Have we met?"

"No, I don't think so."

The doctor squinted at the computer screen in front of the nurse. "And you are...Carl. Carl Dorning." He finally let go of Dorning's hand. "You know, for some reason even your name seems vaguely familiar. Are you sure I don't know you?"

"I'm quite sure."

"You don't work in the medical field by any chance, do you? I swear you sure look..."

"No, not at all. I'm a...computer programmer."

"Oh. I see." The doctor glanced down and tapped his fingers on the countertop. "Well, Mister Dorning, we did some tests on your son, and discovered something rather...different about him."

"You did? I thought you said he was going to be all right?"

"Yes, he should be. I was just wondering if your son had any kind of operation recently."

"Why do you ask? Is there a problem, Doctor?"

"I was hoping you could tell me. There are indications he had some sort of unusual brain surgery, one I'm completely unfamiliar with."

Dorning took a deep breath and tried to look thoughtful. "Well, you're probably unaware of this, but he's narcoleptic and doesn't respond to medication for the condition. That's why he fell and needed those stitches he had. I adopted Miguel not too long ago, and only recently managed to add him to my insurance. Believe me, because the condition was preexisting, that was quite a fight." He laughed politely. "His primary care physician said a recently developed procedure might help him, and we were fortunate enough to get in on the trials just beginning."

"A procedure? Where?"

"A hospital out of state. We've just returned, but we have to go back in a few days for a follow-up exam. Fortunately, he wasn't required to stay there. And so what does the boy do? He promptly falls off his bicycle, perhaps complicating matters. Boys will be boys, I guess." He gave a strained chuckle.

The doctor ignored Dorning's forced laughter. "Did they explain the surgery to you? I was wondering what they did exactly."

"They tried to explain it, but I don't remember the specifics. It was all dry, hard to follow, medical jargon. Rather boring stuff, I'm afraid."

The doctor dropped his gaze again. "I see. Well, that explains quite a bit, actually."

Dorning noticed the X-ray and brain scans tucked under the doctor's arm. "What are those?"

"Hmm? Oh, I took an X-ray when he arrived, then after discovering evidence of the operation, I performed a PET scan since I was very concerned about what I found. The boy's scans came out rather peculiar, but frankly, I'm no expert at reading them. Perhaps the fact he's narcoleptic and had an operation I'm unfamiliar with could explain the results. I just don't know."

Dorning was impressed. "This clinic has a PET scanner? I wouldn't think such a small facility could afford one."

The doctor grinned a genuine grin. "The clinic owner found a used one for a terrific price, and couldn't pass it up. It's our one claim to fame. Who knows? Maybe someday we'll give the Mayo clinic a run for their money."

Both men chuckled.

Dorning coughed pointedly. "But Doctor, aren't you suppose to obtain written permission from the parents or guardian of patients under the age of eighteen before performing such a medical test—particularly one involving nuclear material—no matter how slight the risk? At least, that's what I thought." Dorning's expression was oddly blank, despite the seriousness of the question.

The young doctor drew back in apprehension, not answering right away. "Well, technically, yes, that's correct. But given the potential seriousness of his head injury, I felt it couldn't wait for your permission, despite the regulations. I hope you can understand." It was now his turn to twitch. "I mean, you're not officially complaining, are you?"

Dorning's apathetic, nearly bored expression remained. "No, of course not. Your explanation makes perfect sense. Only a fool slavishly follows the rules." He had a sudden realization, and feigned a slight interest in what the doctor was holding. "Can I see those, if you don't mind? Just out of curiosity."

"Well, sure you can. Here you go." He immediately handed them all to Dorning, relieved to be exonerated so easily.

Dorning ignored the X-ray and studied the scans instead. His excitement grew. "Remarkable. Absolutely remarkable. Why, the entire cerebral cortex is positively..." He caught himself and shot a glance at the doctor.

The doctor stared back at him. "Yes, the entire cerebral cortex is highly active, unusually so. Apparently you know a lot more about PET scans than most people do, Mister Dorning."

Dorning stiffened. "Well, they did perform other scans like this on him, just prior to his operation. That's why I knew the regulations. I do remember some of the things the doctors explained to me, if not everything."

"Were those scan results similar to these?"

"No, they showed depressed activity, which they said is typical of narcoleptics. This looks better. Much better."

The doctor nodded. "That makes sense, I suppose. And I would imagine if this experimental procedure turns out to be a cure for narcolepsy, it would be tremendous news."

"They didn't use the word cure, Doctor. They said it might help." Dorning set the X-ray and scans down away from the doctor, purposefully ignoring them. "Can I see my son now? It's getting late and I'd really like to take him home."

The doctor turned to the nurse, who was still busy on the computer. "Are you almost done, Nancy?"

"Almost," she said cheerfully. "I'll go get him just as soon as I'm finished. You'll have to sign a few papers for me, Mister Dorning. They'll be ready in a moment. And I have some patient instructions for you as well, so you can do some neuro checks on your son to make sure he's all right."

The doctor had an idea. "I'll get the boy, Nancy. You stay right here with Mister Dorning."

Dorning stiffened again, then watched the doctor hurry back down the hall.

He tried not to stare at the unguarded X-ray and scans. "If you'll excuse me, I have to run out to my car for a moment." he said. "I'll be right back."

The nurse didn't take her eyes off the printer as it clattered out a long form. "That's fine, Mister Dorning. Take your time."

As he turned to walk away, he quietly scooped the X-ray and scans off the countertop and hid them in front of him as he hurried to his car.

Natalie looked at him anxiously, still wishing he had let her come inside.

"Is Miguel all right?"

"Yes, he's fine, but the inexperienced, young doctor on duty thinks he knows more than he really does. He's asking far too many questions. Here." He gave her the X-ray and the scans. "Hold on to these for me. Put them under the front seat. The doctor was kind enough to do some valuable tests. I might find these useful. I should be back with Miguel in just a few minutes if all goes well."

Dorning returned to the admittance desk to wait for the papers to sign, glancing with suspicion down the hallway where the doctor had disappeared.

❧❧

The doctor walked up to the boy, smiling as he pulled up an empty wheelchair to sit down in front of him.

"Your father's here to take you home pretty soon," he said.

Marlowe didn't flinch.

"My father. Good."

"I just had an interesting conversation with him. He told me all about your operation, the one on your head."

The professor blinked twice. "He did?"

"Yes. It sounded fascinating, since it's still experimental. What can you tell me about it, Miguel? I'm curious."

He hesitated. "Not too much. When I woke up, it was over."

"Do you feel it helped your problem?"

Marlowe cleared his throat. "Yes. Yes it did."

"And, what was that problem again?"

"I...don't remember the name for it."

"Well, what was wrong with you?"

"I'd...rather not talk about it. I'm sure my father told you all he wanted you to know."

The doctor nodded slowly. "Yes, I guess he did. I was just concerned about what was happening to you Miguel, that's all. I've never seen such an unusual operation before. It just looks, well, very, very strange." He laughed uneasily as he stared at the large bandage on the boy's head. "And for some reason, I had the feeling your dad wasn't telling me the whole truth about it. How about you, Miguel? Are you telling me the truth?"

The professor raised his head, his gaze clear and strong. "Yes. Yes I am."

The doctor hesitated, and then stood up and patted the boy's shoulder. "All right. Never mind. Come on, you're going home."

He wheeled the boy back down the hall.

"Here he is, Mister Dorning." The doctor's smile was artificial.

Dorning hastily finished signing the long insurance forms. "Son! How are you feeling?"

"Just fine...Dad."

The nurse took the wheelchair from the doctor, who was reluctant to let go of the handles. She wheeled the boy through the automatic glass doors to Dorning's waiting car.

The doctor followed them into the cool, cloudy night.

Natalie got out of the car and opened the rear door for the boy.

His face brightened immediately when he saw her. "Natalie!"

She gently patted his shoulder. "I'm so glad you're okay," she said, and buckled him in before returning to her own seat.

Dorning faced the doctor. "Thank you for your concern about my son."

"You're quite welcome. I hope the experimental operation the boy had turns out to be a success."

"Me too, Doctor. Believe me, me too."

They briefly shook hands once more.

Dorning hurried to the car, and got behind the wheel with a farewell wave to the nurse. He started the engine and sped away from the emergency room entrance.

The doctor and nurse watched them go. A light rain began to fall. In the distance, lightning flashed and thunder followed slowly.

"I don't know, Nancy. Why do I feel so uneasy about letting that boy go?"

"You can't keep him here if there's no medical reason to."

He followed her back inside. "I know, but I almost wish there was. Maybe I should have made something up. Hey!" The doctor grabbed the countertop and looked around. "Where's the X-ray? Where are the printouts? Don't tell me the boy's father took them?"

"He probably thought you were giving them to him when you let him see them."

The doctor groaned. "Well great. That's just great. What's his phone number? I'm going to call and leave him a message to bring them back." He picked up the phone behind the counter, anxious to start dialing.

"Are you sure you want to do that? If Williams sees those scans, he'll read you the riot act for not following procedures. And probably me too." She stared at him with brief resentment.

The doctor ran a hand through his hair, paused, and then hung up the phone. "Well, maybe you're right. But I would like to get that X-ray back. Maybe if Williams saw it, he'd insist on doing his own scan of the boy's head."

The nurse laughed once. "So the boy can tell him you already ran him through the machine? What are you going to say then, Doctor? You're probably lucky his father took everything. If I were you, I'd just let it go. And please, follow the rules and regulations from now on, okay? Just because you're willing to come in here and work a shift nobody else wants, that doesn't make you indispensable. I like you, Doctor, but if you ever do anything like this again, you'll leave me no choice but to report you." She gave him an even sterner look then her expression softened. "Besides, I thought his father was very nice man. He seemed very sincere to me. You know, not too many people are willing to adopt an older child with a serious medical problem. It takes a very special person to do that."

The doctor sighed, and then stuck his hands in the pockets of his lab coat in defeat. "I suppose you're right. It's just that I had the strangest feeling that Dorning and his son didn't want to tell me the truth. I'm convinced they were hiding something." He stared out the window to where Dorning's car had been just a few minutes earlier. "What the hell was that bizarre operation all about? I'm not sure I believe the whole story about narcolepsy and a new procedure. You know what? I should have asked Dorning for the name of that out of state hospital, that's what I should have done. Then I could have called them to verify his story. And why did Dorning look so familiar? I swear I've seen him before, or maybe his picture somewhere."

The rain fell harder, and the lightning and thunder grew more intense.

The nurse let out an exaggerated sigh. "I guess we'll never know, Doctor. We'll just never know."

꧁꧂

Marlowe sat quietly in the back of the Mercedes as it sped home, the rain drumming furiously on the car roof. Each flash of lightning illuminated the interior and his fierce, steady gaze.

He raised his hands until they were just inches from his face, then turned them over and flexed his small, limber fingers, still fascinated by them.

"Astonishing," he said. "Simply astonishing."

Dorning glanced at the professor in the rearview mirror. "I can't tell you how good it is to see you again," he said. "I've been waiting for this."

"It's good to see you again, too, Doctor," the professor said.

Natalie turned around as far as she could to look at the boy. "All I can say is, thank goodness you're not seriously hurt this time, Miguel. You really are accident prone, aren't you? I guess I'll have to watch you a lot closer from now on."

Marlowe and Dorning looked at each other in the mirror, sharing a secret grin as lightning cracked all around.

Chapter Sixteen

Dorning burst into the room, carrying a tray full of food. "Good morning, Percival," he said brightly. "I made your favorite breakfast in celebration of your return. Scrambled eggs with pepper, fried ham, black coffee, unbuttered toast. See? I remembered. " He laughed lightly as he set the tray near the side of the bed. "Sorry to wake you so early, but I could hardly sleep last night. I told Natalie I'd give you your breakfast so we can talk in private. I only have about a million questions." He pulled up a chair next to the bed and the figure stirring in it, and then opened the notebook tucked under his arm and uncapped his pen.

Miguel looked at the clock on the nightstand. It was six a.m.

He sat up abruptly. "Wait a minute. What happened yesterday? Did I have an accident? Is my bike okay?" He looked at the breakfast tray, then back at Dorning. "Hey, did you just call me Percival again?"

Dorning's bright expression faded. "You mean you're not?"

"No."

"You were last night."

He took a sharp breath, went wide-eyed. "I was?"

Dorning slowly nodded.

"You mean it's really starting to work?"

"Yes, but apparently you've reverted back this morning." He looked away, clearly disappointed. "I suppose I should have anticipated the possibility. It could take a while for the implanted memories to fully assert themselves." He considered the boy with renewed interest. "Not to worry. I'm sure the Professor will return. In the meantime, why don't you tell me how you felt yesterday? It could be nearly as interesting to record your impressions of the events." He sat with pen poised over a blank notebook page.

"My impressions?"

"Yes. How did you feel as the Professor came back? What did you think?"

Miguel pulled his pillow into his lap as he tried to remember. "All I know is I was riding my bike fast, trying to get home before it got dark, when I must have hit something, because when I looked up, my bike was gone and some man was talking to me in the grass. He brought me home to tell you he thought you should take me to a doctor because I might have been hurt. But when I got to the front door...when I got to the front door..."

Dorning finished his furious writing, and then looked up at the boy for more to write. "Yes? What happened when you got to the door?"

"I don't remember. It was like I was just, I don't know...gone, I guess."

"Huh," Dorning said, and wrote down the boy's remark. "And when were you aware you were yourself again?"

"When you woke me up just now."

"You mean you have no memory whatsoever of the time in between, when the Professor was in control?"

Miguel shook his head.

Dorning tapped his chin with the pen. "Hmm. I would have at least expected some vague or confusing memories during the transition period if not the domination phase, but apparently that's not the case. The transition is apparently quite abrupt. Interesting." He finished writing and closed the notebook, no longer looking dejected. "Well! I'm glad you did come back. Your remarks add a great deal to my research."

The boy was silent a moment, his eyes wide again. "So...that's it? That's how it's going to be?"

"What do you mean? I don't understand." He set the notebook and pen aside.

"I mean, every time the Professor takes over my body, I'm just going to be gone? Like I don't even exist anymore, like I'm...dead?"

Dorning looked alarmed. "Dead? Hopefully you won't be dead. The Professor would be dead too. You're in this together now, you know."

"But what happens to me?"

"I'm afraid I still don't follow you."

"What about my own future?"

Dorning snorted in disdain. "Your future? What future did you have being homeless and uneducated? Chances are you wouldn't have lived to see middle age. The Professor's future will be a wonderful future for anyone. Consider yourself fortunate."

Miguel felt the corners of his mouth begin to tremble, but was powerless to hide it. "I want my own future, not the Professor's. I don't want to be gone like that. I want to live."

Dorning looked thoughtful. "Well, if it's any consolation, I suspect it's possible your personality will reemerge briefly on occasion, at least until the professor's memories are fully integrated. Your memories aren't gone forever yet, just subjugated. At least, that's the indication I have from my animal tests, but frankly it's only conjecture. We'll find out soon enough, I suppose."

"What does that mean? That the Professor and I will share my body back and forth?"

"At first, yes, to a small degree. But eventually the Professor will be the primary consciousness as long as we keep his memory associations strong, which we will." Dorning looked puzzled. "Why are you asking me these questions at this late date? I'm sure I made all this perfectly clear to you when you agreed to participate."

Miguel crawled to the edge to the bed, still trembling. "No, you didn't, or if you did, I didn't understand. I thought it was just going to make me smart like the Professor, and I would remember some of his old memories."

"In a way, that's exactly true."

The boy pounded his pillow. "But it's not! It's not! I don't remember anything about last night! I don't want to live like that!" He sobbed, wiping his eyes with the backs of his hands. "I would rather die. I would. Can't you at least make it so the Professor and I share my body? Can't you? Please?"

Dorning saw the boy's agitated state and considered the ramifications of his threat.

His voice took on a reassuring tone. "Very well, if that's what you wish. You and the Professor can share. I will plan another operation for you to make that possible."

The boy looked skeptical. "You can really do that? Are you sure?"

"Oh absolutely. It's actually quite easy. I'd prefer not to, but if you insist, I will."

"When?"

"Soon. Very soon, all right? I promise. I just need some time to prepare the lab, that's all."

The boy sat back and calmed down. "Okay. You're not kidding me now, are you?"

"No, of course not." Dorning kept his perfect poker face. "I would never mislead you about something like that."

Miguel nodded in relief, then decided to make one more demand, encouraged by his apparent victory. "Okay. And another thing. I want to go see my mother again. I haven't seen her in weeks."

"I'm sorry, Miguel. I'm afraid that request is totally out of the question. But I will do this—I'll make absolutely sure she knows where you are, and that you're safe, and I'll even provide for her financially until she's able to provide for herself. How's that?"

The boy thought the offer through. "Okay. But I would still rather see her myself."

"And someday you most certainly will, once things have settled down a bit. It won't be too much longer, I promise." Dorning waved a hand, anxious to change the subject. "Say, why don't you eat now? We can't let all this good food go to waste. Besides, you must be getting hungry."

The boy sniffed, wiping his eyes one more time. "Yeah, I am." He picked up the fork from the tray and looked down at the food. "So, this is what the Professor used to eat?" He made a sour face.

"Yes. It was his favorite breakfast, but unfortunately it was a bit too spicy for his delicate digestion as he grew older. I know he missed it, so I thought it would be a pleasant surprise."

The boy looked sad then took a bite of the eggs. His sour face returned. "Guess I better get used to it."

Dorning got up to leave. He smiled cordially as he backed away towards the door. "See? Things aren't so bad. I think all we really need is a just little time to adjust to all these changes, Miguel. Just give it some time, and I'm sure you'll agree everything has worked out fine."

He left the boy to the professor's meal, relieved by the knowledge there shouldn't be too many more relapses back to Miguel. And when they did occur again, his fervent hope was they would be brief.

Chapter Seventeen

Miguel lifted his baseball cap, scratched his fuzzy scalp where the bandages used to be, and then put the cap back on.

Dorning noticed the boy's actions. "Does it itch?" he asked.

"A little."

Dorning laid his head back down on the beach blanket in the shade of an outcropping of rocks. "That will go away soon."

Miguel sat on top of the rocks, surveying the ocean. He watched in amusement as a few seagulls wrestled over a small fish washed ashore.

"I really like it out here," he said

"Well, since you can't bicycle anymore, I thought this would be all right as long as you were supervised. I would rather have you watch TV or play video games though, like most boys your age."

Miguel shook his head. "I never liked video games much. Probably because I didn't grow up with them. I like being outside better."

"That's certainly healthier for you."

Miguel looked down at Dorning, laughing silently to himself at the doctor's girth and the baggy plaid swimsuit that couldn't quite disguise it.

"You should get outside more often yourself."

Dorning patted his flabby stomach. "Yes. Well, if you're implying I'm horribly out of shape, I've had no time for regular exercise, I'm afraid. I've been much too busy."

Miguel saw the biggest seagull had won the fight for the fish, and was flying away with it.

"Aren't you worried that the Professor hasn't reappeared in a while?"

"Somewhat. Not too much."

"I'm not." The boy laid down on his stomach, his head and arms dangling over the edge of the rock, and spoke straight down to the doctor. "When am I going to get that operation you promised so the Professor doesn't take over completely when he does return?"

Dorning stirred uneasily, trying not to show it. "Well, since the Professor hasn't made a recent reappearance, I guess it's much less of a priority now, isn't it?"

"Just don't take forever, that's all. I don't want it to end up too late."

"No, no, of course not." Dorning sat up and stretched.

"I was thinking of something else, too...if you promise you won't get mad."

Dorning looked up at the boy. "All right. I promise," he said. "What is it?"

"Well, are you sure you talked to my mother and told her I'm okay? I mean, she does worry about me if I don't see her once in a while. And did you really give her some money like you promised you would?" Miguel looked hopeful. "She could sure use some since she doesn't have a job."

Dorning's piercing gaze was unflinching. "Oh, absolutely. She now has enough money for all her immediate needs. And she said to tell you she loves you very much, and she completely understands why you can't see her just yet. You should try to accept that too, Miguel. Your mother has."

The boy's hopeful expression turned sad. "Well, okay." His face brightened again. "If I can't visit my mother, can I at least go see my old friends?"

Dorning was puzzled by the request and frowned in disapproval. "Those hooligans? Why on Earth would you want to go back to that wretched part of town?"

"I don't know. I guess I kind of miss them. I'd just like to see what they're up to."

"They're undoubtedly up to no good. I can tell you that right now. Don't forget they refused to go with you to the emergency room when you banged your head on my car. I wouldn't consider anyone like that a very good friend. They were only concerned about themselves."

Miguel sad expression returned, but he said nothing.

"Why don't you just enjoy this beautiful day we're having, and stop dwelling on the past?"

The boy scrambled down from the rocks. "Okay. Can I go into the water up to my waist?"

Dorning looked at the rolling waves and saw the ocean wasn't too active. "You may go in, but just up to your knees, no further. I'll be watching."

"Deal."

Miguel ran the short distance into the retreating surf.

Dorning sighed, still wishing the boy wasn't so fascinated with the water.

A wave rushed over his legs and the boy laughed. "Come on, Doctor, you should try it. The water's not too cold."

Dorning slowly shook his head. "No thank you. I never cared much for aquatics."

A stronger wave struck the boy from behind, first pushing him forward, then dragging him back a few steps as it withdrew. The water surged around the boy's waist.

"Be careful now," Dorning chided him. "You're getting in a little too deep."

"I'm all right. I think."

A towering wave suddenly reared up behind the boy and rushed towards him.

Dorning scrambled to his feet. "Look out!"

The wave swept Miguel's hat off and knocked his legs out from under him, then pulled back, taking him with it. His arms flailed in the air, his head barely visible.

"Help...me!" The words were sputtered, and then Miguel was gone.

Dorning charged into the churning water.

"Percival? Professor!"

There was no answer, and no Miguel.

Then further out, Dorning saw the boy's head briefly reemerge and spit a fountain of water like a whale.

The doctor launched himself forward in a belly flop, paddling as best he could until he was able to reach out and grab Miguel by the leg.

"You mean you can't swim at all?" Dorning asked.

A wave poured over the doctor's head, leaving him hacking.

"No. Can you?"

"No," Dorning gasped.

He put his hands under Miguel's arms and threw him as hard as he could towards the shore. "Try," he ordered, and slipped under the water.

A wave lifted the boy up, speeding him toward the beach. Miguel kicked until his feet touched bottom in the shallower water, where he found a foothold. He fought to walk, the water dragging heavy against his legs, until the wave pulled back and he made it safely to the shore, breathless but unscathed.

He immediately turned around and scanned the water for the doctor.

For a moment, all he could see was the frightening, empty surface of the ocean, rocking up and down.

Then he saw the doctor burst up halfway out of a swell, as if thrown. Dorning splashed down on his back, crying out to him before disappearing once more.

"Save yourself, Professor!"

The boy stood wide-eyed in disbelief, arms outstretched as if to command the doctor to come forward. Then his arms began to droop, and his head sank to his chest. His eyelids fluttered.

When his head rose moments later, he pinpointed Dorning still flailing helplessly, further yet from shore.

Marlowe gasped in astonishment at the sight and took a step forward. "Dorning? Is that you? What the devil are you trying to do, you idiot? You don't know how to swim."

He ran and knifed cleanly into the water, swimming with fast, precise, well-practiced strokes to where Dorning bobbed up and down, his arms only infrequently rising to signal help.

When he arrived, Dorning had rolled on to his stomach. Marlowe turned him over on his back again. The doctor coughed and gulped.

"First of all, Dorning, stay on your back. And second, stop thrashing about, will you? That doesn't help matters at all."

Dorning opened his eyes.

"Percival?" he wheezed.

"Yes, yes. Who else would save you? Now keep your head above water and I'll get us home."

The professor wrapped his right arm around Dorning to tow him to shore.

"Good thing fat floats, Dorning, or you'd be in big trouble."

"Yes, Professor."

Marlowe propelled them to shallow water. "Try to stand up. I don't want to scrape your back on the jagged bottom."

Dorning slowly rose to his feet in the knee-high water, standing bent over a few seconds, his hands on his thighs.

"That's a good boy, Doctor. Now let's have a nice walk together up the beach, shall we?'

The professor guided Dorning ashore. The doctor staggered to the empty beach blanket and sat down heavily in the shade, his legs drawn up to his chest, his head on his knees.

He caught his breath before speaking. "It's good you have you back again, Professor. I sincerely hope you don't intend to leave anytime soon."

Marlowe looked surprised. "I was gone somewhere?"

Dorning raised his head and smiled weakly. "Yes. Tell me something, Percival. What time do you think it is?"

The professor looked to the sky, shielding his eyes from the sun. "It seems to be about midday. Why do you ask?"

"Do you remember anything at all about this morning?"

Marlowe looked thoughtful. "That's odd. No, I don't."

"What do you remember last?"

His thoughtful expression remained. "I remember coming home from the clinic with you and Natalie, then going to bed in my own room. That was Sunday night if I'm not mistaken."

"So you think today must be Monday, correct?"

"Yes, I do."

Dorning slowly shook his head, his weak smile remaining. "You're wrong, Professor. Today is Wednesday. You reverted back to the boy three days ago. But I knew you'd return. It was only a matter of time."

Marlowe sank down to the sand in front of Dorning.

"Wednesday! Incredible. I remember absolutely nothing about

those missing days." He glanced behind him at the rolling waves. "But I apparently picked a good time to make my grand reappearance. Lucky for you."

Dorning stared at the ocean. "Yes, indeed. This certainly isn't how I planned it, but I would say the shock of nearly seeing me drown was enough to trigger the swimmer in you. It brought you back to us."

"Well, I was the best one in school." He looked down at his lithe frame. "And I guess I'm a good one again, aren't I? So, what were you doing out there, Dorning? I don't understand."

"I was trying to save you. I mean, the boy. He was inadvertently pulled in by the surf."

"You mean he can't swim either?"

"No. It was foolish of me to let him go in the water at all. It almost cost you your life, precisely what I worked so hard for so many years to save."

"Not to mention nearly costing you your own life, Doctor."

Dorning grunted. "Yours is far more important than mine, Professor. Let's not kid ourselves."

Marlowe looked dismayed at Dorning's comment. "Your life is every bit as important as mine, Doctor. Why, without you, I wouldn't even be here. Your achievement is truly extraordinary, one for the history books."

Dorning waved a hand. "Yes, at least until the do-gooders discover how I...well, never mind." He stood, picked the blanket up off the sand and gave it a shake. "Let's just go home. I think I've had enough of the ocean for one day. I need something to drink."

The professor got up and followed him. "If that would be a glass of sherry, I'll join you."

Dorning stopped and looked down at him. "Sorry, Professor. I don't believe you're old enough to drink. I could lose my liquor license." He grinned.

Marlowe's eyebrows went up. "My God, I hadn't thought of that. I guess there're all kinds of age related issues for me to consider, aren't there?

"Yes, but they're all meaningless."

The professor stroked his chin thoughtfully as they resumed walking. "Hmm. Try telling that to the women I used to know."

Dorning gasped. "Why, Percival!"

Marlowe laughed. "I'm only joking, Doctor. Don't be so strait-laced. I'll tell you one thing, though. When I go through puberty again, this time I'll get it right. I look forward to the next few years, Dorning. I most certainly do."

"It's not just a few years, Professor. You have an entire new lifetime now, thanks to the boy."

Percival's eyebrows went up again, but this time the eyes beneath them held a hint of misgiving and concern.

Chapter Eighteen

"I still don't understand why we're visiting the University," Marlowe said. "Why, I haven't been there in at least fifteen years. Everyone I knew is either dead or retired."

An elderly woman in the front of the nearly empty bus glanced back at Dorning and the boy quizzically, but said nothing.

"Percival," Dorning warned softly.

"Yes, yes. I know," he replied. "Afraid I'm having a little trouble remembering my thoughts no longer match my new, abbreviated appearance. Please bear with me, Dorning. Eventually I'll learn to keep my mouth shut until I look old enough to know what I'm talking about."

"Good. We don't want the wrong people asking questions, now do we? I really wouldn't want you to gain notoriety as some kind of 'boy wonder.' We've agreed you'll simply continue your work in private until some future date when people are finally ready to accept who you really are. Then you can say whatever you wish in public. But until that time..."

"I know, I know," the professor cut him off. "That was our agreement. I'll abide by it, really I will. I don't want to be viewed as some kind of sideshow freak either."

The bus gave a tired hiss as it came to a stop in front of the soaring stone arch framing the entrance to the old campus.

Dorning and Marlowe got off and waited with the rest of the passengers for their luggage. Dorning accepted his large suitcase, and the professor his small one.

The professor hefted his suitcase, and found it easily within his diminished means. "Well, well. Small clothes, light suitcase. I like it. Now, where did you say we were staying?" He looked towards the campus with sudden interest as he walked under the arch with Dorning.

"I didn't. I wanted it to be a pleasant surprise. You'll be delighted to hear that I've managed to arrange a stay in your former graduate apartment for the night."

Marlowe stopped, then threw back his head and laughed. "Oh no! Not that dilapidated old rat-hole? I thought I had escaped that place forever!"

The professor walked along with a bounce to his step now, still laughing softly to himself, the suitcase swinging merrily beside him. "See that?'" he pointed to a squat, one-story brick building, its limestone trim black from decades of soot and rain. "That was the first building on campus. I was one of the last ones to have a class in there, before it became the University archives. When I started as a freshman, half these buildings weren't even here." He swung his head around and came to an abrupt halt. "Oh my God." He dropped the suitcase. "The tree!" He ran off the sidewalk, across the lawn towards a towering oak between two newer buildings.

Dorning picked up the abandoned suitcase and followed him into the shade under the long, high limbs.

"What is it, Professor?"

"It's our tree, the class tree. We donated it to the University when I graduated. It was just a sapling. I helped plant it."

Dorning craned his head back to look up at the tall, soaring branches. "No offense Percival, but you *are* old, aren't you?"

Marlowe smiled. "Yes. And you know what? I might actually outlive the class gift. I would have never even considered that possibility before." He glanced down at himself. "But now look at me, full of youth and vigor once more." The professor turned to Dorning. "I might still have some misgivings about what we've done to that poor boy, but it's wonderful to have a second chance, Doctor." He gazed up at the tree. A breeze made the leaves rustle softly in unison. "Just wonderful." He ran a hand over his head, feeling the short, uniform length of his hair. "Thank you."

Dorning grinned wryly. "Professor, it was my honor to give you that second chance. The world will benefit greatly from all the scientific contributions you'll undoubtedly make. But for now, let's go find that apartment of yours. Your suitcase is light, but I'm afraid mine is getting quite heavy." He headed back towards the sidewalk.

Percival looked up one last time at the tree. *Thank you, too, Miguel,* he thought. *Sorry you can't enjoy the moment with me. Or are you?*

The only answer was the tranquil sound of the leaves in the mild wind.

He turned and hurried to catch up with Dorning, who was trudging purposefully down the sidewalk. "Now just a moment, Doctor. How can your suitcase be getting heavier if you're not adding mass to it? That flies in the face of the laws of physics, you know."

Dorning laughed. "Oh, Percival, you know exactly what I meant." He paused, looked down at the professor. "It's so very good to have you back, to be able to talk to you again like this, you know. I hope I haven't failed to make that clear."

"No, you haven't failed me at all, Doctor. In fact, you've done more for me than anyone could have ever imagined."

Dorning nodded once. "Thank you. But really, the pleasure was all mine. All mine. Now, where's that apartment?" He pulled a folded college map out of his shirt pocket to get his bearings, squinting at it under the noonday sun.

The professor laughed lightly. "Forget the map, Doctor. Just follow me."

They made their way past the library with its dozen Romanesque front pillars, and the chapel with its twin bell towers, to a plain woodsided building tucked away at the edge of the campus. Behind it was the silvery dome of the University observatory.

Percival stopped and grinned at the dome. "Well, what do you know. It's still there. You have no idea how many hours I spent glued to the eyepiece of that turn-of-the-century Clark refractor, freezing my ass off in the winter."

"Sounds perfectly dreadful."

The professor stared happily at the observatory. "No. Those are some of my fondest memories of this place." He turned his attention to the apartment building, and his grin disappeared "Well, for God's sake, they're still painting it that same awful salmon color."

Together they went inside. Dorning reached into his shirt pocket again for another piece of paper.

"Don't bother," Marlowe said. "It's apartment number six upstairs. This way." He took the stairs two at a time.

Dorning followed, still carrying both suitcases. He set the suitcases down in front of the door where the professor waited anxiously.

"Better let me do the talking since I made the arrangements. And by the way, don't believe everything I'm about to say."

"Understood."

Dorning knocked on the door.

Seconds later it flew open, revealing a skinny, shirtless college student with a toothbrush stuck in his mouth. "Ah!" He removed the brush. "You must be Doctor Dorning. And you must be Percival Marlowe's nephew. Good to have both of you here." He stepped aside to let them in.

"Pleased to meet you." Dorning picked up the suitcases and carried them inside.

The professor followed slowly, gazing quietly at everything in view.

The student noticed the boy's interest.

"Sorry about the apartment. I guess it's kind of a dump." He resumed brushing his teeth.

Percival peered into the familiar kitchen, seeing it had hardly changed. Even the old-fashioned gas stove was familiar. "I know," he said.

The student removed the brush again and laughed. "You know? How could you know? Is it that obvious? Hey, we try to keep a clean place, but it's hard what with studying and all." He went back to vigorous brushing, clearly amused by the boy's remark.

Dorning secretly tapped the professor on the shoulder to warn him.

Percival realized his mistake and put a finger to his lips to signal he would be silent.

The student tossed the toothbrush aside, grabbed a t-shirt from the dining room table and pulled it on. "Glad you showed up on time. I don't have any classes tomorrow, so I'm getting an early start on the weekend and cutting out. I'll give you my keys; you can leave them with the apartment director. He lives in apartment one."

The professor nodded, but said nothing.

"Good. Thank you so much for allowing us to stay in your place tonight."

"Not a problem, especially since I don't own anything worth stealing." He laughed, and then looked serious. "Besides, anything for the nephew of Percival Marlowe. He was a great, great man, wasn't he? I'm glad you wanted to see where your uncle lived when he went to school. You know, this may sound crazy, but ever since he died, sometimes it's like I can almost feel his presence here late at night, like he's come back for some mysterious reason." The student's hands went up and his eyes grew slightly misty, as if he could see the apparition now.

"Really?" Dorning replied dryly. "That does sound crazy."

The student dropped his arms, and his acne-scarred face turned slightly red. "Oh. Sorry." He looked apologetically at the boy. "Didn't mean to scare you or anything. Anyway, here's my keys. I better get going. There's food in the fridge if you're hungry."

"Thank you. We'll compensate you for it."

"That's okay. It's my roommate's. Enjoy your stay. See you later sometime."

The student hurried from the apartment.

Dorning grunted as he closed the door. "Percival Marlowe's ghost," he said scornfully.

The professor grinned. "Here I am. Boo." He mimicked the student's expression.

Dorning laughed. "If he only knew the truth, eh? Now *that* would scare him."

Marlowe's grin faded.

"Why are we here, Dorning? You said something about renewing old ties, but I was quite serious on the bus. There's literally no one left here that I know."

"I didn't mean ties with people you used to know, Percival. I meant ties with the University. I thought coming here from time to time might assist you in obtaining a scholarship someday."

"Isn't it a little early for me to consider where I'll go to college? And why this particular university? I know it's my alma mater, but is there another reason I should be aware of?"

Dorning nodded reluctantly. "Yes, there is. Let's sit down, now we can talk in private."

They went to the living room and sat across from one another.

"Are you hungry?" Dorning asked. "I could see what there is to eat."

"No. I would just like an explanation for this field trip we're on."

Dorning took a deep breath, folding his hands as if in prayer. "I want you to remember being the Professor, to have as many old memories triggered as possible as soon as possible. I thought this would be an excellent place to start."

"Does this have anything to do with ensuring I remain the Professor?"

"Yes. My experiments with...uh...my other test subjects..."

"You mean your animal experiments—the mice, the guinea pigs, the primates you were able to procure."

"Yes. My tests with animals showed there were far fewer relapses back to the recipient when the environment was familiar to the subject whose memories were implanted. For example, if the test subject had learned a maze, and then those memories were transplanted, by putting the recipient in the same maze, the subject's memories were restored sooner, with fewer, shorter relapses than test subjects not exposed to familiar surroundings."

Marlowe nodded. "And so here I am, running us through the maze of the sprawling campus like an obedient, well-trained rat so I won't have a relapse. How very thoughtful of you." His humorless gaze was unyielding.

Dorning shrank a bit, his hands still folded. "I do not equate you with the mice, Professor. You know very well many medical procedures are first tested on animals before human trials begin."

"Yes, that's true, Doctor. But I'm afraid that doesn't prevent me from feeling like one of those test animals, particularly since I'm the first and perhaps the last person to ever undergo your procedure." He rapped his knuckles on the coffee table between them. "So, is that it? You want me to take in the sights, reminisce about old times? I can do that. Is there anything else I should know about?"

Dorning hesitated. "Yes. You should probably be aware I had a little problem with the boy."

The professor's mouth fell open. "Problem? What kind of problem? Not medical, I hope. I've already had more than my share of those."

"No, no. You're in excellent health. The boy was just reluctant to allow you to have—shall we say—full-time access. He was apparently unhappy his own memories and personality will eventually be supplanted by yours, and demanded I create some kind of impossible time-share arrangement, if you can imagine that," he scoffed lightly. "I told him from the very beginning what was involved and he willingly went along with our plans. I didn't understand his objection considering I'm sure I went through great pains to explain his role in the procedure."

Marlowe's expression turned mournful. "How could you expect the boy to really understand, Dorning? He was just a boy. How many adults would have really understood the sacrifice you were expecting? Being told what would happen, and then actually experiencing it, can be two very different things." He stared past Dorning, his gaze now anxious. "I wish I *could* do a time-share with him. He basically gave up his chance to have his own future so I could continue mine. When I realized you had somehow managed to perfect your technique, I tried to tell him I was sorry. Now I wish I had had the courage to tell him to run away just as fast as he could."

The professor suddenly looked puzzled as he focused his attention on Dorning again. "You know, you never did explain to me how you overcame what seemed like an insurmountable problem with your technique. What did you do at the end there to finally achieve complete memory transfer instead of partial, which is what I thought would happen? Your results are nothing short of phenomenal, Doctor. If you were willing to publish them, you would easily win the Nobel Prize for medicine. You could be a giant, like I was."

"And will be again," Dorning added cheerfully. Then his optimistic expression faded. "I'm afraid I can't publish my research just yet. Remember, we're trying to keep you under wraps for a while, until people are ready to accept the wisdom of what we've done. In the meantime, my research will continue. There are still some difficult issues that...need to be addressed. Then I'll publish."

Marlowe shrugged then looked anxious again. "All that doesn't help the boy much, does it? I'm glad to be alive, but some people would argue the cost was too high, and it would be very hard to argue they were wrong."

"Nonsense," Dorning replied. "As I've said before, there are any number of people who would have volunteered to do exactly what the boy did so you can continue your invaluable research." He proudly held up an index finger. "After all, there's only one Percival Marlowe in the world."

Percival eyed him coolly. "And there was only one Miguel," he replied.

Isn't that right, Miguel? he thought defiantly.

But his only answer was the doctor's indifferent gaze.

Chapter Nineteen

"So, why don't you show me the sights, Professor, since these are your old digs?"

They strolled together away from the apartment, towards the heart of the campus. The morning air was cool and still and the sky cloudless, making the campus look like a picture postcard.

Percival pointed to a limestone building that framed the west side of the center quadrangle. "There's the old science building where I had most of my physics and astronomy classes, first as a student and then as a teacher. I'd like to see Room Three. That's the room where I realized astrophysics was the one true love of my life."

Dorning looked impressed. "All right. Let's go."

They pulled open the tall, solid wood doors and walked down the worn marble hall to the last door on the left. Several students hurried by them into the room.

"Here it is," the professor said with reverence. He poked his head inside, saw the students taking their seats and opening their books. He glanced around at the condition of the room. "New window shades, new periodic table on the wall," he whispered to Dorning. "Otherwise, it's exactly as I remember it. How wonderful."

The professor noticed an empty seat in the front row. "That's where I always used to sit when I was a student. I'm going to try it out."

Before Dorning could protest, Marlowe was in the room and in the chair. Several students smiled at the sight.

A tall, middle-aged man with thick eyeglasses and an armload of papers brushed by Dorning. The man went straight to the teacher's desk and plopped the stack down.

"Okay, I have your graded tests here, ladies and gentlemen," the teacher said.

The class murmured.

Dorning stood just out in the hall, frantically signaling for the professor to get out.

Marlowe ignored him and stayed put, turning to talk to a student two chairs away instead.

"What class is this?" he asked.

"Astronomy 101."

"That's great."

"My, my. Who do we have here?" the teacher asked, with a nod to the boy in the front row. "You know, these freshman look younger and younger every year, don't they?"

The class laughed.

The teacher stared at the professor. "Who are you?" he asked directly.

Dorning stepped into the room. "I'm sorry. He's here visiting the campus with me. The boy has an interest in science. He's...somewhat of a prodigy."

"Really? Well, he can stay as long as he's quiet. You can have a seat too, if you like," he said to Dorning. "We certainly welcome visitors to our picturesque campus."

Dorning meekly squeezed into the chair closest to the door.

The teacher turned to address the class. "Now, I promised a brief but fun session today since your test results weren't too bad. They could have better, but they weren't bad."

The class murmured again.

"Let's talk about the possibility of detecting life on other planets in the galaxy, since that's a popular topic nowadays. Where do you think we might find extraterrestrial life? Anyone? And I'm not talking about little green men, either, just rudimentary life."

A smattering of hands went up.

"Yes, Michael?"

"I would think towards the center of the galaxy, since there are so many more stars and possible solar systems."

"Good thought, Michael. I would have to agree with that. Anyone else?"

Percival was the only one to raise a hand.

The class laughed.

Dorning tried to signal the professor to put his hand down, but finally realized it was no use.

"Okay, young man, what do you think?"

"I think that's exactly the wrong place to look for extraterrestrial life."

The teacher's face registered his surprise. "Really? Well class, it appears our young guest disagrees. Perhaps he has a better idea. Let's hear what our budding Einstein has to say about the subject. Would you care to come up here and elaborate?"

The professor immediately hopped out the chair and walked to the front of the room.

Dorning lowered his head and rubbed his eyes in disbelief as the class twittered in amusement.

The teacher sat down behind his desk, bemused himself. "See? I told you this would be a fun class today. Okay, the audience is all yours, young man. It's an audience for Einstein. Go right ahead."

"Thank you," Marlowe said. He slowly rubbed his hands together as he gathered his thoughts, eliciting more laughter.

"The galactic core is a violent place. The closer to the center, the more unlikely life is to exist. Why? Partly because we now have strong evidence there's a massive black hole at the very center. Black holes are strange creatures. They gobble up matter and spew out high-energy radiation across the spectrum, including deadly X-rays. Anything unfortunate enough to be caught in the grasp of a black hole eventually meets a horrible fate. It is literally torn to atoms that, in their death throes, are further split into subatomic particles that are sucked down to we know not where, only to leak out eons later in an unrecognizable, garbled mess.

"As this stream of particles first crosses over the point of no return—the event horizon—the center of the galaxy takes notice because it's bombarded with the extreme radiation that's released. For that reason, no life can exist within the gravitational pull of a black hole, a lifeless zone that extends for millions of miles. But even those solar systems near the galactic core lucky enough to be beyond the influence of this destroyer of worlds cannot harbor life.

"Why? Because the neighborhood's too crowded. All that jostling and bumping and spinning around—" He wiggled across the floor, making the class twitter again, "—is not inductive for the development of planets. The gas clouds that surround stars as they develop, the dusty remnants of their own birth, don't have the chance to coalesce into planets with stable orbits if those clouds are tugged in all directions by nearby stars. And those stars that are able to create solar systems are likely to have planets with relatively short lives, because all that conflicting tugging and pulling from gravitational attraction will eventually send those planets sailing away in the absolute cold of space, or crashing into each other or their star, or stretch them into some useless elliptical orbit that broils the planets in summer and freezes them solid in winter. For life to form, you need planets in stable orbits for a very long time, something less and less probable the closer you approach the galactic core, you see. No, there's only one place in the galaxy where you'll find those steady state conditions—right where our own solar system resides, in the safety of the spiral arms.

"Here, there's solace. It may be lonely, being so many light years away from our nearest neighbors, but unless a rogue celestial body comes out of nowhere and disrupts our solar system—which could happen, but isn't too likely—we enjoy the stability of orbit needed to allow life to take hold, and flourish, and evolve undisturbed, right up to my talking to you here today.

"And that's where we should look for life, among our peaceful, safely distant neighbors in the calm waters of the spiral arms, not towards the raging storms of the galactic center where only chaos reigns."

The classroom was silent.

The teacher sat bolt upright in his chair, his mouth hanging open, and his gaze far away. He finally looked at the boy, then at his watch.

"Wow," he said. "I guess we've all been taught a lesson today. I don't have anything to add. Besides, that's a hard act to follow. Anyone else?"

No hands went up.

"Then don't forget to pick up your quizzes. Class dismissed," he said softly.

As the students filed out after grabbing their graded papers, each one stared back in awe at the professor, and spoke in excited whispers as they drifted out of the building.

Dorning sighed and scratched the back of his neck. He knew they had some explaining to do.

The teacher stood up, came around the desk and stared down at the boy.

"Who *are* you?"

The professor hesitated, his head slightly bowed. "I'm...Miguel Marlowe, Percival Marlowe's nephew," he replied.

The teacher went bug-eyed. "His *nephew*?" He nearly doubled over in laughter. "Well, no wonder you're so smart! Wow! Percival Marlowe's nephew! Why didn't you say so before? It's a pleasure to meet you, Miguel." He stuck out his hand. "You know, come to think of it, you do sound an awful lot like your famous uncle."

The professor stood up straight and nodded politely as he shook the teacher's hand.

The teacher's exuberant expression disappeared.

"Sorry to hear he passed away recently. He was certainly a major influence in my life."

"Really? How so?" Marlowe asked.

"I heard one of his last lectures when I was in high school, before he retired from the University. I was undecided whether or not to major in science. That speech not only convinced me to pursue a physics degree, but I attended this very university, and now I teach here."

"That's wonderful. I'm very...I'm sure my uncle would have been very pleased to hear it."

"Well, good day." Dorning stepped between them and firmly shook the teacher's hand. "Thank you so much for permitting us in your class, but we really must be on our way now."

"My pleasure. Thanks for the impromptu lecture, Miguel. Come back anytime you want. You know, I'd really like some of my friends to meet you if you don't mind."

Dorning stiffened. "Perhaps some other time. Goodbye."

He quickly ushered Marlowe out the door, down the hall and out of the building.

Once a safe distance away, Dorning stopped and turned the professor by the shoulders to face him.

"Now you listen to me. Don't ever do anything that asinine again. The last thing we need is to draw undue attention to you."

"Stop squeezing my shoulders, Dorning, and stop talking to me like I'm a child." He lifted Dorning's arms up, then stepped back and let them fall. "I might look like one now, but I was old enough to be your father, if not your grandfather."

Dorning bowed apologetically, but his stern expression stayed. "I'm sorry, Professor, but you simply cannot do whatever you wish. Not yet, anyway. I know the chance to lecture again was probably irresistible, but you run the risk of prematurely revealing who you really are. Claiming you're Percival Marlowe's nephew will help to open some doors to your past, as it did here, but overused, someone will eventually discover your brother never had children, and then the probing questions will begin. We must use that nephew business judiciously. Agreed?"

Marlowe ran his hands over his short hair and nodded wordlessly.

"Good. And by the way, although I certainly don't want to encourage you to do that again, your mini lecture was excellent, as I might have expected."

"Well thank you, Doctor. It was good to stand in front of a class again. I nearly forgot how much I enjoy that."

"You will have the opportunity to lecture as much as you want in just a few short years, Professor. I promise."

They walked side by side down to the cobblestone path leading to the oldest part of campus.

"By the way, Doctor, I was wondering something about you the other day. You were a highly respected neurosurgeon making a considerable income, isn't that right?"

"Yes, but that was many, many years ago. So?"

"So, you just walked away from it all to pursue your memory theory? We've talked a lot about your experiments, but never why you pursued them so vigorously. What was it exactly that compelled you to devote your life to such uncertain research, Doctor? What was the impetus?"

The doctor half-smiled as he glanced up at the bright sky. "Believe it or not, inspiration struck me right in the middle of a delicate operation to remove a massive tumor from a patient's brain. It was a tantalizing idea for transferring memories I knew would be difficult to achieve, but certainly not impossible. I completed the operation—successfully, I might add—changed my clothes, typed up my resignation and handed it in all within the hour. The next day I was busy renovating my basement to create my research lab, and the chase was on to prove my theory was right."

"And that was it? You were out of a job and on your own, with no guarantee of success? That showed a lot of confidence, Doctor, a lot of faith in yourself."

"Not really. I was absolutely convinced my theory was sound. All I had to do was find the techniques to make it work."

"But that took you much longer than you ever thought it would, didn't it?"

"Admittedly, yes. I had quite a few setbacks, actually. That's why I came to you for funds. I knew at the rate I was spending money, I would burn through my life savings well before I achieved success."

"How did you know I would help you?"

Dorning smiled faintly. "I didn't. I just knew you were wealthy, had no heirs waiting for your money, and that my research could benefit you personally since you were getting up in years."

"So it was a gamble that paid off. But why me? Why an astrophysicist, Doctor? There are lots of wealthy, elderly people out there who would have been glad to bankroll you for a shot at another lifetime."

"I didn't want just anybody. I wanted someone who I admired, someone who had the intelligence and creativity to change the course of civilization. That person was you."

The professor was silent a moment. "I guess I should feel flattered, but to be perfectly honest, at times when I was signing all those huge checks for you I wondered if I wasn't squandering my fortune in a foolish pursuit, if I wouldn't have been better off giving my money to some charity, or maybe establishing a few scholarships here at the University." He looked around at the stately buildings on either side of the path. "Weren't you ever discouraged, Doctor, particularly when it seemed your research had hit a dead end? Did you ever consider giving up and going back to active practice?"

"No, never. I knew I would eventually find a way around any problems I was having. It just took almost every waking moment for years on end to do it, that's all." He stared down sternly at the path beneath them.

Marlowe looked at Dorning with concern. "Your dedication is admirable, Doctor, worthy of a Thomas Edison. But I wonder if the effect it's had on your personal life wasn't too high."

Dorning's face brightened. "Why, thank you for the comparison. Edison was one of my favorite childhood heroes. At least I can honestly say I never squandered my time or talent." He glanced at the professor with brief disapproval. "Total dedication to a lofty goal is worth almost any price, isn't it?"

Marlowe hesitated. "Not to me. I always remembered to take time out to have some fun and let off a little steam."

Now Dorning hesitated, avoiding eye contact with the professor. "Yes. I witnessed some of that so-called fun of yours, unfortunately. If you don't mind me sounding impertinent, perhaps the world would have been better off if you had applied your remarkable intellect to conquering equations rather than the frivolous, fawning women who practically flung themselves at you."

Marlowe laughed at the suggestion. "Never, Doctor. After all, if I had accomplished all my life's goals the first time around, your research wouldn't have seemed nearly as important or urgent, now would it? My unfinished business helped push you to find that elusive memory transfer method you ultimately discovered somehow. Now isn't that right?"

"Yes. Yes, I suppose it did," Dorning said, and abruptly looked away.

The professor looked away as well, his jovial expression quickly fading.

"And that, I'm afraid, was the beginning of the end for you, Miguel," he said.

Dorning slowly turned back to the professor to stare at him askance. "You mean you *talk* to the boy? Is this a joke?"

Marlowe shook his head. "No, I do that from time to time, out loud or to myself."

"Why? He's not going to answer, you know. And if he does, you're in big trouble. Either he's about to make an unwelcome return, or else something's gone terribly wrong with the operation."

The professor shrugged. "I don't know why I do it. I guess since I thought for years I would be the one who would be remembered only occasionally, the least I can do is remember Miguel every now and then. Without him, I wouldn't be enjoying all this again." He looked around the stately campus with nostalgia.

"True enough, and while I seriously doubt just thinking about the boy could cause a relapse, if you talk to yourself too loudly in public, they may have no choice but to lock you away."

Marlowe half-grinned.

"No matter," Dorning said. "I imagine in time you'll forget about the boy, and this silly desire to converse with him will come to an end."

The professor stared at Dorning, his expression thoroughly humorless now. "Never, Doctor. I see Miguel every time I look in a mirror. What makes you think I could ever forget him?"

"Because in time it will be *you* who you see in the mirror, not the boy. You will eventually grow accustomed to your new appearance and rarely ever think about him, particularly as you age and look less and less as you do now."

Marlowe shook his head again, more emphatically. "I hope that doesn't happen, Doctor. Miguel deserves to be remembered for what he's done for me. Always."

"Oh, but it will happen, Professor. You might not want to believe me, but it will. As the years go by, you'll slowly forget there ever was a boy. I'm quite sure of it. It's inevitable. Inevitable."

Marlowe was silent, his straight-ahead gaze now fretful.

As they passed the chapel, both bell towers rang solemnly in sequence, signaling the hour.

The professor looked up at the two spires, and saw pigeons flying away from where they had been roosting near the bells. "All right. Just one more question for you about the boy, Doctor, and then I'll shut up about him. Right now, I'm Percival Marlowe. What happens if I suddenly do become Miguel again? Is our little vacation over, or would you continue it? And how do you explain to the boy you still haven't arranged for a time share with me?"

"I'm quite certain he won't be making a reappearance. Your memory associations have been so strong here that you're firmly in control right now. What's needed is to keep your associations coming, and to avoid any of the boy's, so you remain in control. As I said before, my research has shown reversions back to the recipient become less frequent with time, and the relapses don't last for very long without reinforcement. What I would need to do is immediately find something that triggers some of your strongest memories to help get you back as soon as possible. Oh! I almost forgot. I brought something along with me." He dug in his pants pocket, pulled out a circular object, and handed it to the professor. "This should do nicely. It was the first object that triggered memories of you in the boy. I brought it along just in case."

Percival took the object and laughed loudly when he realized what it was. "Oh my God. Dorning, where did you find this? I haven't seen this in years. My old swimming medal. I won this when I was a couple of years older than the age I am now. At the time, this seemed like the pinnacle of success. I thought I'd never achieve greater glory." He smiled widely as he studied the medallion closely.

"It was packed away in the attic of the beach house. I specifically looked for things that might help restore your memories. Believe it or not, this was the best one. Not even your Nobel Prize medal was as effective, which I would certainly have remembered if it were me."

"I'm not surprised. I was inordinately proud to have won this. The moment I did, my entire reputation changed both at home and at school. I was no longer just a brainy bookworm, I was a Renaissance man, an athlete-scholar, a force to be reckoned with. Kids started to come to *me* for advice. And the girls! My goodness, the girls flocked around me like I was Rudolph Valentino. It didn't take me long after that to lose my innocence, I can tell you. Unless, of course, that's more than you wanted to know."

He stopped. Dorning stopped too.

Percival brought the medal up to his nose, briefly closed his eyes, and inhaled deeply. "I always liked that smell," he said in a quiet voice, staring at the medal. "It reminds me of victory and happier times."

He resumed walking.

Dorning caught up to him, grinning to himself. "I know, Percival," he said just as quietly. "I know."

Marlowe slipped the medallion into his own pocket. "Sorry, Dorning, but I'm going to keep it."

"Certainly, Professor. Look at it often. Remember, remember. Just don't lose it. Please."

The path ended in front of the plain, single story archives building the professor had pointed out the day before, the first campus building.

"Shall we go in?" Dorning asked.

"Might as well, since we're here."

To the professor's dismay, he saw almost all of the interior walls had been removed, and everything had been modernized. Behind tall glass cases lining the walls was the neatly organized and labeled history of the University—pennants, football jerseys, freshman beanie caps and other mementos now faded and mute.

Marlowe frowned. "This is it? Rather static and dull, isn't it? You would think they could do something to make the University's unique heritage come more alive."

As if on command, the door to one of the few rooms left in the building sprang open, and a custodian pushing a mop and bucket came out. He was stooped and gray haired, his stained shirt untucked and his gait unsteady.

The professor gasped. "I know him," he whispered to Dorning. "He was a young man when I still taught here. Now look at him; time hasn't been kind. I'd like to see if he remembers me. I mean, Percival Marlowe, that is."

"All right. Just make sure you choose your words carefully," Dorning warned. "Remember our agreement." He stepped over to a display to keep a wary eye on the custodian.

The professor approached the custodian cautiously, watching him struggle to wring out the mop.

"Hi," Marlowe said.

The custodian turned around. "Hello, young man. Didn't hear you come in."

The professor struggled for something meaningful to say. "So, how long have you worked here at the University?"

The custodian grunted. "Why? Who wants to know? Too long, if you ask me."

"Did you know Percival Marlowe?"

"Sure did." He pulled the mop out of the wringer and plopped it on the floor.

"Is there anything on display here about him? I'm interested in science too."

"Probably. Look around." He glanced at the boy, then sighed and leaned the mop handle against the wall. "Oh, hell. Here, I'll show you. It's not much."

The professor followed him to a display case.

"See that picture of the observatory? Look closely at the guy standing in the doorway. That's Percival Marlowe."

"Oh yeah, that's...him all right. Is there anything else here about him?" The professor looked around.

"No, thank goodness."

The custodian returned to his mop.

The professor followed, keeping a respectful distance. "Why did you say 'thank goodness'?"

The custodian grinned a tight, bitter grin. "Why? Because he was one of the most arrogant, self-centered, my-shit-don't-stink bastards who ever taught here, that's why. You won't believe how many people were glad when he finally retired."

The professor grew pale. "What did he do?" he asked softly.

"What did he do? What didn't he do? He was cocky and unapproachable. He had an air about him that said he was above anyone who hadn't won a Nobel Prize like he had, which was everyone else on campus. He never said hello to me or anyone on staff, even if you walked right by him on the sidewalk and said hi first. It was like he didn't even see you. Once I was late putting out a lectern for a speech he was giving, and he cussed me out right in front of everyone, practically the whole school. I felt about this big." He held up his hand, his thumb and index finger nearly touching. "But he didn't care. He was the great Percival Marlowe, kiss his royal butt." The custodian began mopping vigorously.

Marlowe swallowed hard, his expression one of remorse. "That was thirty-five years ago," he said, then realized his mistake and looked at the custodian with alarm.

The custodian did a double take at the boy, then kept mopping. "Yeah, it was about that long ago. But so what? I remember it like it was yesterday, that's all that counts. You don't forget an injustice like that. And he was someone you would never want to forgive, either." He glanced at the boy as he swung the mop back into the bucket. "Oh, look, son. Don't listen to me. I'm just a bitter old man who would retire if I had only saved some money. I'm sure Percival Marlowe did a world of good, only I never saw it, that's all. And now he's dead, he can't embarrass nobody no more. I guess that means the old children's story is true." He wrung out the mop and resumed mopping.

"What old story is that?" the professor asked, fearful of the answer.

The custodian paused, looked up and stared steadily at him with eyes both angry and sad. "Why, the mighty emperor had no clothes. No damn clothes at all."

Mouth sagging open, the professor backed away, slowly at first, and then faster, until he finally turned around and nearly ran to where Dorning waited.

"I heard that," Dorning said in a hushed-but-annoyed tone. "Don't pay any attention to him. He doesn't know what he's talking about."

"Let's get out of here, Doctor. Our little vacation is over." He nearly panted.

"Oh, but what about your beloved observatory? I thought you wanted to make arrangements to use the telescope tonight if you could?"

"No. I just want to go home. I'm afraid I've lost all my enthusiasm. Being here isn't going to help matters anymore. Trust me, it won't."

Dorning glowered at the custodian. "Why that foolish old man. I should report him to his superiors for talking to you that way."

"You will do nothing of the kind." Marlowe's gaze was steely. "Let's just go."

They went straight back to the apartment to pack their belongings and turn in the room key. Then they hurried to the stone arch where they had arrived the day before, making it just in time to catch the next bus home.

As Dorning snored softly in the seat next to him, Percival stared out the window at the countryside rolling by, turning the worn swimming medal over and over and over in his small, smooth hands.

Chapter Twenty

He couldn't sleep after the long journey home.

He slipped out of bed, grabbed his tattered old address book from his desk and crept down the hall. He heard Natalie's harsh snoring as he went past her room and relaxed a bit. Dorning had returned to his own house for a few days, so the professor paid no attention to the empty guest bedroom as he lightly padded the rest of the way to the kitchen.

He dialed the phone by the meager light coming through the windows, squinting to read the numbers on the handset and the ones he wanted from the book.

The phone on the other end rang half a dozen times before he finally heard it lifted.

"Hello?" The voice was drowsy, annoyed.

"Hello, is this Professor Kingston?" Marlowe asked quietly. The name sounded strange in his higher voice.

"Yes, this is he." The long-distance call crackled with faint static.

"Professor, my name is...Miguel. I'm doing a homework assignment about Percival Marlowe and would like to ask you a few questions about him if you have the time."

"How did you get my phone number?"

He paused to glance at the worn address book he had owned for half a century. "The University gave it to me."

"Really? I'm surprised they did that. Actually, I guess I'm surprised I'm still in their phone directory. I retired years ago, you know."

"Yes sir. I know."

"Just a minute."

Marlowe heard fumbling on the other end, imagined his old friend sitting up and putting on his wire-rim glasses.

"Good God. Do you know what time it is, young man? Shouldn't you be in bed? Can't this wait until tomorrow?"

"I'm sorry, sir. The assignment's due tomorrow."

He heard Kingston respond with his familiar throaty laugh. "Well, all right, as long as there aren't too many questions. Wouldn't want you to get a failing grade because of me. But I'm sure you're aware you could have called much earlier."

"Sorry, Doctor Kingston. Thank you. I was just wondering what your impressions were of Percival Marlowe."

The professor turned around and leaned back against the cool kitchen wall.

"Impressions? Now there's a vague question. Hmm. Impressions. Let me think."

Marlowe hung his head, eyes closed, waiting for the answer but half afraid to hear it.

"Well, he was easily the most brilliant mind I ever met. But I guess that goes without saying. He had a sharp wit, and wasn't afraid to use it. No one lasted long in a verbal joust with Perc, that's for sure."

The professor opened his eyes and smiled briefly to hear Kingston's old nickname for him again. "I see. What else do you remember about him?"

"Well, he was a challenging teacher, brought lots of attention to the Physics department—not to mention money—and he won the Nobel Prize, of course. But you probably already knew that, didn't you?"

"Yes sir." Marlowe took a breath and closed his eyes again. "What was he like as a person? Was he a nice man? A kind man?"

"Perc? Oh sure, sure."

The professor waited for Kingston to say more, but that was all.

"No, really. What was he like? You can tell me. This is important."

There was a considerable pause. "Well, he's dead now, of course, so I would hate to speak ill of someone who can't defend himself, but I suppose it would be fair to say he could be a little difficult to deal with at times."

The professor raised his head, his eyes wide. "What do you mean, exactly?"

"Oh, I probably shouldn't tell you this, but it was hardly a big secret on campus. He was mainly known as...Perc the Jerk. That may sound cruel, but it was true, so there you have it." His laughter rumbled along. "Hope you find that funny, young man. We sure did. I don't really want to tell you why, but we all called him Perc the Jerk."

Marlowe took a sudden step forward, gripping the handset tighter. "Who called him that? You and the rest of the Physics faculty?" His expression was nearly frantic.

"Good God, not just the Physics faculty. The entire faculty, as well as the students, staff and everyone else who knew him. As far as I know, no one ever dared say it to his face, although I nearly did once by mistake." He laughed gruffly again.

"When was that?"

"Oh, does it really matter? Well, if you must know, I believe it was at a faculty birthday party. Now whose party was it? All I remember is turning around, thinking the Birthday Boy was behind me, and starting to ask where Perc the Jerk was. You can imagine my surprise when I found Marlowe standing there instead. Fortunately, I don't think he heard me, although he did give me a very puzzled look." His rumbling amusement followed once more. "Say, is any of this information really useful to you? What kind of assignment are you writing, anyway? Is this an expose or something like that? I probably shouldn't be telling you all this, young man, but you caught me half asleep here."

The professor didn't answer right away. "Holloway," he finally said. His gaze was mournful now.

"Pardon me, young man? What did you just say?"

"It was Frank Holloway's fiftieth birthday party," he replied softly.

There was only the hiss of static for a moment. "Good God. You're right. It *was* Holloway's party. How did you know that? Who is this really?"

"I'm very sorry for the way Marlowe behaved sometimes, Harold. I really am. I'm afraid he deserved the ridicule, didn't he?"

"Who *is* this?" Each word was an anxious note.

"It was good to hear your voice again, Harold. I have to go now. Goodbye, my friend. Take care of yourself. And thank you for finally telling me the truth."

"Wait! I want to know how..."

Percival gently hung up the phone.

He stood in the kitchen a few seconds, arms folded, then slowly walked through the semidarkness back down the hall and through his room, out onto the patio. He stood still, listening to the waves wash ashore.

It was all true—what the custodian said, he thought. *They couldn't wait until I retired. What do you think of that, Miguel?*

There was only the relentless sound of the surf in reply.

He turned and went to his bed, sat down heavily in the middle of it, staring straight ahead. When sleep finally caught up to him an hour later, he drifted off where he was, his head bowed down to his chest as if he were ashamed now even in his dreams.

Chapter Twenty–One

"Thank you for agreeing to drive me at nearly the last minute, Doctor. I would have taken a cab, but since I still don't have an allowance, I'm afraid I'm broke."

Dorning grinned briefly, but didn't take his eyes off the road. "Even if you did have money, Professor, I couldn't let you go alone. Beside the usual safety concerns, without an adult chaperone there would be no reason for them to even let you through the door. Even with my presence, I'm still not convinced they're going to allow you to participate in the event. Unfortunately, I'm sure there will be plenty of drinking and all the rowdy behavior that goes with it."

"I hope so. That is, if they learned anything at all from me."

Dorning grinned again as he turned the Mercedes into the already crowded restaurant parking lot and parked.

"How many were invited?" Dorning asked as they got out and headed to the front entrance.

"I'm not sure. All the invitation said was it was going to be a 'big bash.' Both words are relative, I suppose. I'll tell you one thing, though—I'm sure glad I finished going through all my old mail this morning. Otherwise I would have missed my own party."

"And you're absolutely sure they're going to go through with this even though they think you're dead?"

"Absolutely. I called the number on the invitation and was told that instead of a birthday celebration, it would be a celebration of Percival's life. Sort of an Irish Wake, I imagine." He smiled in anticipation as he hurried his pace. Then his smile disappeared, and he slowed down as his expression turned faintly desperate. "I need a celebration after the last few miserable days, Doctor. At least these people truly appreciate me, even if few others do."

Dorning scoffed. "What are you talking about? Lots of people not only appreciate you, they greatly admire you for what you've accomplished."

Marlowe looked unconvinced. "Not everybody, Doctor. That's for sure."

They arrived at the front doors. As Dorning held one open for the professor, he had a sudden thought. "Wait a minute. If the only ones attending this 'big bash' are your former graduate students, just how many of them are there?"

Percival stopped and laughed lightly. He stared straight at Dorning, bemused by the question. "Why, after more than forty years of teaching, they're legion, Doctor."

He went in, and Dorning followed.

The professor pulled the invitation out of his back pocket and glanced at it. "The party is in the King's Chamber, whatever that's suppose to be. Ah!" He saw the sign above the arched entranceway and pointed at it. "Here's my room," he said, with an excited grin.

The professor and Dorning entered together.

The room was decorated like an English pub, with dark paneling and booths, dartboards on every wall for flavor, and a green slate floor. A few dozen people were milling around in the front by the bar, shaking hands and talking excitedly.

The professor nodded, pleased, and his smile returned. "An appropriate place, don't you think?" he said to Dorning over the oldies music pouring from an antique jukebox in the corner.

A few more people came bustling in, brushing right by them in their haste.

"Come on, Doctor. We're missing all the fun," Marlowe said, and went to join the burgeoning crowd.

Dorning frowned at the blaring jukebox then slowly followed the professor.

A woman with long brown hair who seemed about Dorning's age came up to him and blocked his path. She looked puzzled. "Excuse me sir, but who are you?"

"I'm Carl Dorning. Doctor Carl Dorning. I was the Professor's personal physician and a close friend."

"Did you receive an invitation, Doctor?"

"Well, no, but..."

The professor appeared at her side and wordlessly held out his invitation to her.

The woman took it. "Where did you get this?" she asked when she realized what it was.

"It was Percival's invitation," Dorning answered for the professor. "He wanted us to come if he couldn't. Unfortunately, you know the rest."

The woman's eyes widened, and she brought the invitation up for a closer look. "This was *Marlowe's* invitation? Oh. Well, okay then, I guess." She smiled kindly down at the boy. "And is this your son?"

"Yes, he is. He idolized the Professor too. I hope you don't mind he tagged along."

She suddenly looked unsure. "Well, things might get a little bawdy, you know. I don't know if our language is going to be too appropriate for him."

A little smile flashed across Percival's face and his eyes twinkled.

Dorning nodded. "I warned him of that, but he still insisted on coming."

Now it was the woman's turn to nod. "Oh, what the heck. The more the merrier, I guess. Let's go." She took the boy by the hand and guided him toward the noisy crowd.

The professor, clutching the woman's hand tightly, looked back at Dorning and raised his eyebrows twice in quick succession, then winked. A wide, lopsided grin appeared on his face.

Dorning slowly shook his head to make his disapproval clear.

The woman soon abandoned the professor to join in a conversation a few steps away. Dorning stood awkwardly next to him, arms folded and frowning again.

"I think I remember her," Marlowe said confidentially, tapping his chin. "She wasn't one of my stellar students—pun fully intended—but if I'm not mistaken, I believe she's teaching somewhere. And I see Raymond, who's done some valuable neutrino work at Fermilab, and over there is Victor, who said in a letter I finally opened recently he would soon be on his way to CERN in Switzerland. I can't wait to talk to all of them, although I'm going to have to bite my tongue hard not to reveal who I really am. This is wonderful, Doctor, just wonderful, I tell you." He sighed. "This is very rewarding, seeing so many of my former students and knowing not only that they're successful, but that I played no small part in their success." He raised an index finger, shook it proudly. Then the faint desperation appeared again on his face as he looked around at the boisterous group.

"Of course you did, " Dorning replied, his tone dry and matter-of-fact. "They should be very grateful indeed for all you've done for them."

The brown-haired woman who had held the professor's hand suddenly raised both of hers into the air.

"Okay, ladies and gentlemen, why don't we get this party started?"

The chatty crowd gathered around a long table set with plates, forks and napkins, but nothing yet to eat.

The woman cleared her throat, seemed barely able to contain her glee. "As you know, poor old Percival Marlowe passed on to another dimension recently, a few weeks after this birthday party for him had been planned. And I think we all know which dimension he went to." She pretended to fan herself, and the crowd chortled. "After some discussion what to do, we decided to go ahead with the celebration, but since the Birthday Boy's dead, we've turned it into a farewell and so-long party for the Professor to give him an appropriate send off. And since we had already paid for the cake, we decided to change that too, to better reflect the new theme for today." She finally laughed out loud, as did two other members of the party as they brought out a massive single-layer cake from behind the bar where the liquor was flowing freely into outstretched glasses.

"And here it is, ladies and germs," the woman announced. "Our tribute to Percival Marlowe!"

The two cake presenters held the cake high, and everyone raised their glasses in salute. Then still laughing, the presenters brought the cake down with a flourish to the table, where everyone waited anxiously to see it.

The crowd doubled over and roared.

The professor stood in the back, hopping up and down in a hopeless attempt to see over the considerably taller guests. "Come on, it's my turn," he said, and tried to force his way in.

A former student who Marlowe only vaguely remembered looked down at him.

"I'm not sure you're old enough for this, little buddy," the man said, the weepy amusement in his eyes now tinged with concern.

"Why not?" the professor demanded to know, and finally squeezed his way to the front.

He stared down at the cake as the crowd continued to laugh, his eager, happy anticipation replaced at once with shock and horror.

There, in garish frosting colors, was a crude caricature of his former self, wearing only shoes and a mortar board cap, chasing a scantily clad young woman. In the background, a telescope poking out of an observatory was examining the young woman intently with a single enormous, quivering eyeball at its end, and above that were the words, 'Goodbye, And Thanks For All The Lessons, Professor!'

"No," he whispered with a gasp, his eyes round and frozen in disbelief. "Please, not them too."

The brown-haired woman raised her glass into the air again. "Here's to the late, great Professor Marlowe, who—if he were still teaching today—would be sued six ways to Sunday for harassment and probably end up in jail!"

The crowd roared again. "Hear, hear!" they cried.

"And here's to the most brilliant, arrogant jackass to ever win a Nobel Prize!" someone else toasted.

"Hear, hear!" the crowd replied again in kind.

"Ah, but he was *our* arrogant jackass," still someone else said.

The glasses went towards the ceiling simultaneously once more. "Hear, hear!" And the laughter continued unabated.

The professor suddenly felt his head spinning and grabbed the edge of the table for support, not sure what was happening. "No, not now," he said to himself. "You can't see this, Miguel. You can't."

The queasy feeling slowly passed.

The brown-haired woman finally noticed him and quickly lost her bright smile. She set her drink on the table to tend to him.

"Oh, doggone it. Sorry, little guy. I thought this might be a little too intense for you. I guess we shouldn't have let you see this. That's my fault, I'm afraid." She patted him on the shoulder and gently turned him away from the cake.

Dorning, who was red with outrage, immediately confronted her. "What's the meaning of this? Don't you realize who Percival Marlowe was, what a great man he was? How dare you, all of you." He glanced angrily to either side.

The crowd fell mostly silent.

Now the woman's expression reddened. "We know how brilliant he was, mister. You don't have to tell us that. But we also know he had a huge, trampling ego that wasn't very flattering or easy to live with. Sorry if that bursts your bubble about him, but that's the way it goes. I'm afraid you didn't know him nearly as well as you'd like to believe." She handed the professor over to Dorning. "Maybe you should both just leave." The woman looked at the boy in sympathy then bent down to talk to him. "I'm sorry. We didn't mean to upset you. We really didn't." She patted his shoulder again. "Sometimes people like Percival Marlowe aren't what they seem or pretend to be, you know. We're just having some fun pointing that out as we remember him today, that's all. Understand?"

The professor nodded, but said nothing. He avoided looking her in the eyes, too ashamed now to do so and distressingly reminded of Miguel.

And he was humiliated to be lectured in front of his former students by one of them in such a condescending tone, even if they didn't know his true identity.

"This is still an outrageous affront to the memory of the Professor," Dorning protested. "He made more contributions to society than all of you put together ever will." He glanced around the room defiantly, his chin lifted in accusation.

The woman gave him a weary look. "Just go, will you?"

Dorning turned away and guided the professor out the room, as a fresh round of laughter started behind him from another sarcastic toast the professor couldn't quite hear.

They left the restaurant and made their way across the warm parking lot towards Dorning's car. Marlowe's knees suddenly felt weak, and his forehead grew clammy.

"Wait..." The professor broke away from Dorning, hurrying to a drainage ditch nearby.

He bent over and threw up. Twice.

"Oh my God," Dorning said quietly, and glanced away.

Marlowe slowly straightened and caught his breath, his eyes closed.

"Feel better now, Professor? Would you like to go back and get a drink of water?" Dorning tried to sound merely helpful instead of overly concerned.

"No to both questions," he replied, eyes still shut. "I just want to go home." He finally looked at the doctor, his expression drawn, his face pale. "Funny how our little excursions lately all seem to end in disaster isn't it, Doctor?"

They made it the rest of the way to the car without incident, got in and drove off. The professor settled back in his seat, then closed his eyes again and covered them with a hand as if in pain.

Dorning finally broke the uncomfortable silence. "That horrible, vulgar party was extremely unfortunate and totally uncalled for, Professor. You would think your former students would have outgrown such childishness by now, especially considering some of them looked almost as old as I am. They'll regret this someday, Percival, I'm sure of it. You didn't deserve such crass, disrespectful treatment, didn't deserve it at all."

Percival lowered his hand and opened his eyes, then raised his head slightly and stared at the road, his gaze uncertain.

"Didn't I?" he questioned.

Chapter Twenty-Two

"Biologically, yes, you are correct, madam. I should not be drinking. But chronologically speaking, I can drink as much as I want, when I want." The professor poured himself another glass of sherry. The tan beret he had found in his closet slipped a little further to the right, a few sizes too big for his smaller head.

Natalie sat across from him at the kitchen table, looking uneasy. "I'm sorry, but I still find all this just a little hard to believe. You mean to say you have the memories of the Professor, that the Doctor somehow put them into Miguel's brain so the Professor can continue his research. Is that right?"

"Yes, or at least most of those memories. I don't know yet. Time will tell. So what's so hard to believe?" He picked up his glass and took a sip as he stared at her.

She gasped. "I've just never heard of such a thing, that's all. I know there have been some remarkable advances in medicine recently, some of which I just don't understand, but really..."

"But what? Memory transfer wasn't one of them? Why, they're transferring memories left and right, madam, even the ones of arrogant jackasses such as myself. Didn't you know that?"

Natalie's hands flew to her mouth as she giggled.

"Oh, Percival, you..." she stopped when she realized what she had said.

"Good. We're making progress here. You finally called me Percival, which is who I am. More sherry, madam?" He picked up the bottle, pouring her another glass before she could answer. "You know, I remember how we used to drink together like this when you first came here years ago."

She picked up her refilled glass and took more than a sip. "Yes, those were the good...wait a minute. How did you know that? Did the Professor tell you, or the Doctor?"

"Natalie, Natalie, Natalie." He pretended to sadly shake his head. The beret slipped down a little more. "What is it going to take to convince you that I am Percival, and not some silly boy who found out much too late what was really at stake when he 'volunteered'—" He scratched at the air with two fingers from both hands, "—to give up any future he might have had?"

Natalie hiccupped and took another drink. "That poor boy." She looked puzzled. "If it's all true, why didn't the Doctor tell me about it? He just told me the boy was here to eventually take the Professor's place."

"Which, in a way, is true enough. Actually, he didn't feel the time was right to tell you the whole truth. I respectfully disagree. However, he will undoubtedly be furious when he finds out I told you without bothering to consult him."

She looked at the nearly empty sherry bottle. "You think that's bad? Wait till he finds out you've been drinking."

"Oh, piss on old Doc Dorning. He's an old-fashioned, German precision sauerkraut. He wouldn't know how to have a good time if his life depended on it." He took another sip. "Besides, *we've* been drinking, madam, not just me."

Natalie giggled again and drank some more, then looked down into the nearly empty glass. "Yes, we certainly have. In fact, I think I've already had too much." She rubbed her temple. "I can't drink like we used to."

"Now that's better. Like *we* used to. Have I finally convinced you I am who I say I am? Or do you need more proof?" He poured the remainder of the sherry into her glass.

"More proof."

"Fair enough. Let me think. Say, by the way, do you like my hat? I think it makes me look positively debonair."

She sputtered a bit in her sherry, amused. "It's very nice, Professor."

"I know. I have to think of something only you and I would remember, no one else. Would that do the trick?"

"Yes. Then I'll be convinced."

"All right. I have something." He leaned across the table to whisper to her, taking her hands in his. "When you first came here, drinking wasn't the only thing you and I used to do. Remember the time on the patio?" He gazed into her eyes. "You're still an attractive woman, Natalie. I don't think there's anyone out on the beach tonight, if you'd like to visit the patio again with me."

She put a hand to her mouth to contain her laughter. "Oh, Percival! Do you really think we should risk...?"

She stopped, freed her hands and immediately stood up, a look of horror on her face. "No, this can't be. This isn't right. You might be the Professor, but you're also just a boy. I can't, Professor, don't ask me to. I can't..."

She spun around to run from the room. The back of her hand hit her glass of sherry, tipping it over and sending a red river racing across the stark white tablecloth.

The professor leered after her as she went, his vision in one eye partially obscured by the beret.

"I'll be right here when you change your mind," he called out loudly after her.

The front door slammed.

He sat there calmly sipping his sherry, waiting for her to return as he was sure she would, eventually.

Chapter Twenty–Three

When Dorning entered the quiet house, he was surprised at the mess in the usually spotless kitchen. He picked up the empty sherry bottle and tossed it into the trash, then shook his head at the sight of the red-stained tablecloth and the stack of dirty dishes in the kitchen sink.

"Natalie?"

There was no answer. He went and looked into her empty room.

"Natalie? Are you here?"

There was only silence.

Dorning hurried to the professor's room. He knocked twice. There was no answer. He went in.

"Percival?"

The small figure under the bed sheet was facing the wall, unmoving.

Dorning tentative shook the boy's exposed shoulder, wondering who would awake.

"It is you, Professor, isn't it?"

The figure groaned.

"Percival!" Dorning shook whoever it was with more force. "Answer me!"

"What, Dorning, what?" The professor rolled over, his eyes screwed shut. He grabbed his forehead. "Must you talk so loud?"

Dorning relaxed, but still had questions. "What happened in the kitchen? Where's Natalie?"

The professor opened his eyes and sat up with another low groan. "Natalie. Yes. I believe she resigned last night, if I'm not mistaken. In fact, I'm quite sure of it."

"Resigned? Why?"

Marlowe looked up sheepishly at Dorning. "Because of some memories I probably shouldn't have, given my biological age."

Dorning frowned. "What does that mean? Was she drinking?"

"We were both drinking. And at the end, were quite drunk."

Dorning grabbed his forehead and paced in front of the bed. "She let you drink? I don't believe it. I have no research as to what that might do to you, given that not all of your memories have been restored. I can tell you one thing, though. It probably doesn't help. Why would she allow you to drink? She knows you're not nearly old enough. This is insane."

Marlowe silently watched Dorning go back and forth. "She didn't let the boy drink. She let the Professor drink," he finally confessed.

Dorning stopped, his expression one of shock. "You *told* her? Why?"

"Because she's been my housekeeper for more than twenty years, and she deserved to know the truth, that's why." He looked away, sheepish once more. "Unfortunately, I acted like an old fool, and away she went. I doubt she'll be back anytime soon."

Dorning paced again, faster this time. "No. This isn't just insane. This could be a catastrophe. What if she goes to the authorities? They may not believe her story, but they might show up here just to see what's going on. We can't allow that to happen, Professor. You might be taken away." He made a decision and stopped pacing. "We have to leave, that's all there is to it. Get up." He motioned for the professor to rise. "Pack your things, and I'll pack mine. We're going to my house downtown."

The professor meekly obeyed.

They drove in silence into the city. Dorning maneuvered the Mercedes through the snarled noontime traffic.

Percival sighed repeatedly to himself and gazed out the window at the storefronts as they passed by, holding his aching forehead.

Sorry, Miguel, he thought. *Afraid I'm making a real mess of things. Not exactly what you signed on for, is it?*

The only response was the muted noises from the busy city street.

He cleared his throat finally, and spoke. "She may not go the authorities, you know."

Dorning kept his eyes on the heavy traffic up ahead. "We can't take that chance. I'm not even sure my place is such a good place to hide. Perhaps we need to get out of town completely, maybe even out of state, just to play it safe."

The light turned red in front of him; Dorning came to a stop. He caught a glimpse of a group of teenagers on his right. They were pointing in his direction.

He slapped the steering wheel hard. "Damn! I should have gone the long way home. They recognized my car, and now they recognize you." He pressed all the buttons on the armrest to make sure the windows were closed and the doors locked.

"Who?" Marlowe looked out and saw the group of teenagers making their way towards the car. They were still pointing, seeming glad to see him. "Who are they?"

"Old associates of Miguel's, I'm afraid. This is the neighborhood I rescued the boy from. Just ignore them, Professor. We can't risk a relapse."

Marlowe looked aghast. "I used to live here? With them? God help me."

The teenagers pressed up against the window, pounding on the roof and tugging on the professor's door handle.

"Hey Miguel! Good to see you, man. Looks like you're doing all right," a tall, skinny teen said, his face nearly pressed to the glass.

"Yeah man, is this your sugar daddy?" another teen asked. "Tell him I want some of that money, but I ain't doing no tricks."

The group laughed.

The tall teen tried the door handle again. "Come on, man, open up. Don't tell me you forgot about us? We used to be your best buds, Miguel. Aw come on, don't be this way. Look at me, will you? We had some great times together, hanging out and everything. You know we took real good care of you, hiding you from the police, making sure nobody hassled you, listening to all your stories about your mother. Don't you remember? Come on, you have to remember all that, Miguel. There's no way you forgot about us already."

The group began to chant as they banged on the car windows. "Miguel, Miguel, Miguel, Miguel..."

The professor felt oddly lightheaded looking at them and listening to them call Miguel's name. He turned his head and tried to wave the teens away.

"I feel very strange, Doctor," he said. "Must be the hangover, eh?"

The light turned green. Dorning stepped on the gas and sped off, leaving the teens still chanting and laughing at the corner.

Dorning glanced at them in the side mirror. "Hooligans. Sorry, Professor. Are you all right?"

The professor's head went back, and his eyelids fluttered.

"Percival? Is something wrong?"

The boy doubled over, and then slowly straightened up. "Oh, man, have I got a headache." He looked around in confusion. "Hey, where are we going? I thought we were on the beach." He gasped with re-membrance, spun sideways in his seat to face Dorning. "Are you okay? You saved my life. I saw you drowning, and I didn't know what to do, I just didn't know what to do!"

Dorning drove with one hand as he waved at the boy to calm down. "It all right, it's all right. We're both fine. We're just going to my house for a while."

"What time is it? Is it the same day?" He looked around in wild-eyed confusion.

"No, it's...a day later."

"Just a day? I was the Professor for just a day?"

"Yes, yes you were. And now you're Miguel again. See? You're shar-ing, just like I promised. While you were the professor, I performed the operation to make that possible, just like I said I would. Fortunately, the operation was...non-invasive, so it didn't require another bandage. I'm sure you can appreciate that."

The boy sat back, relieved. "Good. I hope I stay Miguel for a while. A long, long while. I don't want to be the Professor too often." He rubbed his neck. "Man, does my head hurt. What happened to me?"

Dorning decided to play a hunch.

He licked his lips. "Miguel, let me tell you something. The Professor is the one who saved my life. When you became the Professor, back there on the beach, he swam out and rescued me. You see, the Professor was a superb swimmer when he was your age. Check your pockets. Let's see if I can prove it to you."

Miguel stuck his hands in his pockets and pulled a brass medallion from one of them. "Oh yeah, I think I remember this."

Dorning gave the boy a calculated, sidelong glance. "You have the medal? Good. Why don't you read it? Take a close look at it, a very close look."

The boy held the medal in front of his face. "Cambridge, 1924." He turned it over. "First place," he read. "That's all it says."

"Are you sure?" Dorning asked. "Study both sides of the medal carefully now. Hold it very, very close. The Professor was very proud of that award, you know. All his classmates thought he was a hero, admired him and came to him for advice. Remember how even the girls suddenly found him attractive, and how much he liked them in return? That medal meant a lot to him, more than anything else you ever achieved in your life, even more than the Nobel Prize you won. Don't you remember? Cambridge, 1924, and you were proud, so proud. First place. *First place.* Even your teachers and family were so proud of you. It was the greatest achievement of your life up to then, the greatest. Why don't you take a whiff of it? It has an interesting metallic smell, remember? One I believe you found very pleasing, very pleasing and unique. Try it. Go ahead. I'm sure you'll really like it."

Miguel blinked, then brought the medal up to his nose to do as he was told, his eyes unfocused and his mouth drooping slightly.

Dorning tried to suppress a grin. "You wore that medal to class every day with its red and white ribbon. Remember the ribbon? Don't you? Red and white? That medal means more to you than anything in the world, Professor. More than anything. It changed your life around, Professor. Changed your entire life for the better. You were so very, very proud, so incredibly, justifiably proud. It changed your life forever, Percival. Forever and ever and ever."

Dorning saw the boy's head nod. Several minutes later the doctor pulled into the driveway to his house.

The medal slipped from the boy's grip and landed with a thud on the floor.

Dorning shut off the engine, came around to the passenger side, opened the door and peered inside.

"Professor? We're here now."

Marlowe raised his head and rubbed his eyes. "Already? Did I fall asleep? Damn, this hangover! Do me a favor, Dorning. Next time I decide to drink, remind me that my bodyweight is only a fraction of what it used to be, and that I should limit my alcohol intake accordingly." He swung his legs around to get out of the car.

"Hold it. I think you dropped something." Dorning pointed at the medallion.

"I did? What is it?

Marlowe retrieved the fallen item, smirking when he realized what it was.

He turned to face the doctor. "Good heavens, it's my precious swimming medal. I sure don't want to lose this, now do I?" He flipped it up in the air, caught it tight and waved it happily at Dorning.

Dorning grinned cordially as he opened the trunk to retrieve their luggage. "No, you certainly don't, Professor. I know how much it means to you," he said, pulling out the first suitcase. "Just how very much."

Chapter Twenty-Four

The detective arrived at headquarters to find his two new understudies in the foyer, both red-faced and almost breathless from laughter. He stared at them in disbelief, then through the window of the closed interrogation room behind them at a woman sitting quietly alone.

"What the hell's going on? What's so funny?"

One of the young officers came forward and put a hand on the detective's shoulder to steady himself.

The detective scowled at the hand and the young officer immediately let go, straightened up and caught his breath. "Sorry, sir. It's just way too funny. Wait till you hear this mad woman's story." He looked at his partner and turned red-faced again. They tried to stifle their fresh laughter behind their hands like two schoolgirls at a slumber party.

The detective glanced at the woman again. She seemed nervous and upset.

"Who is she? Knock it off already, will you guys? Just talk to me."

Both officers finally settled down a bit.

"Sorry sir. She came in voluntarily to make a report, but what she had to say was just absolutely ridiculous, that's all."

"So who is she? Damn it, just tell me what's happening here, will you? I'm not gonna play some stupid guessing game with you."

"Yes sir. Sorry. Her name is Natalie Swyrinski, and she said she was the housekeeper for...Percival Marlowe."

Both young officers turned red yet again, as they struggled mightily not to laugh.

The detective stared at the woman, tapping his chin. "Percival Marlowe. Percival Marlowe. Hey, wasn't he the famous astronomy guy who died not too long ago? He was like a million years old or something, wasn't he? A real old timer."

The two young officers chortled.

"So why is she here? What did she have to report?"

One of the officers sighed deeply. "Sir, we would really appreciate it if you would talk to her, rather than hear it from us. Her story's...pretty amazing, to say the least. We couldn't do it justice. No pun intended, of course."

They glanced at each other and chortled again.

The detective eyed them with disgust. "You know, if you two keep this up, I'm going to start to wondering if I picked the right new guys for the job. This is a very serious business we're in, you know, protecting children. Just looking at her, I'd say it's entirely possible she was the old astronomer's housekeeper."

"Oh, we don't doubt that, sir. It's the other things she claims we have to wonder about."

"Like what?" He held his arms out, waiting for an explanation.

The young officer sighed again. "Sir, if you don't mind, could you just interview her? There's just no way we can tell you her story and keep a straight face. We just can't." He wiped away his tears, and the other officer followed suit. "Sorry, sir."

The two of them stood there still looking amused, but now also apprehensive.

It was the detective's turn to sigh. He scratched the top of his bald head. "You mean you can't even manage to give me a hint what this is all about?"

"No, sir. Please, just trust us on this one. You have to hear it for yourself."

He nodded. "Okay. Fine."

"Thank you, sir."

He didn't look at either of them. "Don't mention it." He put a hand on the doorknob, and paused. "Is there a blank tape in the tape recorder?"

"Yes, you're all set. Good luck, sir."

The detective ignored them, still angry at their childish behavior. He opened the door and stepped into the room.

He smiled kindly at the woman, wondering what he was getting into as he shut the door behind him. "Natalie Swyrinski? Hi. I'm Detective Davis. Do you mind if I call you Natalie? I assume you're here to report a suspected incident of child abuse." He came forward and sat down across from her.

She looked up at him sullenly. "I heard your men. They think I'm crazy, don't they?" Her expression was pained. "The way they ran from the room, laughing at me behind my back after I told them the truth was shameful, just shameful." Her chin quivered as she brought a crumpled tissue up to her face to dab at the corners of her moist, bleary eyes—eyes that looked like they hadn't slept well for days.

Then he was surprised to see more than a glimmer of resolve in her tired features, a kind of sad determination to make someone listen and believe her.

He gazed at her with sudden sympathy and respect. "Don't pay any attention to them, Natalie. It doesn't matter what they think. Only what I think." He promptly switched on the tape recorder and made sure it was working. "Now, why don't you start over again for me? I'm very interested in what you have to say. Please state your full name for the record."

She smiled faintly in appreciation, put the tissue down and took a deep breath to begin her story once again.

≈≈

They settled into their new routine in the doctor's house, the professor never venturing outside during daylight. Dorning bought him a small telescope he set up in the fenced backyard, where the professor spent hours on clear nights stargazing and re-familiarizing himself with the Messier objects visible from their location. Meal times were unplanned events, unlike Natalie's clockwork preparations. The two of them ate whatever they could find in the refrigerator and cabinets, and when they were low on food, Dorning would make a hasty trip to the grocery store, where he would grab as many items as he could remember they needed. On occasion, Dorning would stop by the now-abandoned beach house and pick up a few of the professor's books and papers and bring them home at the professor's request, until there was almost nothing left to retrieve. Soon Marlowe's bedroom in the city house resembled his former bedroom in the beach house, with books and papers strewn about on the dresser, nightstand, desk and floor.

Dorning surveyed the jumble, which was in stark contrast to his own more orderly living quarters down the hall.

"Too bad I couldn't change a few things about you, Professor. One thing I would have definitely given you is a sense of basic cleanliness."

Marlowe looked up from the massive tome he was reading on the bed. "I'm glad you didn't. I have better things to do than sweep and dust all day. I guess that's your job now that Natalie's gone." He jotted part of an equation down in the notepad by his side then returned to the book. "After all, it is your house."

Dorning was about to chide him again for driving Natalie away, but decided to forgo the lecture. Instead, he stared at the professor and how he read while stabbing the air with a pencil as if fencing with the stubborn math.

The professor finally sensed the doctor still standing in the doorway. He raised his head and held the pencil at bay. "Something wrong, Doctor?"

"No, it's just that while I'm fully aware you're Percival Marlowe, looking at you and the filthy way you live, sometimes I would swear I have a typical American son."

"If it's any consolation to you, Doctor, I've always been a slob. Too bad you couldn't ask my dear, departed mother." He glanced around the messy room. "Sometimes I even wonder if my slovenly habits didn't contribute in some small way to her early, unfortunate demise."

"Now Percival, that's no way to talk about your mother. I think she was a saint if she put up with this."

"Indeed she was. A role you play well now that you're our house-keeper. At any rate, if you don't mind, Doctor, I would like to read this so I can finish a paper I began several years ago. I've recently realized where I went astray in my calculations, and have a few ideas how I might get it back on track." He jotted down a few more numbers, and then turned his attention back to the book.

Dorning nodded. "Of course." He turned to leave, then came forward again.

"Professor?"

"Yes?" He didn't look up from the book.

"I can't tell you how good it is to see you back at work. It makes up for all the frustrations, all the troubles I've endured."

Marlowe slowly raised his head again and closed the book on his hand. "And I still can't thank you enough for all you've done. It's wonderful to have the interest and stamina once more to wrestle with these incredibly difficult equations." He glanced at the nearly filled page on the notepad. "That's really what old age robbed from me, my enthusiasm and my vitality." He looked away, and his voice grew quieter. "It's odd, but I don't remember when I lost them exactly. I guess time just kept chipping away at them until they were finally gone. It's been a while since I've felt this rejuvenated, this able to focus and make a contribution again." His gaze returned to the doctor. "I guess what I'm saying is, thank you for giving me back Percival Marlowe."

Dorning's eyes turned misty, and he struggled to speak in a steady voice. "Professor, that's exactly what I hoped to hear one day, what kept me going all those difficult years."

He turned and strode rapidly away so the professor wouldn't see the tears that started to fill his eyes.

Percival put the pencil point to the notepad, paused, and then lifted his head.

"And thank you, Miguel," he whispered sincerely. He stared straight at nothing, his expression hopeful. "If it has to be this way, the least I can do is be successful, and make your sacrifice as worthwhile as I can. Okay?"

There was only the stark silence of the cluttered room in reply.

He returned to the lengthy equation, finished it off with a few bold, inspired strokes, sad but determined now to do the very best he could.

෴

The next morning, the professor sat reading the paper while Dorning made a pot of coffee. The unexpected sound of the doorbell made both of them jump.

"Who the devil could that be?" Marlowe asked. "Are you expecting someone?"

Dorning hastily dried his hands. "No. No one." He hurried to the door and peeked through the peephole to see who it was. In the driveway was a white sedan, and at the door was a short, bald man in shirt sleeves and tie who Dorning didn't recognize.

Dorning's lips curled inward. "Damn," he said softly. He glanced behind him. "Get in the basement, Professor. Hide in the closet where I showed you. This doesn't look good."

Marlowe ran from the table. Dorning waited until he heard the basement closet door shut before he opened the front door.

He stuck his head out and around the screen door, trying his best to seem unperturbed. "Yes? Can I help you?"

The man held up a gold badge in a leather case. "Hi. Are you Doctor Carl Dorning? I'm Detective Davis from the County Child Welfare Agency. Mind if I come in and ask you a few questions, Doctor?"

"Why no, not at all. I was just making some coffee. Would you like some?" He stepped aside and held the screen door open.

The detective stepped in and casually looked around. "No thank you, Doctor. I've had plenty already today."

"Well, come in, come in." He motioned the detective into the kitchen then pulled back the chair the professor had been sitting in not a minute before. "Have a seat."

The detective sat down. Dorning took the chair on the far side of table.

"So what can I do for you, Detective?"

The detective cleared his throat as he leaned forward, his arms folded and elbows on the table. "Doctor, I'll get right to the point. Did you employ a housekeeper named Natalie Swyrinski at the home of the late Percival Marlowe, who had also employed her prior to his death?"

Dorning didn't twitch. "Yes, both Professor Marlowe and I employed her for housekeeping services. She quit unexpectedly almost two weeks ago; I haven't heard a word from her since. Is she all right? I've been worried about her."

"She's fine, Doctor."

Dorning feigned relief. "Good, that's good."

"But she doesn't want to work for you anymore, Doctor, or even see you again. She says you're an evil man. She even says you're a...proverbial mad scientist."

"What? What's that suppose to mean?"

The detective laughed a little and unfolded his arms. "Doctor, she told us quite an unusual story, one that—well, frankly—we have a hard time believing completely. Now she admits on the night she supposedly discovered you were an evil, mad scientist she was drinking to excess, but all that's not the reason I'm here. One of the things she claimed is that you have, or had, a Hispanic boy named Miguel living with you, a boy you brought home for Natalie to take care of shortly before Percival Marlowe died. And that when Percival Marlowe did die, you moved into his house with her and the boy. Now as far as Natalie was aware, this Miguel was not related to either you or Percival Marlowe in any way. She never heard you talk about the boy's parents or legal guardians, nor did she ever see or talk to the boy's parents or guardians. Apparently at one time you said, and I'm quoting Natalie here—" He pulled a notepad from his shirt pocket, flipped through the pages and read from it. "'He's going to take the Professor's place one day,' and she further said you instructed her to take unusually good care of the boy, that you didn't want anything bad to happen to him. But one day, when the boy was lost after a bicycle accident— requiring medical attention, as you later discovered—you refused to involve the authorities to assist you in locating him despite your concern for his well being, preferring instead to spend nearly an hour looking for him yourself. Finally, Natalie claims that you told her— and again, I'm quoting here—" He read from the notebook again. "'I'm going with the boy on a short trip. We shouldn't be gone for more than a couple of days,' which, according to Natalie, is exactly what happened. Not only that, but when the boy returned with you, she said he seemed sullen and upset, not his usual cheerful self. A couple of days after that is when she and boy apparently had a few drinks for some odd reason and she ran away, claiming the boy was—well, let's just say—not himself anymore." The detective closed the notebook and stuffed it back in his pocket, regarding the doctor with a cold gaze. "Could any of this possibly be true, Doctor?"

"I don't know what she's talking about. She's the one who sounds mad."

The detective lowered his gaze. "Doctor, we did a little investigation into your background when Natalie came to us with her story. This is what we found out. Please correct me if any of this is wrong." He glanced up at the ceiling and took a deep breath. "You were a highly respected neurosurgeon who, for some unknown reason, quit your job suddenly about twenty years ago and dropped completely out of sight. Now, with the salary you were earning, it could be you just retired early, but you never said so to anyone, and you haven't drawn from either Social Security or your considerable pension fund despite becoming eligible recently to do so. You never married, have no family or close friends we could discover—other than the late Percival Marlowe—never travel anywhere or, frankly, seem to do much of anything anymore. All this seems very unusual for someone who once had the drive and ambition to be a neurosurgeon. What have you been doing all these years, if you don't mind me asking?"

"I did retire. I simply haven't yet needed any outside assistance to live very comfortably. I don't mind saying I like reading, watching television, stargazing, bird watching..." His voice trailed off.

The detective glanced at the telescope behind Dorning in the living room. "I see. Well, that certainly makes sense, Doctor. But why did you retire so suddenly? Everyone who knew you back then was shocked. They thought you were very happy with your job."

"That may be what they thought, but sometimes outward appearances can be deceiving, as you undoubtedly know. I was tired of the tremendous stress, the daily grind. I felt just terrible all the time, had to drag myself to work, so I quit before the job could kill me."

The detective nodded, and then scratched the top of his bald head. "I can buy that. All right, Doctor. We checked with some of your neighbors and they've never seen a boy here, not even once. If he is here, you've done a great job hiding him. And we don't have any current reports of a boy named Miguel missing from the county, if that was really his name."

"I can assure you, Detective, there is no boy here." His gaze was steady.

"Well, thanks for your time." The detective stood up.

"Um, Detective, just out of curiosity, why did Natalie consider me a mad scientist, if you don't mind saying?"

The detective laughed a little again and put his hands on his hips. "Well, in her highly agitated state, she claimed Miguel was no longer Miguel. She said the Professor's spirit or soul, or something like that, was somehow transferred by you from the Professor into the boy. So basically, the boy was gone and the Professor was alive again. She was absolutely convinced this was true, based on what the boy told her."

Dorning tried to look incredulous. "And you believed *anything* she had to say after that incredible story?"

"Not especially. Neither did my two trainees, who interviewed her first." He shook his head at the thought of them. "But my job is to protect children, Doctor, and she said just enough plausible things to bring me out here to talk to you. Just enough."

"Well, then. Sorry it was a waste of your time."

"No, it's never a waste of my time to get to the truth, Doctor." His cold stare returned.

Dorning stirred uneasily. He couldn't help but turn away from the detective's unflinching expression as he cleared his suddenly tight throat. "That's certainly a commendable attitude, Detective. Well, good day."

"Good day, Doctor Dorning. I can let myself out."

Dorning followed him to the door anyway, and locked it the moment the detective was outside. He peered intently through the peephole, waiting until the detective got back in his car and drove away before hurrying down the stairs to where the professor was hiding in the back of the closet.

He threw the closet doors open, and saw the professor sitting on the floor. "I'm sorry, Professor. We have to move again. Tonight, late."

Percival sighed and lowered his head, not saying a word.

Chapter Twenty-Five

They packed their bags and loaded the trunk of the Mercedes in the garage with the overhead door shut. Dorning peeked out of the closed front window curtains every few minutes, looking for any signs of the detective's return. An air of tension was palpable, preventing them from conversing except in brief utterances—questions, answers, commands.

When the trunk was full and shut, the professor finally said what bothered him the most. He stood side-by-side with Dorning as both stared at the waiting car.

"This disrupts my work just horribly, you know. Is this how we're going to have to live from now on, constantly on the run? How am I to accomplish anything meaningful under these circumstances? It's impossible, just impossible."

Dorning took a deep breath, sympathetic yet angry. He didn't hesitate this time to say what he had avoided saying the day before. "I'm very sorry about your work, Professor, more so than you can imagine. But it was you, not I, who decided to let Natalie know about my research and experimentation. This is the price to be paid for that moment of indiscretion."

Marlowe bowed his head and ran a hand through his lengthening hair.

Dorning's hard stance softened. "This won't be forever. When you're legally an adult for the second time, I imagine whom you associate with will no longer matter to the police. After that, I plan to carefully and slowly reveal elements of my research to prepare society to accept you. Once that happens, I'm sure you'll enjoy celebrity status, and perhaps return to lecturing at the University if you wish, maybe even become a member of the faculty once more."

Percival half-grinned, his first sign of amusement that evening. "The faculty? God help me. All those meetings, committees, and cap and gown processionals in the miserable heat, cold, and rain...I think I'll just ask to be a guest lecturer, and stick to my theoretical work this time around. I've had my fill of pomp and circumstance."

Dorning patted the professor's shoulder. "Whatever you wish,

Professor. But in the meantime, we must not let them take you away. Your work will virtually come to a halt if you find yourself in some restrictive foster home, away from all your books and papers."

Marlowe nodded. "When do we leave, Doctor?"

"Let's wait a little longer; I want to be sure no one sees us."

The professor looked puzzled. "Where are we going, anyway?"

Dorning hesitated. "I really don't know. We'll see where the road takes us."

Marlowe looked surprised. "*That's* your plan? You disappoint me, Doctor. I would have expected something more definitive from you."

Dorning shrugged. "That's far better than finding out the hard way the police guessed where we were headed if we had a place to go. Let's just consider this the chaos theory of travel planning and let it go at that, shall we?"

Percival grinned once more.

✍ ✍

Dorning peeked outside one last time, then sighed and turned out the living room lights. He walked through the semi-darkness to the lighted, closed garage, where the professor waited in the back seat of the car.

Dorning got behind the wheel and took a deep breath. "Remember now, stay out of sight until we're well out of town. I'll let you know when I think it's safe to get up. Are you ready?"

The professor got down on the floor. "I'm ready."

"Then here we go."

Dorning pressed the remote control on the sun-visor, and the overhead door rolled upward. He started the Mercedes, turned on just the parking lights, and slowly backed down the driveway.

A white car with a single blue light flashing on top of the dashboard came silently but quickly down the street and pulled up behind him, blocking the path. Dorning hit the brakes, narrowly avoiding a collision with the front of the unmarked squad.

Dorning slapped the steering wheel before slumping back in his seat in defeat.

"What is it?" Percival asked, still on the floor.

"The worse news possible," the doctor replied as Detective Davis got out of the unmarked squad, flashlight in hand, and casually made his way to the driver's side window.

Dorning hesitated then pressed the button to lower the window. He turned off the parking lights and the engine.

The detective aimed the flashlight at Dorning's ashen face.

"Good evening, Doctor." he said brightly. The detective glanced at his watch. "Or should I say morning, since it's now well past midnight? Where are you going so late? You know, except for the owls, the birds are all asleep so you can't be going to watch them, and since it's

cloudy out—" He pointed the flashlight to the sky. "—I guess you won't
be stargazing, either. I'm surprised you're not inside, reading or watching television, your other two hobbies, or—like most people at this
ungodly hour—sleeping. Wherever you were going, it must be mighty
important."

Dorning didn't answer.

The professor quietly sat up. The detective turned the flashlight
on him. "Well, well. You must be Miguel, I presume, the eleven-year-
old boy who was absolutely not here. Are you okay, Miguel?"

He nodded, said nothing.

The detective turned the flashlight back on Dorning. "You know, I
think it would be a good idea if I had a private little talk with the boy,
if you don't mind. In fact, I'm afraid I must insist on it." There was a
hard edge to the detective's voice. "Stay right here, Doctor. Don't move;
I'll be watching. Miguel, why don't you get out of the car and come with
me?"

Dorning stiffly turned his head to look at the professor. "Yes,
Miguel. Go ahead with the Detective." He nodded steadily.

The professor obeyed, following the detective to the squad. He
waited by the back door for the detective to let him in.

"No," the detective said. "Get in the front seat so we can have a
little chat face-to-face."

The professor got in the passenger side. The detective switched
off the flashlight, slipped into the driver's side, and turned on the
dome light.

The detective relaxed and smiled. "You know, you look just as
Natalie described you, except you seem a little scared. Are you scared,
Miguel? If you are, you don't have to be. Not anymore. I'm only here to
help you."

"I'm not scared."

"Good. That's good. So tell me, how did you end up living with the
doctor? Are you a runaway, Miguel? If you are, nobody's reported you
missing."

"I'm not a runaway. I was abandoned, living on the streets."

"What's your last name, Miguel?"

"I...don't know."

"You mean you have no idea who or where your parents are, or
even if they're still alive?"

"No sir."

"How did you survive on the streets? You weren't doing tricks,
were you? I sure hope not."

"Tricks? Oh, absolutely not. I think I used to beg for money."

"You think? You mean you're not sure?"

"Yes, I was a beggar."

"A beggar? Is that what you call yourself? Huh. That's kind of an
old fashioned thing to say, isn't it?" Davis thought of Natalie's incred-

ible story, staring wordlessly at the boy for a moment. "In fact, that sounds an awful lot like something only an elderly...well, never mind. That can't be." The detective shrugged the thought away, then glanced back out the windshield with a nod towards Dorning. "So how does he fit in? Where did he come from?"

"He hit me with his car by accident. No, actually, it was entirely my fault. He drove me to the emergency room and realized I was homeless, so he took me in. I guess he just felt sorry for me, didn't want me to have to return to the streets."

"But didn't you actually go live with Percival Marlowe for a while, the famous scientist who died?"

"Yes, I lived in his beach house."

"Why? What did he have to do with all this? Why didn't you just live here with the doctor?"

"Because the doctor wanted me to get to know the professor. The professor had no family either. I guess the doctor felt sorry for him too."

"Okay, now let me ask you the million dollar question, Miguel." He turned as far sideways as he could to face the boy directly. "Did either of them hurt you in any way? And I mean in *any* way, if you get my drift."

"Absolutely not."

"Not even once?"

"No sir."

The detective sighed and scratched his head. He looked over at Dorning still sitting in the Mercedes. "If that's true, this is all very odd. Why would a retired neurosurgeon persuade a homeless boy to move in with one of the most..." The detective stopped, his puzzled expression gone. "Wait a minute. You said the professor had no family. You mean no brothers, sisters, uncles, aunts, nephews, nieces, nobody?"

"That's right. He had a younger brother, but his brother was killed in the Second World War." Percival shrank a bit, and his eyes filled with sadness. "That was the last of his family."

"He told you that? Huh." The detective scratched his head again. "You know, somebody like Percival Marlowe, when they get up in age, sometimes they don't have all their wits about them anymore, but they still have their money. And if they don't have any family, all that money could end up in the pockets of somebody who doesn't deserve it. What was it Dorning said? He said he didn't need Social Security or his pension money. Even if you were wealthy, why wouldn't you take what was coming to you, unless you planned all along to get your hands on an even bigger pile of cash? What if you devised an inheritance scam that required a pawn, someone like a homeless boy nobody misses? Or would miss, if he then conveniently disappeared?" He looked at the boy with renewed concern. "Tell me something, Miguel. Did the doctor ever offer you anything besides food and shelter? Did he ever

talk about money? Come to think of it, why would Natalie be so convinced you were actually the professor, unless the doctor had you acting that way to steal the professor's estate?"

"No. No! You're completely wrong. The doctor would never do
anything like that. Never. He had absolutely nothing but the professor's
best interests in mind. I'm quite sure of it."

The detective stared steadily at the boy, his look of concern replaced with suspicion. "Why do I suddenly no longer believe you,
Miguel? Maybe you're not as innocent as Natalie assumed, and me
too. You sure don't talk like an innocent kid of eleven. How old are you
really? Thirteen, fourteen, older? That would sure help to explain what
happened between you and Natalie the night she quit working for the
doctor. Maybe you're quite the street hustler, in on some clever scheme
to steal the professor's estate. Am I right Miguel, if that's even your
real name?"

"No, you're wrong, absolutely wrong." Marlowe shook his head
emphatically.

The detective ignored him. He clenched his jaw and stared hard
at Dorning. "Wait right here. I want to ask the doctor something. This
whole thing is getting way too bizarre." He stepped out of the car and
marched over to the Mercedes.

The professor waited until the detective lowered his head to talk
to Dorning, then quietly opened the car door. He slipped out, dropped
to all fours, and scrambled across the yard.

When he made it to the sidewalk, he stood up and ran as fast as
he could.

The detective heard the sound of rapid footsteps, swung the flashlight around and saw the squad was empty, the front passenger door
ajar. "Hey, Miguel! Get back here right now!" He skipped in the direction of the footsteps, pointing back at Dorning. "Stay! I'm not through
with you yet." And he bolted after the boy.

Davis shook his head as he ran. "Damn!" he said to himself. "Why
didn't I see this coming? I should have thrown him in the back and
locked the doors."

Percival glanced behind him and saw the detective in pursuit. He
cut across a driveway, picking his way through the dimly lit hodge-
podge of bushes and fences in the backyards, trying to avoid a dead
end.

The detective laughed, not far behind. "I've got you now, Miguel.
You're not getting away. That's right, go ahead and run into a fence too
tall for you to climb and I've got you."

The professor saw two wood picket fences up ahead, nearly back
to back, with only a narrow easement between them. He turned his
shoulders sideways, ran with the fences rubbing against his chest and
back. The front of his shirt caught on a nail and tore. He kept moving
until he reached the other side, then veered off back towards the street.

The detective tried squeezing between the two fences, but found himself stuck immediately. "Damn it!" He swore. He could only watch as the boy disappeared between two houses. "You're in big trouble now, young man," he yelled. A dog in the house behind him barked. "You hear me? I'm still gonna find you. You ain't gonna hide from me."

The detective kicked the fences in frustration then turned to go back and finish questioning the doctor.

Percival kept running until he was convinced the detective had given up. He paused in a thicket to catch his breath, and then pressed on towards the center of town, hiding any time slow headlights came his way. By sunrise, he was on the main city street, his feet and legs aching from the long hike. He was in the heart of the city because he knew there was only one group who could help him survive until he could find Dorning again.

The trick, he knew, would be to convince them he was still Miguel, to pretend he knew more about the boy's life on the street than he really did.

"I'm Miguel Sanchez, Miguel Sanchez, Miguel Sanchez," he repeated, so he wouldn't call himself Percival.

He suddenly felt oddly disoriented, put a hand to his head and closed his eyes. People hurrying to work streamed around him on the sidewalk as he stood wavering for a few seconds.

The strange feeling passed as fast as it had come, and he continued searching for the unfamiliar intersection where the friends he didn't know made their home and living.

Chapter Twenty-Six

He found them in the worst part of town, the four of them sitting on plastic milk crates in an alley behind a bar. Two of them were smoking and talking with their heads hung low, and the other two were playing some kind of fast card game, throwing their cards on the ground and pulling fresh ones from the deck that sat between them.

Percival was sure they hadn't seen him yet. He peered around the corner, hoping to hear a name or two before making his presence known so he could better pass himself off as Miguel. But the distance was too great to hear anything except an occasional loud obscenity from one of the card players, or a peal of laughter from the smokers.

He took a deep breath to brace himself, then stepped around the corner and walked straight towards the four teens.

If Dorning was ever going to find him again, the professor knew this would be one of the first places the doctor would look. In the meantime, these teens were his best hope of surviving on the streets until Dorning finally arrived.

One of the card players saw him first, and jumped up yelling Miguel's name. All four were soon rushing to greet him, skipping like boys rather than acting like the young men they were. They picked him up under the arms and carried him to where they had set up home. He laughed in spite of himself at their greeting.

Then their questions began.

"Man, did you run away from that guy who hit you with his car?"

"Yeah, we saw you a few days ago still with him and you acted like you didn't even know us. Our feelings were hurt man, really hurt," one complained with an exaggerated pout.

The other teens laughed.

"So what did that old guy do to you? Are you still a virgin?"

They all laughed again. The tallest teen grabbed him by the chin and turned his head one way, then the other.

"Looks like he took pretty good care of you, except for that shirt." He examined the large hole ripped by the fence nail.

"So what happened, punk? You gotta say something."

They waited for his answer.

"Not much. We rode around a lot. I lived near the ocean."

The teens laughed louder yet.

"The ocean? Oh man, he's a surfer dude now."

"Fancy car, ocean view, and he comes back here to us."

"Yeah, why did you leave your free ride, man? I won't have if I were you."

He sought a reasonable explanation, one both vague and short. "There was some...trouble with the police."

The teens all ah-ha'ed in unison, then shook their heads as if they expected that answer all along.

"Man, old guys picking us up is always bad news in the long run. What'd I say?"

"You're lucky he didn't hurt you, man."

"Yeah, he better not come back here if he did."

"Did you at least get any money?"

They fell silent again, waiting for his answer.

"No. He never gave me any money. Just free meals."

They all groaned and playfully waved him away.

"Then it was all for nothing, man, all for nothing."

"Hey, free food ain't bad. I'd take it."

"So you got nothing to show after all that time?"

"Hey man, you hungry now?"

"Yes." The professor answered the last question immediately, grateful for something to eat.

The teen who asked pulled a sandwich out of a paper bag at his feet, tore off a hunk and handed it to him. "Here you go. We take care of our own around here."

"Yeah," said another teen. "It's good to have you back because your sad little puppy face always gets us plenty of extra change from the sweet little old ladies driving by."

The group laughed again, but this time not too loudly, as if they all knew it was only too true.

Marlowe finally realized why they had missed Miguel. He took a bite of the sandwich, wondering how much Miguel's absence had cost the teens in handouts.

"Hey, how's your mother doing?"

"Yeah, is she getting better?"

The professor froze for a few seconds then slowly lowered the sandwich from his face. "My...mother. I don't know. I guess I...haven't seen her in a while."

The teens groaned their disapproval.

"Man, at least you've got a mother."

"Yeah, or at least one that's still willing to see you, anyway. Mine won't."

"You better go see how she's doing, man. They gotta be close to letting her go pretty soon."

Percival thought a moment. "Do you know if she's still in the same place?"

"You're asking us?"

"Yeah, how would we know?"

They stared at him with looks of disbelief.

That wasn't the answer the professor was hoping for. He decided to try a different approach. "Well, would one of you guys mind going with me?" He wanted to see Miguel's mother for himself, if only to satisfy his own curiosity about her.

"Why? Afraid of running into your old man? Can't say I blame you, the way he smacks you around."

He froze again, stunned to learn both of Miguel's parents were still alive and in the immediate neighborhood. He tried not to sound too surprised. "Yeah, that's it. I sure don't want to see him again, do I?"

"I'll go with you," the tallest teen said. "Got nothing better to do."

"Great. When can we go?"

The teen pulled a wristwatch missing its strap from his baggy pants pocket. "If we go now, we can be back in time to catch the lunch traffic. Don't wanna miss all that fresh loose change."

"Okay."

They hurried from the alley into the street. The professor hung just far enough behind the teen not to make it obvious he was following him.

At one intersection, he anticipated a right hand turn and took it, but the teen went left instead.

"Hey, where you going?" the teen called after him.

Percival sheepishly caught up with his guide. "Sorry."

They continued on their way.

The teen glanced at him with scorn. "Man, how long ago was it you last visited your poor mother? She used to be all you ever talked about."

They arrived at the rehab center, a dirty building with crumbling facade like all the others on the block. At the front desk, a nun sat talking on the phone. When she saw the boys, her face brightened. She hastily ended her conversation and hung up.

"Miguel! Where have you been, child? We were so worried about you. Your mother has been asking about you for weeks." Her face darkened a bit. "And your father has been here looking for you too."

"Uh oh," the teen said.

The nun got up. "Follow me. Your mother has her own room now."

The professor was relieved he no longer had to pretend to know where he was going.

They climbed a flight of poorly lit steps then entered a hallway that smelled of urine. The nun opened a door and ushered them in. "She'll be so glad to see you."

She left the room, closing the door behind her.

He stood there, staring at a woman sitting up in bed. She seemed pale but alert as she watched a soap opera in Spanish on a small color TV.

The teen gave him a slight shove in her direction. "Go on, man. She's right there. Say hello."

Percival approached her slowly. "Mother?" he said. The word sounded hollow on his lips.

She turned in surprise, letting out a cry of glee at the sight of him. She motioned him closer and pulled his head down onto her bosom, which heaved as she repeatedly called Miguel's name.

Percival closed his eyes, his face smothered by the woman. "We had no right," he whispered. "This isn't right."

She straightened him up and looked him over. "What did you say?" she asked.

"Nothing...Mother," he said. He tenderly touched her face, sorry Miguel wasn't here to savor the moment.

She kissed his hand, then her expression turned stern. "Miguel. Shame on you for not coming to see me for so long. You know how I worry about the men taking you away, putting you in a new home. The police brought you here once and I had to promise them you would stay off the streets, beg them not to take you. I was afraid they caught you again and I wouldn't see you anymore. Don't scare me like that, Miguel. You come and see me more often, okay?"

"Yes, Mother. I understand."

Her stern expression dissolved into tears and she pulled him close once more.

Go ahead, Miguel, he thought. *This is your time.* He held his breath, concentrating on letting Miguel take over.

Nothing happened.

He hung his head, patted the woman's hand. "I'm sorry," he said softly. "I'm so very sorry."

"That's okay, Miguel, as long as you don't do that to me again. You're a good boy. Did Sister tell you? I'm getting out soon. Then I'll get a job and we'll be back together, just like before." She reached for a handkerchief on a tray besides her to dab at her tearful eyes.

The professor saw something on the tray among the woman's belongings that caught his full attention.

"Wait a minute. What is that?"

The woman looked at him, confused. "What do you mean?"

He pointed at the object, a thin, rectangular box. "That. I think...I think I know what that is somehow, don't I?"

The woman's face brightened. "You mean this?" She took the box, held it out to him. "Of course you know what it is, silly boy. It's yours."

Just as he reached for it, had it nearly in his grasp, he heard the door behind him bang open, and the teen cry out a warning.

Someone grabbed him by the ear, and twisted him around. He yelled out in shock and pain, trying helplessly to free himself. When he looked up to see who was doing this to him, he gasped and nearly forgot about his throbbing ear.

He saw his own new face, twenty years from now. The man reeked of alcohol and had coarse stubble on his chin, but it was his face nonetheless, staring down at him in a drunken rage.

"Father?" he asked.

"Who else would it be, you ungrateful, little...where have you been? Don't you know I've been looking for you?"

The woman leaned out from the bed, her arms outstretched, both of them just out of her reach. "Jose! Jose, no! He's just a poor boy, my poor boy," she sobbed.

"Leave him alone!" The teen charged forward and shoved the man away, then stood between them.

"So you have a bodyguard now? Is that it?" the man asked, unsteady on his feet.

"Just leave him alone," the teen replied.

Percival couldn't take his eyes off the man. He suddenly felt lightheaded, a feeling he now understood.

"Yes, that's it," he said, as his eyelids fluttered. "That's it."

He moaned and doubled over, then slowly rose again.

"Look what you did to him," the teen said.

Miguel looked around the room in confusion and put a hand to his aching ear, unsure why it hurt. Then he saw his father and mother, his father glaring threateningly and his mother beckoning him to safety.

"Mama!" he said. The boy ran and threw his arms around her. "Mama, guess what? I was...I was..." he stopped, realizing he could never explain it, didn't even know where to begin.

She pulled him close and rocked him back and forth. "It's okay now, Miguel. Everything's going to be okay."

The teen opened his hard fists.

Miguel's father looked sullen. "You haven't brought me any money for too long," he said to Miguel. "What good are you?"

"Jose, please," Miguel's mother pleaded. "He's just a boy. When I get out, I'll get a job, and we'll be a family again. You'll see." She stroked Miguel's hair, smiled kindly at him. "We'll have plenty of money, and find a nice place to live, and things will be like they used to be. Okay, my Miguel?"

"Yes, Mama."

Miguel's father looked unconvinced. "You better get a job," he said. "Because nobody will hire me. God knows I've tried."

"If you stopped getting wasted..." the teen began.

"Stay out of this," the father warned. "You're just a bum like Miguel. That's all either of you are ever going to be."

"No, I'm not," Miguel said. "When Mama gets a job, I'm going back to school."

"School?" His father laughed. "What makes you think they can still teach you anything?"

"Because I'm not stupid like you say. I can have a good future."

His father's expression turned sullen. "A future? There is no future. There's only today." He turned to go.

Miguel left his mother's side and ran towards his father. The teen put an arm out to stop him, but Miguel brushed it aside.

"Papa. We can try. At least...we can try." He looked up at his father, wanting to hug him but afraid. "But first you have to try not to be so angry all the time. That's what keeps us apart."

His father raised his hands in surprise as if unfamiliar with Miguel's words, then lowered them and roughly rubbed the boy's head. "Ah. So you want to be the new man of the family, is that it? Tell us what to do? You?"

"I just want us to be a family again, like Mama said. You were a good father to me before you lost your job and got so mad about it. You used to play catch with me in the alley, and take me to parades and the circus and even the movies. I remember all that, and want it all to happen again. So does Mama, I'm sure. Don't you, Papa? Don't you want those days to return, when we were all so happy?"

His father looked at his mother, who sat with a hand covering her mouth.

He rubbed Miguel's head again, more gently this time. "Maybe someday those days will come back. We'll see what happens," he said, and abruptly left the room.

Miguel stepped out in the hallway and watched his father walk away and disappear into the stairwell.

The teen came up behind him.

"Man, I thought you hated school. Were you serious about going back or were you just kidding?"

"Serious," Miguel answered firmly. "I want to be smart on my own."

꧁꧂

That evening, after begging for handouts and dodging the police who tried to keep the panhandlers away from the commuters in a rush to leave the city, Miguel ate at a nearby deli, his first full meal all day. He kept enough change to buy a thin pad of paper and a pen at a convenience store. Then, with the darkness, said goodbye to his friends and returned to his secret hiding place in the park. He hadn't been there in weeks, and was dismayed to find that his blanket—left out unprotected in the rain—was moldy and decayed. He tossed it in the trash, hoping they would give him another free one at the Salvation Army shop tomorrow.

As he bunked down on a pile of leaves for bedding, he pulled out the notepad and opened the pen. It was only a matter of time before Dorning found him, he knew, and whatever trick Dorning had used to make him become the professor the last time he was bound to try again. To prepare for that event, he decided to write a letter he would keep with him at all times.

He stared at the blank page under the faint light of the distant streetlights, and then laboriously began to write his earnest message to the professor as the crickets chirped and the moon slowly rose in the calm evening sky.

Chapter Twenty-Seven

Miguel worked the lunch crowd at the busy intersection, knowing how to fade away when squads came down the block without drawing their attention. If a suspicious car came along too late for him to casually make it to a hiding place, his friends would hide him by pretending to be window-shopping, their backs to the street with him in front, nearly pressed up against the glass. The teens were just tall enough not to draw more than one glance from the officers in marked or unmarked cars. They looked just old enough to always get the benefit of the doubt that they weren't underage as long as he wasn't seen with them.

He made sure all of them had enough money to buy something to eat at the end of the day, since drivers often singled him out for a little something extra. If the driver got a little too friendly or started to ask the wrong questions, his friends would intervene and create a distraction so he could quickly disappear.

When the handouts started to dwindle and the storeowners began to complain about their presence, they went a few blocks over to work a brand-new crowd.

He was more than glad to share what he got in exchange for one small favor: "If the guy in the black Mercedes comes back, you've got to hide me," he told them. "And if he asks you where I am, you have no idea. Deal?"

"Sure, man," the oldest teen said. "Nobody's taking you away again. Not if we can help it."

Miguel felt somewhat reassured by the promise, but still knew that Dorning was bound to show up, and sooner rather than later.

☙❧

He was returning from visiting his mother one Saturday morning when he saw them coming towards him in a hurry, blocks from where they were panhandling. He could tell immediately from their worried expressions something was terribly wrong.

They grabbed him by the arms and carried him through a revolving door into a department store. Two clerks immediately frowned at them; they stopped where they were and set him down.

"What is it? Cops?" he asked over the Muzak pouring from the speaker directly above them.

The tall teen shook his head, and Miguel instantly knew.

"It's him, isn't it? Did he talk to you?"

"No, we ran when we saw him. I'm not even sure he saw us. But he's around. We thought you might want to take the rest of the day off."

"Yeah," said another teen. "Go back the way you came."

"Just get the hell away from here before it's too late."

Miguel followed them out the door and looked fearfully up and down the block. He didn't see the familiar car.

"Want me to come in case he finds you?" the tallest teen asked.

"No," Miguel said. "I've been thinking about some places to hide. I'll be okay."

"Good luck, man," another teen said. "See you later."

Miguel walked briskly away, head down, trying to use the sparse crowd on the sidewalk as a shield from the street.

"Crap," said the tallest teen, watching him leave. "He better be okay. We don't get half the money without him."

The other teens nodded somberly in agreement.

Miguel walked straight past the rehab center where his mother was, certain the doctor would look for him there. He decided to keep walking, to get as far away as he could from where the doctor expected to find him. All the familiar churches and shelters in town were out of the question—Dorning was bound to call or visit them all.

He finally decided to go to one of the last places the doctor would ever think to look for him, the industrial park. With only trains and truck traffic, it was no place to panhandle or even hang out. And since it was the weekend, he could easily find a place to hide all day among the loading docks and trailer yards because there would be few people around.

Miguel took the alleyways, guessing they were too slow and diffi-cult for Dorning to maneuver through, but kept a sharp eye out for the Mercedes whenever he had to dash across a street.

At the sight of the factories up ahead, Miguel began to feel safe. He passed by rows of dumpsters and trash compactors, looking up at the nearly windowless buildings on either side that were each blocks long. Without the sound of traffic or the bustle of people on the side-walks, there was only an eerie silence, as if the factories were giants fast asleep.

He heard the unexpected squeal of tires behind him and spun around.

There was nothing there.

Miguel kept walking. He found a recessed loading dock with a long row of tall overhead doors and saw one door had been left open as if forgotten. He walked up the slight incline, cautiously peering into the bay.

"Hello?" he called. His voiced echoed in the empty chamber.

No one answered.

He boosted himself up and decided at once it was just the right place to stay.

Then he heard the squeal of tires again. He gasped to see the black Mercedes slowly drive past the loading dock, stop and back up, then turn into the bay as if Dorning had read his mind and followed him here. Miguel stood tight against the inside wall so he couldn't be seen.

He heard the car door open and close, then approaching footsteps on the asphalt that stopped when they reached the dock.

"Clearly you're not the professor," he heard Dorning say. "Percival would be looking for me, instead of running away. You're probably wondering how I found you, aren't you, Miguel? Actually, you made it ridiculously easy. I simply thought to myself, 'Where would I hide if I were the boy?' and came to the same answer you did—where the doctor would never think to look. And so I drove by the factories a few times after failing to see you with your friends—who seemed quite nervous, by the way, which told me they had tipped you off—and sure enough, there you were, in plain sight, just walking along all by yourself for the whole world to see. And when I saw this open door, I realized you would think this was the perfect place to hide, when in reality, it's the worst because it's much too obvious. And that's how I found you, as I knew I would in time. You might as well come out, Miguel, because I'm not leaving until you do. There's no place to run anymore. The game is over."

Miguel tensed himself, then burst out of hiding and leapt over Dorning's astonished head, landing hard on his feet then running as fast as he could. Behind him he heard the car door slam and the squeal of tires once more. The car engine roared as if furious he wouldn't do as the doctor said, surrender without a fight.

Miguel heard the Mercedes coming up fast. He made a sudden left turn at an intersection, knowing Dorning wouldn't expect it. The Mercedes sailed past, the brakes screeched in protest, and the car came around to pursue him again.

His lungs burned and his legs grew wobbly. Miguel saw another intersection up ahead, gambled on turning right this time.

He ran into a dead end with stark, windowless walls all around, and collapsed in a heap to catch his breath.

The Mercedes blocked the exit. Dorning got out, his expression grim.

"That was foolish, very foolish Miguel. You could have been hurt. Percival could have been hurt."

"I'm not Percival," he replied when he could speak. "I'm Miguel, and I want to stay Miguel."

Dorning stepped forward. "I'm afraid that's impossible now. You know full well how important it is the Professor continues his work. Why, that's exactly what he was doing before the unfortunate incident with the police. I didn't spend the last twenty years of my life trying to save the Professor's life for nothing, Miguel. You can't just walk away."

Miguel finally turned his head and looked at Dorning, surprised to see the doctor in a rumpled shirt with his hair unkempt.

"You can't make me be the professor if I don't want to."

Dorning laughed bitterly. "Make you? No, the professor 'makes you' because he wants to live too, you know. Here, let me show you something." He reached into his pocket and pulled something out. "I'll prove it."

"No!" Miguel scrambled backwards on all fours into a corner. "What is it, the same trick you used before to make the professor appear?"

"No, it's not a trick. It's just a little something I'd like you to look at, that's all." Dorning came forward and opened his hand, revealing a brass medal. "Here, take a look, and I'll tell you all about it. It won't hurt you; in fact, it has a very interesting story."

"No! Get away!" The boy closed his eyes, covering them with both hands.

"Miguel, I'm growing weary of this. I just spent a small fortune on bail for trumped-up Obstruction of Justice charges, and I've been reduced to living in a seedy hotel room. I don't have time for this."

"I won't. I won't do it," Miguel said, and curled up tight into a ball, his hands over his head.

Dorning stood in front of Miguel, staring down at him. "The police are looking for you, Miguel. You'll be arrested too, for running away from them. You won't have much fun or freedom in jail. Is that what you want? But the professor is smart, Miguel, smarter than you and me. He can find a way to keep you out of jail. He can keep both of us out of jail. I need the professor right here and now and so do you, whether you like it or not."

"No. Please. Why are you doing this to me?"

Dorning dropped to his knees in front of the boy, his teeth bared. "Stop this nonsense! I've wasted enough time. You will look at this."

Dorning dropped the medal and grabbed Miguel arms. He forced them behind the boy's back and held them there with one hand.

Miguel yelled as loud as he could, his eyes still tightly closed. "Help! Police! Help!"

"Shout as much as you want, there's no one around to hear you."

Miguel sobbed and buried his head as far in his chest as he could.

"All right," Dorning said, "if that's the way you want it, let's try this instead."

Dorning grabbed Miguel by the back of his hair. He forced the boy's head forward, just inches from the medal on the ground.

"What are you doing?" Miguel asked, still afraid to look.

"Listen to me then, if you won't open your eyes yet. On the ground is something the professor was very proud of, something that meant everything to him when he was about your age."

Miguel shook his head. "No! I won't listen to you." He sang to drown out Dorning's words. "Hush little baby, don't say a word..."

Dorning yanked on Miguel's hair; the boy winced and cried out.

"*Don't* sing. You will listen to me, or I'll pull your hair even harder the next time. Now, what it is you're refusing to look at is a swimming medal the professor won. It's brass, about two inches in diameter I would say, and on one side it has a picture of a swimmer diving into the water with the words 'Cambridge, 1924' underneath, and on the other side it says 'First Place'. Do you remember that medal, Miguel?"

Miguel whimpered softly, his eyes still closed.

"Good. Now the reason why this medal meant so much to the professor is because his whole life changed for the better after he won it, just like your life is going to change for the better once the professor returns. You see he was always smart, but not so popular when he was a boy. But once he won this medal, with its impressive red and white ribbon, everyone wanted to be his friend, and he wore the medal all the time to show people how grand he was now. Even his family looked up to him like they had never done before. All the kids at school followed him wherever he went, eager to see and hear what he was going to do and say next. They came to him with all their problems, and he helped solve them, winning even more respect and admiration, like a true hero. His teachers suddenly found him fascinating too, and the grades they gave him were always excellent. But that's not the best part. You know what the best part was?" He put his mouth closer to Miguel's ear, talked softer to him. "It was the girls. All the girls flocked to him, loved him, wanted to be with him. He could pick and choose, and you did, professor, you did."

Miguel opened his eyes a little and gazed down at the medal through narrow slits.

Dorning put his mouth even closer to Miguel's ear, nearly whispering now. "That's right. Now notice the familiar smell the medal has. Doesn't that bring back fond memories? Of course it does. It wasn't long after you won that medal you lost your innocence to a beautiful girl, a girl you always wanted. Remember? She was so beautiful, and you had her, you had her as you always dreamed you would. And there were others, there were many others that followed, all so beautiful. Remember, Percival? That was when you knew you were no longer a boy, but a man. A man, Professor. A man. So very, very proud to finally be a man."

Miguel's arms and head went limp; Dorning let go and patted the boy's shoulder. "That's right," he said. "Believe me, this is for your own good."

Dorning sat back, picked up the medal, and put it in his pocket.

The boy groaned low, slowly straightened up.

"Good afternoon, Professor."

Percival raised his head and looked at the factories around him. "What? Where the devil are we now?" He smoothed his hair down on the back of his head. "And why does my neck hurt? What did you just do?"

"That doesn't matter. All that matters is that you're back."

Percival stood up and put his hands on his hips, towering over the doctor for a change. "Dorning, why didn't you tell me?"

Dorning remained seated, not understanding. "Tell you what, Professor?"

"The boy. He has a mother. And a father. They're here, Dorning, in this city. He's not an orphan like you led me to believe."

Dorning stood up and dusted himself off. "I never said he was an orphan. I said he was homeless. And he is. Or was."

"But that could have changed. He could have had a meaningful future. I saw the possibility of the family reuniting, or at the very least the boy could have finally had a roof over his head with a mother who genuinely loves him."

"A possibility? I suppose anything's possible outside the laws of physics, but the certainty is your future will enrich civilization to a vastly greater degree than someone who merely achieves a roof over their head, no matter who loves him." He motioned towards the car. "Come on. We can debate this on the way home." He turned to go.

The professor sighed and followed Dorning. "Is that the only way you can justify what we've done? That I'll achieve more than the boy would?"

"That's not a bad reason, is it? In fact, I think it's terrific."

Percival opened the passenger door then stopped. "I wish I could be as certain as you, Doctor. But I'm no longer convinced any reason can ever justify it." He looked to the city behind them. "What I really wish is that I *could* share somehow with the boy on a regular basis, like he wanted to."

Dorning took a deep breath. "Professor, I think we've already had more than enough of that talk. You have no idea."

They got into the car. Dorning carefully backed out of the dead end, no longer in any hurry.

"So what happened after I ran away?"

Dorning drooped, then glanced at the professor. "I'm out on bail."

"You're kidding. Are the police still looking for me?"

"Oh, yes. Most definitely. In fact, they were convinced I knew where to find you."

"I had the distinct impression that detective thought I was in on some kind of scam with you regarding my own estate."

"That's their theory."

"Hmm." Marlowe tapped his mouth. "There must be a way out of this. I may have to rearrange a few financial matters, see if I can still pull a few strings somehow." He watched the city disappear from view as Dorning entered the highway.

Dorning finally allowed himself to grin a little. "Professor, I'm counting on it. That's why I went through all that trouble to help you return as soon as I could."

"Too bad Miguel doesn't have someone helping him return."

Dorning's grin faded. "I'm sorry, Percival, but with any luck, that will be the last time you'll ever have a relapse if I have anything to do about it. I can't take much more of Miguel. I hope the boy is gone forever, and good riddance if he finally is."

Percival was silent as he stared out the window.

Here we go again, Miguel, he thought. *Are you getting as weary of this as I am?*

The only thing he heard in response was the steady purr of the car engine as they sped away from the forlorn factories behind them.

Chapter Twenty-Eight

The neon sign at the motel was mostly burnt out; only the "vacancy" was lit, and even that flickered at times as if uncertain.

"I'm sorry for the accommodations, Professor," Dorning said as he pulled into the pothole-strewn parking lot. "With your estate still tied up in the hands of the lawyers, money's rather tight right now."

As they walked to the room, Marlowe noticed to his amusement that even though Dorning's car wasn't a new model, it was still far better than those of the other residents.

The room was more generous than the professor had expected, with twin beds, two large dressers and a small desk. On one of the dressers, stacked in a precarious heap, were all his precious books and papers.

The professor went to the dresser and patted a thick volume with his name on the cover. "My work," he said. "Excellent. Before all that nasty business with the police, I was very close to completing something major I've left unfinished for years. Something truly wonderful. The solution finally occurred to me in a flash, like they used to."

Dorning sat on his bed, froze taking off his shoes, then slowly looked up at the professor in awe. "Why Percival! That's fantastic news. Why didn't you tell me that before? That's precisely what I meant about achievement, why you simply had to have the opportunity to continue your work. Think of how much this will mean to the scientific community to have Percival Marlowe in his prime again."

The professor stepped away from the book. "Too bad it won't mean much at all to Miguel's parents."

"Ah." Dorning waved a hand. "When all our troubles are behind us, you can secretly provide for the boy's family if you like, since you're soon to inherit the bulk of your own estate." He finished taking off his shoes.

Percival half turned his head. "Now that I've met them, I wonder how his parents would react to what we've done to their son. Probably not well."

"Oh, I don't know. They might grow to love having a brilliant astrophysicist in the family."

"But I wouldn't be their Miguel, even though I look just like him, right down to his fingerprints." He looked at his hands. "It's just not the same, don't you see?"

Dorning shook his head and stood up. "No, I don't. All I see is the shower, which I need to use right now. Then I'm going shopping for some food. The best thing you could do is organize your files so you can get back to work and finish that important paper. Sorry for the mess, I'm afraid I just dumped everything of yours on the dresser. If it's any consolation, I need to reorganize my own research papers too. I didn't want to leave them behind where they might be found." He nodded to the other dresser in the room, which had a more modest stack of books and files, and grabbed a change of clothes from his suitcase. "Now, if you'll excuse me, Professor," he said, as he stepped into the washroom and locked the door.

The professor half-heartedly shuffled a few of his books then decided the tedious task could wait until sometime later. He heard the shower turn on and the shower curtain clatter along its pole.

A notebook on Dorning's dresser caught his eye. The professor recognized it as the journal Dorning had started, then abandoned. He went and picked it up, flipping through the few entries in Dorning's cramped handwriting, then closed the notebook and set it aside. He noticed that underneath the notebook was a manila file folder. With the sound of the water still running in the shower, the professor opened the file for a quick look. The title page of the papers inside grabbed his interest, and he began to read.

The professor felt his knees grow weak. "Oh my God," he said, and took the file over to the desk.

He sat down to read what he couldn't believe, what he had never suspected at all.

～≈

Dorning finished drying off, got dressed and combed his hair. He felt refreshed now, his spirits lifted by the professor's revelation about the nearly completed major new work. Humming faintly to himself, he opened the bathroom door, expecting to see Marlowe busily rearranging the jumble of books or maybe even finishing what Dorning was sure would only be the first of many scientific breakthroughs.

Percival was standing by the desk, an empty folder in his hand. Papers were scattered across the floor, and the professor's eyes flashed at him in anger.

Dorning stopped humming. "What is it? What's wrong?"

"Your technique, Dorning. That's what's wrong. Your solution for ensuring complete and total memory transfer."

Dorning took a sudden step forward and stopped, dismayed by the realization it was too late to intervene. "You shouldn't be reading my personal files, Professor. Those are meant only for me. This is an invasion of my privacy."

"I paid for that research for years, Dorning. I have a right to know where all my money went. Besides, you let me read all your other research except for this little discovery, didn't you? This 'last piece of the puzzle,' as you called it." He threw the empty folder down.

Dorning cleared his throat. "I didn't see what good would come of you being prematurely aware of how I succeeded."

"'Prematurely?' The deed is done, Doctor. When were you going to tell me? When were you going to let me know that to achieve your one hundred percent memory transfer, you had to invade my brain with your instruments while I was still alive and in the process, kill me?"

"You were terminal, Percival. You know that. I couldn't let critical memories be lost forever. The donor brain must be viable for as long as possible for full memory transfer to occur."

"Murderer."

"There was no other way. Time was running out. It was that, or only partial success, which might as well be failure. It's the only way I know how to make the all the fragile memory proteins cooperate."

"Killer."

"Stop saying that! Stop implying I acted improperly somehow. It's the only procedure that works. I simply did what was best for you, the best I knew how."

"The best for me? I could still be alive as myself, not living in a body you stole, Dorning. Stole!"

"I stole nothing. I'm telling you, the boy's sacrifice was absolutely worth it, the best thing he could have done with his miserable life. I would have even sacrificed myself for you if I could. Many people would have. I'm still convinced of that."

"You're not listening to me, Dorning. No one had to make a sacrifice. I wasn't dead. With proper medical treatment, I might still be alive."

"As what, Percival? As what? A shell of a man, fatigued all the time, rolling to and fro in your wheelchair, practically spoon fed until you finally died? Is that your idea of being alive? Look at you now. You have enough energy and stamina again for answers to cosmic questions to spring into your mind, instead of merely trying to remember if you took all your medicine in the morning. Which reality would you rather have, Professor? Which is better for humanity?"

They circled each other, inches apart, the professor's head turned upward, eyes locked with the doctor's.

"Your success—my life—doesn't justify the means, Dorning. No one is so irreplaceable you can resort to euthanasia and then rob someone else—especially a child—of the right to live their own life, even if that life is impoverished."

"You're talking nonsense, Professor. Certainly in a perfect world we would all have the same opportunities to succeed, but that isn't how the world works, I'm afraid. With his social status and lack of education, the boy was going to amount to nothing. Now he can make all the difference."

"Is that all that's really important to you, Doctor? Achievements? Is that how you define a life worth living and one that's not?"

"Yes! Whether it's scientific work, or artistic, or as a leader of industry, what we accomplish is ultimately how we're judged, how we're remembered by others. A life without goals, without passion for some endeavor, is a wasted life. An empty life not worth living."

"You're wrong, Dorning. A person who accomplishes nothing of material significance in their life, but who is kind to others and treats them fairly, who is loved and respected for just being a decent human being, is the most successful person I can think of. That's far more important than all the scientific discoveries ever made."

Dorning blinked and stepped back. "You can't really believe that, Professor. I know you too well. We're kindred spirits, or at least we used to be. We would still be living in caves if any of that were true."

The professor relaxed, but still regarded Dorning warily. "I would rather live in a cave, admired for my concern for others, than live in a world filled with high technology that values life as poorly as you do."

Dorning looked away then finally replied with a hint of resentment in a smaller voice. "I valued your life enough to risk everything I had to save it, Professor. And that's what I did, and we're just going to have to live with it, whether all my many personal sacrifices are appreciated or not."

Marlowe's hard gaze softened. "Dorning. I know your motives were noble, but how you finally succeeded was all wrong."

Dorning bowed politely. "And with all due respect, I couldn't possibly disagree more."

They were both silent a moment.

Dorning stood up straighter as if to restore his dignity. "Now. All that said, I must go shopping if we intend to eat tonight. We have nothing at all. Is there anything specific you would like me to get you?" he tried to sound upbeat.

"Yes." The professor stared at him, his eyes cold. "I'd like my soul."

Dorning took a deep breath. "Very funny, Professor. I'll be back in about an hour." He headed for the door, then stopped and turned around again. "I hope our disagreement won't interfere with the completion of your nearly finished paper, will it? If so, then everything I've tried to accomplish goes completely to waste. It would all amount to absolutely nothing, including the boy's 'sacrifice', as you've called it."

Percival looked towards the dresser. "No, Doctor. I'll finish the paper. In fact, it's nearly done. It won't take very long to complete."

Dorning looked pleased. "Good. I look forward to reading it, even though I'm sure I won't quite understand it. See you in a while, Professor."

Dorning left the room.

Marlowe sighed deeply and rubbed his face. He decided to take a shower too and freshen up.

He kicked off his shoes and started to pull off his shirt when he realized there was something in the chest pocket. He pulled out a folded sheet of paper, opened it and began to read the sprawling print:

Profesor-

If you are reading this, than I am no longr Miguel. I just want you to know that I would like to have my life back if I could, all the time. I am sorry for you, but I did not know I would have to be forgottn in order for you to live again. That is not fair at all. I know you are very smart and can do a lot for the world, but I think if I go back to school and work hard, I can help the world too, as Miguel. I know you are a nice man becase I lived with you awil. We had fun. If you can bring me back, my mother and maybe my father would be a famly again if I'm around becase I want them to. I hope you can do this, becase my mother missis me when I am you. Do not listen to the doctor abot this becase he didnt tell me the truthe, he is meen. Maybe he didnt tell you the truthe to. If you cant bring me back, then Im sorry to bothr you with this note, but I hope you can becase I want to live again, that is all.

Miguel Sanchez

Percival sat down heavily on his bed and slowly bowed his head. When he finally raised it, his eyes were rimmed with profound regret.

"I'm so very sorry, Miguel," he said fervently, ruefully. "Can you ever forgive me for what we've done to you?"

There was only the usual, now completely unbearable silence.

"Enough of this," he said then, and his eyes flashed with renewed purpose and resolve. He immediately went to his book and papers, and began at once to organize the pile, knowing he didn't have much time before Dorning returned.

Chapter Twenty-Nine

Dorning carried the heavy grocery bag across the parking lot to the motel room. He had mixed feelings about leaving the professor alone while he went shopping, but he knew he couldn't keep an eye on him every minute of every day. Their bitter argument had bothered him in the store, however, and on the way home, and it was with growing apprehension now that he hurried to the door, fumbling with his keys, fearful of what he might find—or not find—inside.

What he saw nearly made him drop the bag.

The professor's books were lined up on the dresser, and on the desk were neatly stacked papers arranged in orderly rows.

But the professor wasn't in view.

And then Dorning heard the bathroom door open and saw him step out, wearing fresh clothes.

"Percival!" He beamed. "Thank goodness you're okay. I was worried about you after our little disagreement. It looks like you've been very busy while I was gone. That's wonderful, just wonderful." He set the bag down on his bed.

Percival smiled, but his eyes were cold. "I have an even better surprise for you, Doctor."

The professor opened the top drawer of the desk, pulled out a large envelope.

"My completed manuscript, ready to mail."

Dorning took the envelope and held it with reverence. "How many years did you say this took to finish?"

"Too many," Percival replied. "I haven't completed anything this significant in a quarter century at least. It's some of my best work by far."

Dorning felt overwhelmed, and wiped his misty eyes. "Look at me, about to cry like a silly fool. Forgive me, I didn't expect this so suddenly. See, I knew my faith in you was justified, Professor. I knew you wouldn't let me down, or the world. And here's the proof." He shook the envelope then wiped his eyes again. "They'll wrongly conclude this was a work you completed before you died, but someday they'll know the truth, and rejoice that Percival Marlowe is still alive, and once again at the forefront of science."

The professor patted Dorning's arm, then took the envelope back. "Well, thank you, Doctor. All that's left to do now is to mail it, along with some other letters I've prepared." He picked up a few more envelopes from the desk.

Dorning's eyes widened. "Others?"

"Relax, Doctor. These are rather mundane. They're just some boring financial and legal correspondence."

"What about?" Dorning looked at the smaller envelopes in the professor's hand with curiosity.

The professor smiled stiffly. "Oh, nothing much. You'll see."

Dorning beamed again. "My. We should argue more often if this is what comes out of it, Professor. You've been very, very productive this afternoon."

Marlowe's empty smile remained. "Yes. Well. Now all I need is some money for postage, Doctor. Hopefully we're not that broke."

"Oh no, we have enough to last a while longer. We're not in dire straits just yet."

"Really? Well then if you don't mind, could I get some to buy some supplies, maybe even enough for a few new books I need? I'm afraid they're rather expensive." He stared steadily at Dorning.

"Why, of course, of course." Dorning hastily opened his wallet and pulled out six hundred dollar bills and a few lesser ones. "Here. This is the most I can spare until your estate is finally settled."

The professor took the money. "Thanks again." He slipped the hundred dollar bills into one of the envelopes and stuffed the rest in his pocket.

"Well, you're certainly entitled to it. I only wish I could give you more." The doctor put his wallet away.

Percival briefly lowered his gaze. "I also want to thank you for all you've done for me. I might have sounded ungrateful before, but I mean it when I say the past few weeks have been absolutely extraordinary. Your achievement, although by questionable means, is nothing short of remarkable, Doctor. I want you to know that." He firmly shook Dorning's hand.

Dorning felt his eyes welling up again, and proudly raised his head.

"Percival, this is only the beginning."

"I know. No hard feelings then?"

"No. I'm just surprised by your sudden change of heart. I didn't expect it so quickly."

The professor considered that a moment. "Well, I guess the second chance you gave me allowed me to reexamine some of the beliefs I held in my first lifetime."

Dorning waved a finger at him. "Don't be too hasty to throw away those earlier beliefs, Professor. They served you well for a long, long time."

"Yes. I suppose they did."

He let go of Dorning's hand. They both stood there awkwardly.

Marlowe stepped towards the door, and was the first to speak again. "Well, I have to go mail my letters. They're not going to do any good sitting around here."

"Would you like me to drive you?"

"No, don't bother. I saw a post office just a little ways down the road. You prepare our dinner, and I'll be back soon. You can drive me to get my books and supplies later." He opened the door then remembered something. He closed the door and rubbed the tip of his nose. "Oh, by the way, Doctor. I was wondering. What is it again you use to restore me when I lapse back to being Miguel? I know you showed it to me at the University, but I don't remember." He struggled to sound convincing.

"Use? Oh. This." He pulled the swimming medal from his pocket, handing it to the professor. "You may not believe it, but that old, meaningless award has a very, very powerful pull on you, Professor, far more so than anything else you've ever owned. With it, I'm able to trigger a positive response in you, restore you through a veritable flood of happy childhood memories. We're lucky to have it, since it can help prevent another relapse." The doctor started emptying the bag of groceries onto his dresser.

"Oh yes, now I remember." Percival pretended to examine it dispassionately, but couldn't help but grin. "Odd, but this still means a lot to me, even now." He hefted the medal in his palm. "I can feel it." His joyful expression faded. "Funny how the simplest things..."

He let the thought trail off and looked at Dorning, who was opening a package of paper plates. "Shouldn't I hang on to this at all times, Doctor, and look at it every day in order to help me stay in control?"

Dorning raised an eyebrow. "An excellent suggestion. Perhaps that would have avoided the last unpleasant relapse, when you didn't have the medal with you. Go ahead, keep it. Just guard it with your life, because in some ways, that's exactly what it is." He waved a hand. "You know, I'm a little disappointed at how tenacious the boy was, far more so than any of my other animal test subjects. He certainly didn't give up without a fight, which under normal circumstances I would have considered admirable. But we simply can't afford to ever let him reappear again, now can we?" He looked back at the professor, his expression blank, as if he expected the professor would now fully agree.

Percival squeezed the medal tight in his fist then came around to confront Dorning with one final hunch.

"It's funny you should say that about Miguel, Doctor. Are you sure there isn't something else you aren't telling me about the procedure, something more I deserve to know?"

Dorning refused to look directly at him as he unpacked the groceries slower. "What do you mean, Professor?"

"I mean, even after you thought you had 'perfected' your technique there were problems, weren't there, Doctor? If not, why would you be so opposed to letting Miguel appear every now and then, to share, like he wanted? What happened afterwards with your procedure, Doctor? Why do you seem so afraid of Miguel's reappearance?" His eyes flashed, and he stepped closer for the answer.

Dorning smiled weakly and stopped unpacking, still not looking directly at the professor. "A typically astute observation, Professor, although I'm not actually afraid of the boy." He finally glanced at him, fleetingly. "I'm afraid for you."

"Why?"

Dorning resumed unpacking, slowly again. He didn't answer right away. "Because, to my immense disappointment, I discovered that if there are too many relapses lasting for too long, the final relapse becomes permanent. Unfortunately, that means you could still be lost. If, however, we manage to keep you in control—and with your renewed cooperation today, we will Percival, we will—" Dorning glanced fleetingly at him again. "In time the boy will finally be completely gone, and those damnable relapses will no longer be possible. How long exactly we have to wait for that thankful, happy day I have yet to determine, but it shouldn't be all that much longer. In other words, you aren't quite out of the woods just yet. And that's why I hope the boy never returns, if you really must know. I hadn't told you because I simply didn't want you to worry. I wanted you to tend to your work instead, unencumbered. And that's the only reason." His expression turned less somber. "I'm still hopeful that someday I'll find a better solution to this... stubborn little problem. That is, if I can ever return to my lab." He looked around the motel room with disdain.

Marlowe nodded, secretly pleased to hear exactly what he had long surmised. It was just the information he needed; what he had fully expected to hear.

"Well, Doctor, I guess that means there's really nothing to worry about, at least not as long as I have the medal, right?" He held it up for Dorning to see, then slipped it into his shirt pocket. "I better get going now. It's getting late. See you in a while." He went and opened the door, still staring at Dorning.

His back to the professor now as he prepared their cold meal, Dorning waved at him over his shoulder. "That's fine, Professor. Dinner will be ready momentarily. Be careful now and don't take too long to mail those letters." His voice sounded almost pleasant again.

Percival's expression turned melancholy. "It shouldn't take too long at all. Goodbye, Doctor."

He watched Dorning a few seconds longer, then quietly slipped away.

Chapter Thirty

He arrived at the beach house at sunset and told the cab driver to wait. The professor walked up the drive to the front door and found it locked as he thought he would. He went to the back of the house to try the window off the patio. That lock never worked right, he knew, and if he pushed the window down first and then pulled out and up...

The window slid open. He crawled inside.

Percival turned on the light in the bedroom. All the familiar bedroom furniture was still there, including his pillow and bed sheets, still in disarray on the bed just the way they were when he and Dorning had moved out in a hurry when they thought the police might be there any moment. Without the jumble of books and papers everywhere, the room looked bigger than he remembered it. The professor noticed Dorning had even taken the Nobel Prize medal out of its case on the wall, leaving the glass door open.

He closed the small door and moved on.

In the kitchen, the dirty dishes from his last meal in the house were still in the sink, as was the red stain on the kitchen tablecloth from Natalie's spilled glass of sherry.

He turned on the hallway light and looked into Natalie's room, not surprised to see she had secretly returned to retrieve all her belongings. The room seemed odd without her dozens of family pictures on the walls or her vases filled with bright silk flowers.

The guest bedroom, where Dorning stayed briefly, held less interest. He moved past it back to his old bedroom, walking through it again to the patio to look out at the setting sun. Wispy, bright orange-red clouds dipped down to the horizon, and in the east, the sky was already a spreading inky blue. He had spent years on that patio, first by choice as a young man, later because he had nowhere else to be.

The professor went down on to the beach and walked along the shore up to the water's edge. He gazed far out to where the water and sky met, hoping to see a ship, or maybe even a shimmering mirage, as he had seen so many times before. There was nothing.

As the sky drew darker and the shadows longer, Percival pulled the swimming medal out of his pocket. He looked at it carefully, turning it over and over. Then he suddenly reared back and flung it with all his might at the ocean, watching it sail towards a cresting wave. The medal hit the top of the water, skipped once, and was swallowed up. He stood there a moment, then slowly walked back to the waiting cab.

He got in as if nothing had happened. "I want to go into the city now. I'll give you the address."

The cab pulled out of the long driveway, and the beach house disappeared from view.

As the cab hummed along on the highway, the sky now black, he took the one envelope he hadn't mailed at the post office and made sure it contained all he intended. He licked the flap, closed it, and forced the envelope back into his shirt pocket. The stiff edge wasn't far under his chin.

The cabdriver looked at him in the rearview mirror. "Funny way to carry a letter. You could get hurt that way."

"It's a gift for...a friend," he explained. "I don't want to forget it."

The professor looked out the window up at the moon, and then peered beyond it to the distant stars. He thought of the manuscript he had mailed that afternoon.

I know a few more of your stubborn secrets now, he thought with considerable satisfaction. *And soon everyone will. We did it, Miguel, we did it. We were very, very smart, just like you wanted to be.*

In the city, the cab pulled up to the rehab center. Marlowe paid the driver.

"You don't want me to wait?"

The professor sadly shook his head. "No. With any luck, this is the end of the line."

He watched the cab pull away then went into the well-worn building.

A nun he hadn't seen before scowled at him from the front desk. "I'm sorry, young man, but visiting hours just ended. You'll have to come back tomorrow."

Then the nun the professor recognized came down the steps and motioned him forward. "It's all right, Sister. His mother's still awake." She guided him up the steps. "My, my. Two visits in one day. Aren't you the dutiful son now, instead of disappearing for weeks on end?"

He went alone into the room and saw Miguel's mother sitting up in bed, watching another TV show in Spanish.

The volume was turned so far down, with the soft click of the door latch behind him, she turned her head and raised her hands in surprise.

"Miguel! You should be asleep somewhere where it's safe, not walking these streets at night. Shame on you. Come here."

Percival obeyed, moving stiffly.

She hugged and kissed him. He barely responded.

The woman held him at arm's length and looked him over, worry now etched on her face. "Is something wrong? You don't feel like you did this morning. Are you getting sick?" She put a hand to his forehead.

"No, Mother."

She laughed faintly. "Why do you call me 'Mother' when you've always called me Mama? You did that once before to me. I hope you don't think you're all grown up now, because you're not. Don't try to grow up too fast, Miguel. That's no good. You'll grow up soon enough, much too soon." She brushed back his hair with her fingers, finally noticing the envelope in his shirt pocket and nodding towards it. "What's that you have?"

"Ask me about that later, Mama. It's a surprise for you and Miguel."

She laughed again. "You *are* Miguel, silly boy. Listen to you."

He licked his lips, his shoulders hunched, all his hopes pinned on what he was about to ask. "Mama, you were about to show me something the other day before my fath...before Papa came in and grabbed my ear. What was that? It looked a little bit familiar."

Her face brightened. "Oh yes, you remembered that, didn't you? Here it is." She reached over to the tray on the side of her bed and rummaged through her meager belongings. She pulled out the thin wooden box and handed it to him.

He saw it was some kind of latched picture frame, and had a vague memory of it that made his jaw go slack.

"I know this somehow," he said softly as he examined it. "Tell me about it, Mama."

"Open it up," she said. "You know how."

Much to his surprise, he did. And when it opened, he saw two pictures inside, one of Miguel as a baby, the other a family photo with Miguel a few years older and his mother and clean-shaven father, all smiling.

He saw a small, folded key under his baby picture, lifted it upright and wound it. Music began to play, a child's lullaby.

"Remember now, Miguel? You used to carry it with you everywhere you went when we first gave it to you. We laughed that you even slept with it. You played that song over and over and over again, but then one day I guess you felt you were too old for such a thing, and you put it aside. I'm glad I kept it for you. I knew some day you might like to have it back again." She patted his cheek. "It meant so much to you."

The song started over, and she sang the words. "Hush little baby, don't say a word..."

He stared deliberately at the pictures and listened to the song. The lightheaded feeling returned.

He raised a trembling hand to his forehead. "Yes, Mama, yes.

That's it. That's it exactly. Sing. Sing!"

She sang and he joined in, still focused on the pictures, until his eyelids finally began to flutter and he started to garble the words.

He lowered his head to the woman's shoulder. She cradled him and rocked him, still singing softly by herself.

"Goodbye, Miguel." He could barely mouth the words. "Thanks for everything."

And Percival was gone.

Miguel straightened up with a start and looked around the room in a daze. "Mama!" he said when he finally saw her. "It's you."

She finished the song and smiled. The music stopped.

"Now, what's the surprise you have for us?" she stared at the envelope.

"Surprise?" He looked down. The envelope hit him in the nose. "I don't know." He yanked the envelope out of his pocket and hastily tore the flap open.

He pulled out six crisp one hundred dollar bills and a folded letter.

His mother's hands flew to her cheeks, and she squealed with delight. "Miguel! Where did you get all that money?"

He gave the bills to her. "I'm not sure." He opened the letter and read it to himself, then quickly stuffed the letter back in his shirt pocket. "It's all right, Mama. A nice man wanted us to have that money to help us be a family again. Everything's going to be okay from now on. I'm not going away ever again. Never again." He picked up the picture frame, held it close.

"Now that sounds more like my Miguel," she said, and held her arms out wide.

She cradled him again and he sighed along with her, glad to be with her once more.

Chapter Thirty-One

Miguel and two of his friends stood near an intersection. He stared down at the sidewalk and kicked a loose piece of concrete, unable to look them in their eyes.

"So this is it, eh? This is how it ends. Tomorrow you go back to school."

"Yeah, the poor guy," the other teen added.

Miguel shrugged. "Well, now that I have a place to live, I can register. You know, I want to go to school. I've got some catching up to do."

The two teens laughed and shook their heads.

"Well, don't be a stranger. You know where to find us."

"Oh no, I'll see you. I'll see you all the time, after school. I promise."

The other two teens came racing down the block and doubled over in front of them, nearly out of breath.

The two teens with Miguel looked down the street in alarm. "Cops?"

They shook their heads. "No, not that. You gotta see this. Especially you, Miguel. Come on."

Still panting, they picked Miguel up by the arms and raced with him back down the block to an electronics store, where they burst inside and set him down in front of a towering projection television set. The other two teens followed them in. A commercial blared from the stereo speakers on either side.

The storeowner glowered at them from the register. "Hey! I thought I told you kids not to hang out here no more?"

One of the teens who had brought Miguel in waved at the storeowner to be quiet. "Okay, okay. We want to see this one news story and then we'll be gone."

The commercial ended, and the local news returned.

The teen put his head close to Miguel's. "You won't believe this, man, you just won't believe it. Watch."

The newscasters appeared, a man and a woman. The camera switched to focus on the woman.

"And here's the story we've been promising you. After an anonymous tip arrived in the mail, police raided the inner city home of Doctor Carl Dorning today, a retired neurosurgeon."

The picture switched to the familiar house, surrounded by police vehicles. The police were carrying the empty animal cages and other scientific apparatus out of the house.

"The tipster claimed Dorning was performing unregulated animal tests in the basement of his home, which was described by police as filled with expensive equipment, including surgical tools. His neighbors describe Dorning as somewhat of a recluse, rarely seen in public. Police won't speculate what those experiments were exactly, but they did say some of the equipment was intended for use on humans. One of the items taken away was said to have been a small freezer full of dead, dissected animals. Police reports show Dorning was recently arrested for Obstruction of Justice, but details on that arrest are sketchy. Dorning is currently out on bail, and his whereabouts are unknown, since the home appears to have been vacated days earlier and the tipster didn't provide any information to police as to where Dorning might be found."

Dorning's mug shots from his arrest appeared on the screen.

"See?" The teen said. He elbowed Miguel in the arm. "That's the guy in the Mercedes. He's the one you were with."

The news report continued. "If you've seen this man, police ask you call them immediately. Since there were no records found of what experiments might actually have been performed in the home, they're anxious to talk to him. His court date on the Obstruction of Justice charge comes up in two weeks, and if he doesn't appear, a police spokesman said a warrant will be issued for his arrest. Chuck?"

The camera switched to the man, who looked appropriately concerned. "That's a very disturbing story, Jill." He looked at the camera. "We'll keep you posted as more information becomes available."

The teens let out a collective howl.

"Whoa man, you're lucky he didn't operate on you, Miguel," one of the teens said. He drummed his fingers on Miguel's head.

The other teens laughed.

"Quiet!" Miguel said. He stepped closer to the television. "There's another story."

The man read the news with a smile. "...and the editors of that prestigious science journal said today they've received a manuscript from beyond the grave. Percival Marlowe, the famous astrophysicist who died almost two months ago, was the author of the article, which was dated just days before his death but mysteriously not mailed until recently. The editors are convinced the work is genuine because they described it as a stunning breakthrough in quantum physics bringing us one large step closer to a Unified Field Theory, which is kind of a Holy Grail for physicists everywhere. The editors said only someone as brilliant as the late Professor Marlowe could have written such a work, which rules out any possibility of forgery. That, and the fact the manuscript contained references to private conversations the professor had with the editors decades ago, conversations they're convinced no one else knew about. It's just unfortunate, they added, Percival Marlowe won't be around to see his last major work published. The article is slated for a future issue due out before the end of the year."

"Come on, man. We better go," one of the teens said, eyeing the storeowner, who was reaching for the phone. "The show's over."

Miguel hung his head then slowly followed the chattering teens out of the store.

∽≈

The black Mercedes crossed the state line under the cover of the night. Dorning sat hunched over the wheel, his eyes bloodshot from lack of sleep. He muttered to himself to help stay awake, then turned once more to look at his stack of research papers on the passenger seat as if to make certain they were all still there.

∽≈

Miguel's mother poked her head into his small bedroom in their apartment.

"Are you ready for bed, Miguel? Tomorrow's your big day, you know." She smiled, vibrant again, the way Miguel remembered her. "You need a good night's sleep before starting school."

"I'm ready," he said. He went over and gave her a hug. "When's Papa coming home?"

Her smile faded a little, and she patted his face. "Not for a while, Miguel. The Sisters are helping him like they helped me. When he's ready, he'll come to visit. And if those visits work out, we'll be a family again. It won't be easy, but we'll try. I promise, we'll try very hard."

"I hope so, Mama. I want us to be like we were before."

"Me too, Miguel. Me too. Now you better get to bed. Goodnight."

She kissed his forehead and closed the bedroom door.

Miguel listened until he was sure she was gone, then went to his dresser and removed the letter that came with the hundred dollar bills from its hiding spot under the bottom drawer. He unfolded it and read it to himself once again.

Miguel,

I want to thank you for the chance you gave me to live for a little while longer, but after reading your note, I knew the time had come to say goodbye and respect your wishes that you return for good. I know what it is Doctor Dorning uses to make you become me, and will soon get rid of it forever, where no one will ever find it. I have a hunch how to get you back and—more importantly—keep you back; whatever it is that restores you, you need to keep with you always, and enjoy it every day so you forever stay Miguel. You must surround yourself with everyone and everything you love, all you hold near and dear to you to help you stay just the way you are, and to help you grow up the way you should, as Miguel Sanchez. The enclosed money is a gift from me, but when you're a bit older, you will get an even bigger gift—you will become sole trustee of my estate. I know you don't understand yet what that means, but it will be a truly wonderful thing for you and your family. You might even want to use it to do a little something for your friends, who helped you and helped me too when I needed it the most. I have told my lawyers to find you when the time comes, I'm sure they will. They'll also take the necessary steps to end any lingering problems you might have with the police. And finally, I'm going to make it impossible for Doctor Dorning to ever do to anyone else what he did to you. This must never be allowed to happen again. I'm glad I had the chance to meet your mother and your father, and am certain everything will turn out just the way you want. Be good, get back to school and study hard, and someday maybe you will be famous like I was. My time lasted longer than it should have, but yours, my young friend, is only just beginning.

Percival Marlowe

He stared respectfully at the professor's name as he nodded to himself. "I knew you were a good man," he said softly.

Miguel carefully refolded the letter and returned it to its hiding spot. He picked up the wooden picture frame on top of the dresser and touched the photo of his family. Then he took the frame to his bedside, wound the music box with care and set the frame down gently on a table in the corner of the room. After turning off the lights, he got into bed, closed his tired eyes, and let the soothing lullaby weave its magic spell.

About the Author

Almost from birth, Mark Wakely has had a life long fascination with all things scientific.

Throughout grade school, it was the usual model rockets, telescopes and microscopes that occupied his spare time, along with avidly following the space program.

In high school, he started a science club that earned him the Baush and Lomb Science Award in his senior year, which he followed up by acing the science section of the ACT college entrance exam. Fortunately, despite those achievements, Mark managed to avoid the dreaded "nerd" designation, and swears he never even owned a pocket protector.

By the middle of his freshman year in college, however, he felt something in his life was lacking, that something being artistic expression. That ended his budding science career, but launched a new English major.

It was probably inevitable that Mark found himself drawn to writing science fiction, and after cutting his literary teeth by writing poetry (which he still writes) and several "so so" SF stories, Mark wrote two novels prior to *An Audience for Einstein*, which he considers far and away his best work ever.

Mark is currently a college administrator at prestigious Elmhurst College in Elmhurst, Illinois, and resides in a town nearby with his wife and three children. He is already hard at work on his next novel.

The ChroMagic Series
by Piers Anthony

1,000 years ago Earth colonized the planet Charm. But the population of Charm is now far removed from their ancient ancestors. Technology has been lost over the years but the people have something better--Magic!

Key to Havoc
ChroMagic Series, Book One

Once again, Mr Anthony creates a complex world unlike anything we might imagine.
— Amanda Killgore, Scribes World

Oh my lord, this was a fantastic book!!
— Chris Roeszler, Amazon Reviewer

Trade Paperback • ISBN 0-9723670-6-3
Hardcover • ISBN 0-9723670-7-1
eBook • ISBN 1-59426-000-1

Key To Chroma
ChroMagic Series, Book Two

Chroma continues to fascinate, making readers anxious for the final book in the trilogy.
— Amanda Killgore, Scribes World

Trade Paperback • ISBN 1-59426-018-4
Hardcover • ISBN 1-59426-017-6
eBook • ISBN 1-59426-019-2

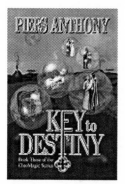

Key to Destiny
ChroMagic Series, Book Three

Piers Anthony is one of those authors who can perform magic with the ordinary.
— A Reader's Guide to Science Fiction

Trade Paperback • ISBN 1-59426-044-3
Hardcover • ISBN 1-59426-043-5
eBook • ISBN 1-59426-045-1

Lord of Wind and Fire
by Elaine Corvidae

A kingdom on the eve of war. A queen held captive. A land in turmoil. A shape-changer's heart. Suchen's life as Steward of Kellsjard is a good one, if uneventful. But the arrival of the exiled wizard Ax threatens to upset her quiet existence.

Wolfkin
Lord of Wind and Fire, Book One

Wolfkin is a superb fantasy shapeshifter romance that will keep you turning the pages.
—Debora Hosey, The Romance Readers Connection

5 Stars! Superb romantic fantasy.
—Harriet Klausner, Amazon.com's #1 reviewer

Trade Paperback • ISBN 1-59426-055-9
Hardcover • ISBN 1-59426-054-0
eBook • ISBN 1-59426-053-2

The Crow Queen
Lord of Wind and Fire, Book Two

Ms. Corvidae shows yet again her penchant for weaving engrossing fantasy tales.
—Kelley A. Hartsell, July 2004

Excellent tale and recommended to all fans of Fantasy! 5 Stars!
—Detra Fitch, Huntress Reviews

Trade Paperback • ISBN 1-59426-058-3
Hardcover • ISBN 1-59426-057-5
eBook • ISBN 1-59426-056-7

Dragon's Son
Lord of Wind and Fire, Book Three

For the lover of fantasy and fantasy romance, this book is definitely for you!

—Amy L. Turpin, Timeless Tales

Trade Paperback • ISBN 1-59426-061-3
Hardcover • ISBN 1-59426-060-5
eBook • ISBN 1-59426-059-1

Printed in the United States
66512LVS00007B/14